THE PERIL OF THE FAE

A CONTEMPORARY SCIENCE FANTASY

RETURN OF THE FAE
BOOK TWO

MARTY C. LEE

Bookaholics Press

Book design, cover, and publication by Bookaholics Press LLC
Edited by Martha Rasmussen
Author photograph by Melissa C. Baxter

ISBN-13: 978-1-950230-36-5 (epub)
978-1-950230-37-2 (paperback)
978-1-950230-38-9 (large print)
978-1-950230-39-6 (hardback)
978-1-950230-66-2 (audio)

Published by Bookaholics Press LLC
Provo, Utah bookaholicspress@gmail.com

Contact the author at MCLeeBooks.com

*For Tad, who is my best ally,
and for my Heavenly Father, my safety.*

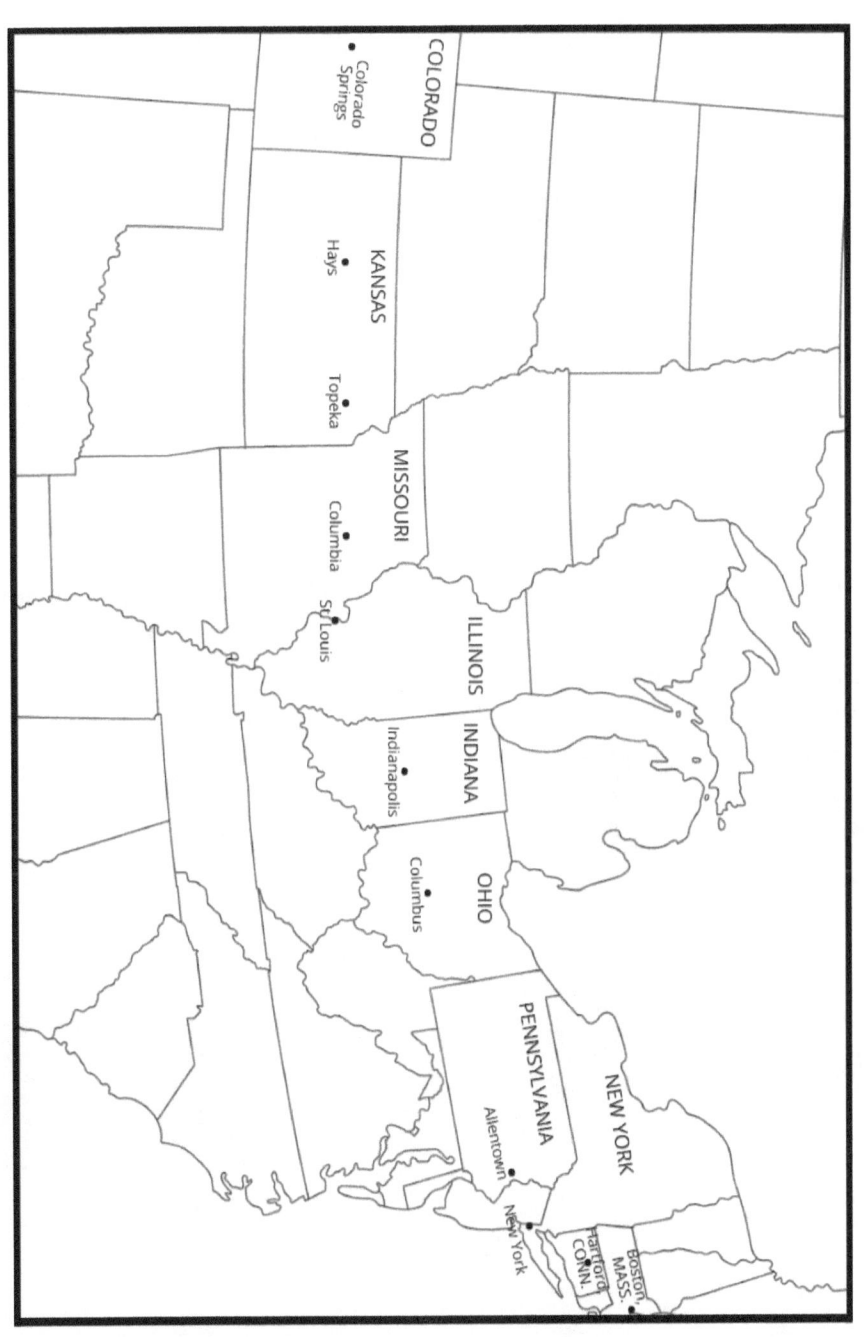

AUTHOR'S NOTE

While I have been meticulous to real life detail and science in some places, in others I could not find information, or changed things for the sake of the story or to protect real people, or simply made mistakes. Most of all, please remember this is a work of fiction. The characters are completely imaginary.

PROLOGUE

_____

IN WHICH THEY MEET THE NATIVES

DAY OF LANDING TO NEXT DAY, SOMEWHERE ON THE DARK SIDE OF KI

THE WHEELED WAGON rumbled to a stop under Gil's feet. He jerked awake and discovered the darkness was still lit by the worldlet in the sky. Would the magic last all night? He didn't know how long he had been asleep since the four natives had picked them up.

Miknon lay beside him, fast asleep, her full belly round under her flounced skirt. For the first time in a long time, he wasn't hungry, either. He took a moment to enjoy the sensation and the thrill of his other form.

Gil crouched low, ducking under the cover across the back of the wagon. When the time was right, he would talk to the natives, but Miknon might as well sleep longer.

Metal slammed, and Gil carefully poked his head back out. The broad, dark-haired Ki native had emerged from the navigation center of the wagon and now entered a large building glowing with lights.

The big pale-haired person shook the little one until it woke and sat up straight. They talked with the other dark one for a few moments, until the first returned and worked the magic to move the wagon to a new location.

They all exited, and Gil examined their silhouettes for clues, deciding to call two of the natives male and two female, though they might be nothing like the people he knew.

The first one, the broad male — if he was male — showed a key and explained something. From the tone of her voice, the pale female protested. Yes, he was nearly sure she was female. The one Gil decided to call Broad shrugged and dangled the key again, explaining more. The tall one with darker hair — also probably female — sighed and untied the cover on the wagon cargo area.

Gil slid over to shield Miknon, lifting his head to speak, but the natives only removed several bags and the box that had held the creamy liquid Gil drank earlier. The little one reached up to pet Gil's fur.

"Nisedaug," he said.

Tall tugged him away and led him through the door Broad had unlocked and was holding open. Gil glimpsed a huge bed and a couple of chairs before the door closed. In a few minutes, the light in the room turned off.

It seemed he and his sister were being left outside. No chance to talk for now.

How could people actually live on the dark side of this world? They ought to freeze on the dark side. But it was warmer than the air had ever been on the ship that had carried his people from their world to this one. Or almost to this one, since *New Kunisu* was now on the worldlet above him and the rest of the fleet was hiding in the ring of stones past the neighboring red world, waiting to hear if they could colonize peacefully or must conquer their new home of Ki before they could settle.

The lords were in favor of conquest, unlike Gil and Shar, the prince still in hiding after an assassination attempt. When Miknon was discovered spying and had to flee to save her life, Gil accompanied her for two reasons. First, he wouldn't abandon his sister to danger. Second, this might be the only chance to make peace with the new world and rescue everyone from their mutual peril.

He desperately needed to talk to the natives, somehow, but it could wait until after their sleep shift. Sleep sounded like another good idea. He closed his eyes and let himself drift into oblivion.

"HAYDAUG," someone whispered, and a soft hand touched Gil's head.

He jerked awake again. Was the sky lighter now? How could that be? His elders told him the dark side of a world was always dark. It must be the worldlet shining brighter, or more magic.

The edge of the wagon lowered, and Miknon scrambled under Gil's chest just before Little stared into Gil's eyes, smiling. Or baring his teeth?

No, that looked more like a smile. He smiled in return, and Little laughed.

"Kumensite." Little reached toward Gil. "Kumboi." He found his necklace and hooked his fingers under it at the back of Gil's neck, tugging gently. "Heerboi."

"What does it want?" Miknon whispered.

"Us to go with him?" Gil guessed, desperately wishing he spoke the language.

"Bad idea," Miknon said.

Little kept pulling on Gil's necklace, tugging him toward the edge.

"I'm not sure I can stop him without hurting him," Gil said.

"Bite it!" Miknon ordered.

"Why?" Gil asked. "He hasn't hurt me, and I don't think he intends to. We have to try talking to them sooner or later. We have a duty, remember?"

And Little didn't look like a monster. Nobody had hurt them yet, and they would have to take some risks to find allies. Miknon muttered something and grabbed the ring hanging from his necklace. Wherever he went, she would go. Her body shivered against his chest, and he hummed soothingly despite his own fear.

By now, Gil was at the edge of the wagon, and another step would take him out entirely.

"Kumonboi," Little urged.

He glanced over his shoulder at the room holding his companions and tugged harder on Gil's necklace. Landing on his head wouldn't help, so Gil jumped down. As he hit the ground, one rear leg snapped, sending fiery pain shooting through his body.

Gil howled and collapsed, careful not to crush Miknon.

It hurt. He tried to breathe through the pain. It really hurt. Apparently, his three shifts since they had landed hadn't strengthened his bones sufficiently to deal with his extra weight on this world. Trying to rise on three legs, he could feel his bones bending. Bad idea. Immediately, he lay down again and concentrated on breathing slowly.

"Ow, ow, ow," he whispered.

Little banged on the door to the room and yelled, then darted back and knelt by Gil. "Ime-saury ime-saury," he wailed, tears welling in his eyes. "Aryuohkay?"

Softly, he stroked Gil's fur until the other natives ran from the room, which now blazed with light. Gil licked Little's knee to comfort him.

All four of the natives argued for several minutes, with Little frequently pointing to Gil. Eventually, Broad crouched by Gil and slowly reached for him, making soothing noises. He didn't seem to have any weapons, so Gil let him approach. Broad picked him up, and Gil tucked his head to keep Miknon hidden. Her weight still hung from his necklace, but she added a firm grip on his fur.

Little ran ahead into the room, and by the time Gil was carried inside, a fuzzy white cloth had been laid on a chair by the window. Broad set him on this, despite his dirty condition, then the natives backed up and stared at him. Though none had embroidery or jewels, they all wore short tunics in various colors, with something like short, loose hose on their legs. Their hair stuck up oddly, and they yawned as if still half-asleep.

Miknon kept her shaking fingers wrapped around his necklace and fur, though she said nothing.

Gil tried to arrange his broken leg in the most comfortable position. At least it was fairly straight and no bone poked through the skin, so a healer could mend it with minimal crippling. He squinted against the blinding light in the room. Was this really the amount of illumination they preferred? In the excessive light, he could see Broad had black hair, while Tall's was brown.

Little tugged on the arm of Pale, who looked similar. Perhaps they were child and parent? That would explain the size difference, too. The child begged, pointing to Gil, pouring out words much too fast to catch any of them.

His mother — presumably — rubbed her head and winced. The other two made various negative gestures, shaking their heads or folding their arms.

So, Little was the only one already on their side. But Gil never expected this to be easy. He raised his head to make eye contact, and Little stopped talking, his mouth hanging open and his eyes wide. He reached under Gil's chin toward Miknon.

Miknon screamed, and Gil jerked backward, slamming into the back of the chair. Little reached again. He must not hurt Miknon!

Shifting would make his leg start healing whether or not it was set properly. The healers would have a harder task, but his sister needed his protection.

Quickly, he shifted to his two-legged form and raised a hand to ward off the child. "Don't touch her, please."

The Ki natives screamed and fell backward.

Chapter 1

Werewolf

Ian Fitch gaped in shock. His dog had turned into a naked boy! And he'd talked, though not in any language Ian recognized. That was surprising, since he spoke seven languages, more or less, and knew what a lot of others sounded like. Though thirteen wasn't old enough to be an expert on anything.

His sister, Alexandria, dropped into a judo stance, hands shaking. Nikolaos Antonakis stepped in front of Mom and raised his fists. Even though they were only unofficially family, Nikos was taking his promises seriously.

But he'd better not hurt Ian's dog! When they rescued the dog last night in the middle of nowhere, Mom had only agreed to drop it at the animal shelter this morning, but he was sure he could convince her to keep it.

Ian jumped in front of the boy and raised his hands. "Everyone calm down."

His own voice squeaked, and he cleared his throat and took a deep breath. After all, his dog hadn't done anything since he turned into a boy, and if he'd wanted to hurt them, he could have bitten them earlier.

"Calm down?" Alexandria said. "Are you crazy? You brought a werewolf into our hotel room! What the—"

"No swearing!" Mom barked.

"He's not a werewolf," Ian denied.

Was he? He had unmistakably been a very big black dog a few minutes ago. Or a wolf? He looked over his shoulder at the equally black-skinned boy, who sat quietly, hands clutching one leg. He had certainly been a dog when Ian had found him last night in an empty field.

"There are no werewolves." Mom's voice trembled.

"What would you call him?" Nikos waved toward the chair by the window, which definitely held a boy instead of a dog.

"A naked werewolf," Alexandria amended, turning scarlet.

"Okay, okay." Ian grabbed a second towel from another chair where it had been drying.

Slowly, he approached the boy, who watched him with narrowed eyes but said nothing. Once Ian was within arm's reach, he tossed the towel over the boy's lap.

"Is that better?" he asked his sister.

Alexandria rolled her eyes. "Only slightly. If he's not a werewolf, what is he? And what is the blue one? Some kind of fairy?"

Ian shrugged. "I don't know what they are. But they aren't threatening us, and I don't think he can move with that broken leg. Can we all sit and relax a little?"

"Yes," Mom said. "I agree."

Alexandria whirled on her. "You do?"

"Yes. They haven't done anything to us. Sit down." Mom edged from behind Nikos and took the other chair.

Reluctantly, Nikos and Alexandria sat on the far end of the bed. Ian flopped cross-legged on the floor, closest to the strangers. If anyone panicked again, he would be near enough to intervene.

Despite the boy's absolutely black skin, his cautious eyes were a brilliant pale blue. As everyone sat, his shoulders relaxed slightly. His little friend, now huddled at his side instead of under his chin, was blue from head to foot and had blue-feathered wings, matching blue hair, and navy blue eyes. She was only a foot high, but obviously a living creature rather than a doll or mechanical device. Both of them had many frizzy braids coming undone. And both were dirty and smelly and shaking.

It wasn't that cold in here, despite the air conditioning. Ian could understand a tiny fairy being afraid, but why would a werewolf fear normal humans with unimpressive teeth and nails? Maybe it was because of his broken leg.

The rising sun lit the window of the hotel room, and the werewolf pulled open the curtain enough to see outside. His eyes grew wide, and he said something to his blue friend in a shocked voice. Both of them hunched as he jerked the curtain closed again.

"It's the full moon," Nikos muttered.

He'd been a Greek exchange student in Alexandria's high school before he invited them to come with him when he left for college, since they no longer had a home and Alexandria was his best friend. Not that Ian cared. He'd rather be with Nikos than with Dad, who didn't love Ian anymore. And Nikos never yelled at him like Dad did.

"Werewolf," Alexandria repeated.

"But the moon is still up, and he's a boy," Ian said. "Doesn't that mean he isn't a werewolf?"

Mom leaned sideways and peeked behind the curtain. "He's right. The full moon is up."

Alexandria threw out her hands. "Then what is he? And where did he come from? Why is he hiding from the moon if it doesn't make him shift?"

"Wait," Ian said. "What if he came from that asteroid on the moon? You know, the one NASA said crashed? What if it was actually a spaceship that landed?"

His sister had obsessively followed the NASA reports on the peculiar asteroid for the last nine months, though unlike Dad, she steadfastly denied the theories of aliens.

"You're kidding me," Alexandria said. "You think we have a space werewolf? What kind of crazy idea is that?"

"Maybe?" Ian said. "You said there aren't any Earth werewolves. Nobody has ever seen a real werewolf, right? So maybe they're new. If they're new, they had to get here somehow. And what else is new and peculiar? The asteroid. You know it was traveling oddly, and the scientists haven't discovered why yet, so maybe it *was* a spaceship instead of another 'Oumuamua. And if he's worried about the moon, maybe it's because he knows something about it that we don't, like a spaceship sitting there."

"That's ridiculous," Alexandria said.

"If myths are real, why not aliens?" It made perfect sense for the crazy situation.

Alexandria threw her hands into the air.

He smirked at winning a point in their argument, then hopped to his feet and pulled the curtain open a crack. He pointed to the werewolf, then the moon, then back to Earth.

"Are you from there?" he asked.

The boy indicated himself and his friend, then drew an imaginary line from the moon to the hotel. Imagine Dad being right about aliens — or anything, for once.

Alexandria rubbed her hands through her hair, making her bed-head worse. "I suppose that explains how we have a mythological creature — two myths — in our hotel room. They're new to Earth."

"It doesn't explain why we have myths of real creatures," Nikos murmured.

He flexed his fingers as if eager to dig into the mystery, which made sense for someone planning on a mythology major.

"We can ask him later," Ian said, "after we have a common language."

A thrill rushed through him at the thought of learning a new language that no one else knew.

"You're assuming we'll be together long enough to learn a common language," his sister retorted.

The werewolf had said nothing since his first words, but he watched each person as they spoke. The blue fairy still huddled at his side, mostly hidden behind his arm.

"What are we supposed to do with a werewolf?" Nikos asked. "Call the police?"

"You can't give my dog to the cops," Ian protested.

He'd wanted a dog forever, but Dad had said no. Now Dad was out of their lives, and Ian had lucked into a dog, and he wasn't giving him up.

Mom sighed. "Ian, he can't possibly be your dog. Look at him. He's a person."

"But not human," Alexandria pointed out. "His palms and soles are also black, and his fingernails look halfway to claws."

"And his facial proportions are wrong," Nikos said with the authority of an art student.

"He's injured, anyway," Mom said. "The hospital seems more appropriate than the police. They can treat his broken leg."

"The hospital would definitely notice he isn't human," Ian said. "They'd call the cops!"

He wrinkled his nose, trying to remember if he'd read about how to set a broken bone. Not something he wanted to try by himself, but what choice did they have?

"That's not our problem," his sister said. "The police can handle this better. Or NASA, or the military, or just about anybody."

"Aren't you curious?" Mom asked. "Why did they leave the moon? How did they get here? Are they alone?"

Alexandria groaned. "Is there an army of werewolves roaming Earth now?"

To head off that question before his sister panicked, Ian turned to the strangers and pointed two fingers at them. "Are you alone?" He unfolded the rest of his fingers and wiggled them. "Are there more of you?" He pretended to look for others around the room and out the window.

The werewolf held up two fingers and pointed downward. He wiggled both hands several times and pointed to the moon.

"So maybe only the two of them here," Nikos said, "but more in their spaceship on the moon. Are they scouts? Or, since they seem afraid of being seen, are they runaways? Hunted?"

"If they're being hunted by something worse than a werewolf," Alexandria said, "we'd better not get in the way! Our own problems are bad enough without involving ourselves in a monster hunt. The police can investigate those questions."

Ian folded his arms. They were ganging up on him. "You can't let the police take my dog."

Mom rubbed her forehead. "Ian, stop calling him your dog."

Ian scowled. "Well, it's not fair to abandon people, either. What would your Diplomacy Club think, Alexandria? Didn't you swear to treat aliens with kindness and consideration and not ruin everything like the movies always do?"

He'd sat in the back of the room for enough of her after-school meetings to already know the answer.

Alexandria rolled her eyes. "It was all hypothetical, because aliens don't exist." She looked at their visitors still shivering in the chair and groaned. "Fine, we can talk to them before we go to the hospital. But I'm not making any promises for later!"

Good enough. Ian would keep wearing down her worries until he had her convinced.

"Where do we start?" Nikos asked.

"With an introduction, of course." Ian beamed at the alien boy, who smiled back, revealing teeth too sharp for human though less fanged than a dog's.

"I'm Ian." Ian touched his chest. "Eee-unn."

"Ian." The boy inclined his upper body in an awkward half-bow.

Ian pointed to his new older brother and used his shortest name. "Nik."

"Nik?" The werewolf's eyebrows shot up, and he babbled something to his friend, who shook her head and scolded him. He laughed, poked her belly softly, and repeated, "Nik." He bowed again, with a huge grin.

"Alex." Ian pointed to his sister.

She folded her arms. "Alexandria."

"Shorter is easier to remember." Ian knew she hated her nickname, especially with her memories of Dad, but five syllables were a lot.

"Alexandria." She scowled at him, and her hazel eyes brightened to sage green.

Okay, it wasn't worth a fight. "Alexandria," he repeated slowly.

The werewolf's eyes widened, and he murmured something to his companion. His bow was much deeper this time, and he very carefully pronounced, "Alexandria."

Ian pointed at Mom, then paused. What should he say? Mom or Mama, like the rest of them called her? Or Helen? Or Mrs. Fitch? Um, no, with the divorce final, it would be Ms. Ellison.

"Helen." Mom touched her chest and copied the werewolf's half-bow.

The boy bowed again. "Helen."

Ian reached toward the strangers. "You?"

The werewolf put a finger on the blue girl's head. "Miknon."

She swatted at him and said something that sounded like a protest, and he talked back for a minute. When she folded her arms and glared, he shrugged his shoulders.

He touched his bare chest and said, "Gil."

"Gill, like a fish?" Nikos asked.

"Gilbert?" Ian guessed.

"Gilmore Wolves?" Alexandria's voice squeaked, and she slapped a hand over her mouth to hide a giggle.

"Is there no wolf in Gilead?" Mom misquoted from the Bible, the corner of her mouth twitching.

"Gil-galad was a werewolf king," Nikos recited, perhaps because Gil's ears were pointed like mythical elves.

Ian bit his lip to keep from laughing. What would Tolkien have said about a real werewolf?

"Calm down." Mom took a deep breath. "It's a coincidence that his name sounds English."

"Before we take him to the hospital," Alexandria said, "can we put him in some clothes?" Her cheeks were still pink, though no longer scarlet.

"I suppose he could borrow some of mine," Nikos said, "but he's taller and thinner. I'm not sure my pants would stay up, and what about his broken leg?"

"He's *too* thin," Mom said. "Look at his ribs."

Ian bit his lip again. Every one of Gil's ribs stood out starkly, as did his cheekbones. Every bone, in fact, could be traced easily. Though Miknon was covered by a tight shirt and ruffled skirt, her arms and face seemed as thin as his. They looked three-quarters starved.

Alexandria waved her hands. "Okay, since he isn't howling about his leg, we can at least feed him first. Who knows how long the hospital would make him wait to eat. Nikos, go get the food crate from the truck, please."

Ian cheered internally. Alexandria never could resist solving problems, and she had a kind heart under her worries. Sooner or later, she'd see his idea was best. Um, somehow.

Mom headed for the little hotel fridge. "When I emptied the cooler last night, I noticed you boys finished the meat and cheese, but we can feed Gil and Miknon cereal, fruit, and PB&J sandwiches."

Nikos saluted ironically and exited the room. He returned in a minute with an empty plastic crate.

"All the food is gone." He tipped the crate to show empty, shredded packaging.

Everyone turned to stare at their unexpected guests, who looked at the empty crate and ducked their heads as if they expected blows.

"If we can't feed them," Nikos asked, "should we take them to the hospital the way they are? They seem peaceful enough."

"You promised we could talk to him first," Ian protested.

Alexandria groaned and hopped to her feet. "Okay, so we need more food. And if we have to go out, we might as well buy him an outfit that will actually fit. I think Nikos would appreciate not putting that stink in his clothes, and we can't take him to the hospital in the hotel's towel. Mom, you come with me so we can move faster and find cheap stuff."

"We're babysitting aliens?" Nikos asked. "What if they attack?"

She raised an eyebrow and pursed her lips. "If his leg is really broken, I don't think he's a danger unless the stink kills you. And who do you want to be here if he does attack: you or Mom?"

Nikos narrowed his eyes at her. "I see your point."

Ian ignored their arguing, because his dog was nice and wouldn't attack anyone. And what if he could improve the stink? Maybe Mom would let him keep his dog then.

"I'll put the crate back." He snatched the crate and keys from Nikos and darted from the room.

After throwing the crate into the back of the truck, he grabbed the collapsible stool from the back seat and hurried back inside. He hid the stool under the table and returned the keys to Nikos.

His sister was still staring at Gil and Miknon. "What size do you think Gil wears?" Alexandria asked.

"I have a measuring tape in my purse." Mom found it and slowly approached Gil, then let her arms sag. "How do I tell him what I want to do?"

"Here," Ian said, "measure me."

He raised his arms and stood still while Mom held the tape measure across his shoulders and arms and around his waist. Alexandria took notes to demonstrate the reason for the process.

Mom knelt to measure Ian's inseam, then paused and grimaced at Gil. "I don't think…"

Alexandria turned pink again. "No way."

"Get shorts," Nikos said. "It's definitely warm enough, and then the length doesn't matter."

"Good idea. They'll be easier to get over his broken leg, too." Mom approached Gil again, tape measure held in front of her.

Gil looked from her to Ian, who nodded vigorously.

"It's okay." Ian held out his arms again to show the measuring position. "Okay."

"Ohkae." Gil raised his arms.

He held still while Mom measured him, but Miknon flew crookedly out of reach. Once Alexandria had the figures in her notebook, she and Mom changed clothes in the bathroom and headed for the door.

Alexandria glared at Ian and pointed a threatening finger. "Just keep them out of trouble."

He smiled back innocently. As soon as she closed the door, he whirled on Nikos. "They do stink, but we can give them a bath. Then the ladies won't be so mad."

"Oh, no," Nikos said. "I'm not bathing a stranger, especially one with claws. And he can't even stand."

"We can't leave them like that," Ian said. "The hospital can't set his leg when it's so filthy. I got the folding stool from the truck so he can sit in the shower."

"And if he doesn't like the water, he can bite off my face," Nikos said.

"I'll do it," Ian volunteered. "He's my dog."

"He's not—" Nikos pinched the bridge of his nose. "He's not your dog."

"Oh, come on," Ian begged. "Would you like to be that dirty?"

Nikos grunted and disappeared into the small hotel bathroom. He emerged a minute later with a stack of towels.

"Spread several of these on the bed, please." Rubbing his chin, he examined their guests. "I suggest we start with Gil. If we're lucky, he can explain to his friend, yes?"

"Yes." Ian felt his ears getting hot. He definitely didn't want to try bathing a girl, even if she was only doll size. Although that brought up another problem. "But we can't put Miknon in the shower."

"No," Nikos said, "I was thinking of the bathroom sink."

"Ah, yes," Ian agreed. "Just her size."

He ducked into the bathroom and checked Nikos's preparations. He had put the stool in the shower and unfolded a towel by the sink. Ian put a washcloth and the hotel sample shampoo on the floor of the shower.

He returned to the bedroom and found Nikos and Gil staring at each other. The way the werewolf was shifting position made him think of something else.

"Uh, Nikos? What about the toilet?"

Nikos winced. "We stick him on it and hope he figures it out, I guess."

Ian grimaced. "Are we ready to start?"

"No," Nikos said, "but if we aren't finished by the time Alexandria returns, we'll be in trouble."

Big trouble, and his sister always knew how to make him sorry.

Both boys took a deep breath and approached the werewolf. This had better change Alexandria's mind about keeping the aliens, because if they left, Ian wouldn't have a dog *or* a new language to learn!

Chapter 2

In Which the Enemy Doesn't Drown Them

Day after landing, Ki

As the two Ki natives approached with grim looks on their faces, Miknon flew farther away to give Gil room to maneuver. With two of the enemy gone, the odds of escape were a little better. If only Gil's leg weren't broken. At least the tall one with the stonegazer's eyes was gone, but they didn't know exactly what magic the rest of them could do.

But her brother didn't move. He didn't shift to wolf, didn't raise his hands. He just watched.

"Gil," she protested, "don't let the enemy take you without a fight."

"We don't know if they're enemies," he said. "They might be allies, and we desperately need friends. Look, the child is talking to us, not threatening."

And indeed, the aliens had stopped a few steps away, and the little one named Ian was babbling frantically, gesturing and pointing. None of it made any sense, of course, and Gil might be completely wrong about their intent.

Finally, Ian stopped talking and looked helplessly at the big one. Nik shrugged and slowly stepped closer. A blue-eye emblem hung on a chain around his neck, like the family crest Gil wore. Nik reached toward Gil, who didn't move, hopeful idiot that he was. First, Nik touched Gil's broken leg gently, gazing at his face. When her brother still did nothing, Nik scooped him into his arms and carried him toward a door in the far corner, carefully maneuvering around obstacles.

"Don't let them take you," Miknon called after them. "They might torture you!"

She slid down from the cold air-blower and crawled across the floor. The light coming through the window grew brighter, but she didn't have time to see what magic was causing it.

"I trust Nik." Gil patted the alien's shoulder.

"It's a coincidence he has the same name as Nikandros." Miknon risked the entire name of the king's secretary because the aliens didn't speak their language. "It doesn't mean you should trust him."

"We have to give them a chance," Gil said.

Miknon almost screamed. The prince had given him authority to try for peace, but right now, it felt a lot safer to let the fae attack instead.

Ian turned and saw Miknon crawling. He crouched at her side, holding out his hands. She cringed away, and he froze, speaking quietly. He pointed toward the doorway and said her brother's name in the middle of an incomprehensible river of words. Then he smiled and held out his hands again.

And what choice did she have? He was dozens of times her size and could capture her anytime he liked. If she played along, could she find a way to escape later?

"If he hurts me," she shouted to Gil, "I will bite him."

"Fair enough," her brother said as he disappeared through the door, which closed behind him.

Was she too late to help Gil? Would touching the alien lead to her own peril? Maybe, but if her brother died, she would rather join him than face this strange world alone.

Miknon sat on Ian's hands and held her breath, but the alien merely closed his fingers halfway, not quite touching her, and tiptoed after Gil and Nik. He waited outside the door, talking all the while. A roar echoed, and Gil screamed.

"Are you hurt?" Miknon yelled, lunging toward the door.

Ian closed his hand a little more, keeping her from escaping but not hurting her. She grabbed the closest finger and prepared to bite it. Nobody was keeping her away from her brother.

"Okay." Gil shouted the Ki word. "I'm just surprised," he continued in their own language.

Miknon let go and waited. The door opened soon, revealing a small room that was all hard and shiny and blinding white. Gil sat right inside, on a tall table with a bucket built into it. The white cloth was loosely wrapped around him.

He pointed to the corner of the room to a funny chair with a hole in it. "That's a compost chair, and it's very noisy."

Ian set Miknon on the near side of the bucket. The table was cold and smooth, and she tucked her flounced skirt under her legs for warmth. Nik pulled on shiny handles, and water flowed into the bucket.

Ian wiggled his fingers in the water. "Wauter."

"Amazing," Gil said. "The water tank must be built into the wall or in the next room."

Nik stuck his hands under the spigot, then rubbed a white rectangle between them. He put down the rectangle and rubbed his hands together, then showed them to Gil and Miknon. Suds covered his skin until he washed them off under the water.

Ian pointed to the rectangle. "Sope." He pointed to Nik, still rinsing his hands. "Waush."

"Ah," Gil said. "They're showing us how to cleanse."

"We know how to wash," Miknon said.

"We didn't know how to access their water," Gil clarified. "And we didn't know the words. See, I told you they were friends."

Miknon looked down at her filthy skirt and bodice. "That would be nice." Both the wash and the friends. But she still didn't believe they were safe.

Ian pointed to Gil, then to the "sope" and water. Obediently, Gil washed his hands. As he turned his hands to rinse them, Ian and Nik yelped.

Nik took Gil's hand, and Ian leaned around Miknon to see the cut across her brother's palm. They had needed blood to stage their death when they snuck away from their ship, but the bandage was too filthy to leave on after their escape. The wound had scabbed over nicely, and now it was clean, so what was the problem? Washing it had only loosened the scabs a little.

And did everyone believe they were dead? If they did, Mother and Ram must be heartbroken. But if their deception had failed, how long would it take the lords to come after them? She couldn't see a happy ending to this escapade, no matter how she looked at it.

The aliens chattered at each other, then Ian darted off. He came back with a black rectangle in his hands, which he tapped frantically for a minute.

"Okay," Ian said.

Nik turned one handle and put Gil's uninjured hand under the water. "Haut."

After a second, Gil yanked his hands back. "Ouch."

Nik turned the other handle, tested the water, then put Gil's hand under. "Coled."

"Brr," Gil said.

Nik turned both handles, checked the water again, then had Gil feel it. "Waurm."

Gil smiled and nodded. "Got it. I'm not sure water temperature is the most vital vocabulary, but I suppose we have to start somewhere."

"And where did you want to start?" Miknon asked. "Please don't kill me? I like that one."

Leaning on his good hand, Gil stretched across to pat her legs. "They haven't hurt us yet. They haven't taken advantage of my injury." After a wince as he sat up and readjusted his leg, he turned back to Nik. "Okay."

Nik nodded and bent to look at Miknon. He pointed to the big room and made a shooing gesture. She folded her arms and shook her head. No way would she leave her brother alone with these strangers.

Nik shrugged and picked up Gil again, but only walked a few steps to the glass compartment along one wall. After setting Gil on a small bench in the middle of the compartment, he again tried to shoo Miknon.

He pointed to Gil. "Waush."

She leaned against the wall and glared at him. If they wanted him to wash, why did they take him away from the bucket? No, she wasn't leaving her brother.

Ian babbled something. She gave him her crankiest look and shook her head again.

Nik shrugged and took the white cloth away from Gil. In its place, he dropped a much smaller cloth and one of the "sope" rectangles. Ian babbled again, but Miknon kept watching Gil. If this was the start of torture, she'd manage to fly. Even at her size, eyes made good targets.

"Haut? Coled? Waurm?" Nik asked Gil, adjusting something up high then reaching for a handle on the wall.

"Do they have *two* water spigots in the same room?" Gil asked. "They must be highborn to have such luxury. Worm. Worm-coled."

With a nod, Nik turned the handle. After a gurgle, water suddenly poured from a high spigot, hitting the wall and running down the shiny surface. With one hand in the water, Nik played with the handle. Finally, he reached up to move the spigot. Water poured over Gil, and he squeaked.

Miknon rolled to her knees, ready to fly to him.

"Okay?" Ian called from the doorway.

"Okay, okay," Gil said. "Hey, Miknon, this actually feels pretty good."

Nik closed the glass door and shooed Miknon again. She stuck out her tongue at him and resumed her seat. He shrugged, leaning against another wall in a position where he could watch Gil from the corner of his eye without staring at him.

Miknon spared a sideways gaze for Nik but spent most of her attention on her brother. After a little experimenting, Gil lathered up and used the small cloth to scrub off the accumulated dirt of conjunctions with little bathing due to water rationing, as well as the recent mess from their escape. Layers of dead skin peeled off with the dirt, so disgusting that Miknon was glad she hadn't eaten recently.

Gil carefully washed his broken leg, hissing as he ran his fingers down the bone. "I think it's just cracked," he called to Miknon.

"You don't know that, you idiot," she responded. "And that's bad enough, anyway."

"But it could be worse."

Didn't anything worry her overly optimistic brother? It could still *become* worse.

Gil knocked on the glass until Nik looked at him. Gil pointed to the soap, then to his hair, and raised his eyebrows. Nik shook his head and opened the door. He poured a thick cream from a little bottle into Gil's good hand, then mimed rubbing it into his hair.

Either the cream wasn't as effective as the soap or Gil's hair was hopeless, because he eventually shrugged and gave up. After he rinsed, he knocked on the door again, and when Nik looked at him, held up his arms.

Grabbing the large white cloth again, Nik opened the door and turned off the water. He squeezed some of the water from Gil's hair, then wrapped him in the cloth and carried him into the bigger room.

When Ian offered another ride on his hands, Miknon accepted in order to be with her brother faster.

The room was even brighter now, and the fabric hanging over the window glowed with light. None of the aliens looked at it, so it must be magic they expected, though she couldn't tell what it was doing.

Gil sat on the huge bed, drying his arms and hair with a second cloth. "I feel great," he told Miknon. He turned to Nik, who was sitting in a chair by the big window. "Waush Miknon?"

"Oh, I'll be fine," Miknon said, ignoring her itchy scalp and persistent stink.

"Waush, okay," Ian said.

He darted into the small room and clattered around. He popped back and grinned at Miknon, offering his hands again. They hadn't hurt Gil, only cleaned him. Her scalp itched again, and she wrinkled her nose at her own stench.

"This was your stupid idea," Miknon told Gil. "If this goes wrong, I'll get you."

Patting instead of rubbing, Gil dried his broken leg, not quite managing to hide his winces. "You'll be fine."

Reluctantly, Miknon let Ian carry her back to the shiny room. At least he was a child — she was pretty sure — instead of the more grown Nik. And she could bathe with her clothes on, cleaning everything at once. It would be a lot better than nothing.

The bucket in the table had been filled halfway with warm water, soap sat on the edge, and a teeny cup overflowed with the hair cleansing cream. Several of the small cleansing cloths sat on the table, and one was already soaking in the water.

Ian put her down and demonstrated how to push down the lever to drain the bucket. He backed out of the room, pulling the door with him. Apparently she would get more privacy than Gil had. Was that because she was a girl or because she didn't need help with a broken leg? Either way, she would accept it.

"Wait," she said.

Ian stopped and swallowed hard, eyes wide. He pulled the door nearly closed, peeking through the crack with a red face.

She pointed to the hair cream and then to her feathers. "Can I use this on my wings?"

He sighed in obvious relief, shrugged, and closed the door.

Not helpful. Well, the extra weight she had on this world meant she needed to exercise her wings before she could fly much anyway, so she might as well get clean. Keeping one eye on the door to make sure it stayed closed, she hurried through a lovely warm bath. Like Gil, layers of skin came off with the dirt and the stink, turning the water a nasty color.

She drained the bucket and refilled it, though she couldn't figure out how to get the water as nicely warm. After unbraiding and washing her hair in the fresh water, she drained and filled the bucket a third time, and pulled her filthy clothes into the water, too.

Ian had left a whole stack of the little white cloths, so she wrapped one around her hair and one around her body, then rolled up her skirt and bodice in a third.

Now what? She couldn't open the door, and her fists were too small to make an audible knock, even if she could reach the door. She was trapped in here.

Don't be ridiculous. They would surely check on her eventually, if only to pursue their own agenda. But why wait? She grabbed the now-empty bowl that had held the hair cream and used it to tap on the wall. In a minute, someone knocked on the door, then opened it the tiniest crack.

"Miknon okay?" Ian asked.

"Okay," Miknon said.

He opened the door slowly, then came in. After rinsing out the bucket and tiny bowl, he screwed the bowl onto a tube of something. Apparently it was some kind of lid. Well, it had been the right size. He glanced around the rest of the room, then pointed to the rolled-up cloth.

She unrolled it enough to show what she had done, and his face lit up. He grabbed the roll, let her climb onto his hands, then carried both to the other room. She sat by Gil, who was struggling to comb his tangled hair. At least the aliens had a comb his size. On the ship, the fae washed and brushed their hair infrequently to avoid loose hairs floating around whenever the weight went off. The braids also helped contain the problem, but ever since the water restrictions, they had done little but pin the old braids tighter to their heads.

For Gil and Miknon, the trip from the worldlet to Ki had been difficult enough to lose most of the pins and leave their braids in total chaos.

"When you finish, will you brush my hair?" she asked.

"Mmm-hm." Gil yanked and winced.

Ian attached something to the wall, and with a roar, air blew from it. He unrolled her clothes and aimed the blast at it, using a judicious finger to keep them from blowing away.

Keeping an eye on the aliens, Miknon unwrapped her hair and tried to get out the worst of the tangles with her fingers. She slowly fanned her wings, trying to dry them.

Ian flipped her clothes and blew air at the other side. The flounces on her skirt fluttered as if they were no longer soggy. A magic dryer? Did it work on things other than clothing?

"Ian," Miknon said, not sure if he would respond. He didn't, but Nik glanced her way.

"Ian," he bellowed. Perhaps the blower was too noisy for the alien's hearing, then.

When Ian turned off the contrivance, Nik said something that started with her name.

"Oh," Ian said. "Miknon okay?"

"Okay," Miknon said. "Can that thing dry my feathers?" She pointed to the magic blower and then to her wings.

Ian raised his eyebrows and pursed his lips. "Okay."

He moved her to the side of the bed closest to him, then turned on the blower again. It was quite noisy from this close. After holding his hand in front of the air with a considering look on his face, he slowly moved it to point at her. Hot air blew from it, instead of cold air like from the box on the wall. They had two kinds of air magic, then.

"Ouch," Miknon said. "Haut."

"Okay," Ian said, and the heat and pressure lessened. "Okay?"

"Okay." She sat quietly and let the warmth soak into her feathers and bones. It even dried the cloth around her.

Just as her wings dried, Gil gave up on his hair, tossing the comb to the bed in disgust. "It's useless."

The door opened, revealing a world at least a dozen times brighter than the ship or the light on the old world that the ship mimicked. How could it possibly be so bright on the dark side of the world? How much magic did they have to squander it so much? Miknon ducked her head to shield her eyes, as did Gil beside her.

The other two aliens entered, arms full of strangely shiny bags which they dropped onto the table and empty chair. When they spotted Gil and Miknon, the tall stonegazer's eyebrows shot up, and she put her hands on her hips and started scolding.

Uh oh, what had they done wrong? They had only obeyed Ian and

Nik. Had they broken some bathing custom? What would their punishment be? Wings twitching, she scooted closer to Gil.

Ian turned off the air-blower and argued back. The older one, Helen, raised her hands and stopped them both with a few words. She looked into several bags, then handed one to Nik and one to the stonegazer. Then she grabbed another and marched toward Gil. After dumping the contents onto the bed, she slowly reached for Gil's injured hand, speaking softly.

The trusting idiot handed it to her, a smile on his face. Miknon scooted under his arm to see better. How better to start torture than with an already weak point?

The woman tilted Gil's palm to the blinding light and squinted at it, then put it back on his knee. She opened several of the packages she had dumped onto the bed, squeezing cream onto a little pad. Then she took back his hand and covered the cut with the pad, pressing its edges. The magic made it stick in place, and she repeated the process with two more pads until the entire cut was covered.

"It doesn't hurt," Gil assured Miknon. "I think she's a healer, maybe."

"But she didn't do anything except cover it," Miknon said.

Gil rubbed her head. "We'll see, then, won't we? At least it will stay cleaner."

At the table, Nik and the stonegazer opened packages and stacked food in layers. Miknon's stomach growled, and she looked away. It wasn't her food, and she didn't know what they would ask in exchange.

Helen dumped her healing supplies back into the bag and emptied another one. She held up clothing against Gil and nodded, dropping it at his side. Next was a small dress, but she frowned as she compared it to Miknon. It was about the right height but much too broad. The woman sighed and handed it to Miknon anyway.

Cheerfully, Ian held up Miknon's almost-dry clothing and turned the air blower back on.

Nik said something, and Helen nodded. After turning off the air-blower, Ian joined them near the table. All the aliens crossed their arms and bowed their heads while the stonegazer talked for a minute. Then they passed food to each other, chattering and laughing.

"I told you they would torture us," Miknon whispered.

She and Gil turned away, mouths watering. At least starvation was nothing new. They had survived it before and could survive it again. Starvation was better than poison, which they would have to suspect if they were fed.

When they escaped these aliens, they could look for food. Somewhere. But how would they travel when their bones were still too fragile to support their weight, much less with Gil's broken leg?

CHAPTER 3

BREAKFAST

June 15, 2022, Topeka, Kansas

"They aren't getting dressed." Alexandria slouched in her chair. And she'd hunted all through the toy section to find a dress that might fit the fairy. Okay, so it didn't, but she had tried. The werewolf's clothes ought to fit, though. Did he not like the colors? Did human styles break some kind of taboo?

Did werewolves never wear clothes? Her ears grew hot. That would definitely not work on Earth.

On the king-size bed, the two aliens watched every move of sandwich to mouth like cats with mice.

"Maybe they need help," Mom said gently from the other chair. "Unfamiliar clothes, broken leg, and so forth. Or maybe they're still recovering from their showers."

She bent a mildly reproachful look at the two boys on the floor. Alexandria echoed the look more forcefully. What had they been thinking, to manhandle a werewolf? What if werewolves hated baths and he had changed back and ripped out their throats?

Nikos shrugged and tipped his head at Ian. Oh, nice; blame the thirteen-year-old. Technically, Nikos was an adult and ought to be more responsible. How had Ian convinced him that bathing a werewolf was a good idea?

Ian stuffed the rest of his sandwich into his mouth and mumbled, "They don't stink anymore."

Which was true, thank goodness. The reek had been awful. Ian reached up to the table and grabbed another sandwich.

The werewolf and the fairy flinched and turned to look at the wall. Gil's pointed ears actually folded down, and Alexandria stopped eating to stare. How flexible were they? She gave herself an internal smack. It didn't matter how much he could wiggle his ears! They had bigger problems.

"Well, if they won't get dressed yet, we might as well feed them," Alexandria said. "Otherwise we'll be waiting forever, and we still need to dump them at the hospital before we leave."

"We can't leave them behind," Ian protested.

"Ian," Mom said, "I don't know if we'll be allowed to take them away from the hospital, and Gil needs his broken leg treated."

Ian crossed his arms and started arguing. Alexandria sighed and put two sandwiches onto a paper plate. She cut one into small pieces for the fairy, then carried the plate across the hotel room.

"Here you go," she said.

The werewolf reached for a sandwich, but when the fairy touched his hand, he stopped. Neither alien looked at her, though the werewolf inhaled and swallowed hard.

Alexandria shrugged. "Okay, well, if you want it."

She put the sandwiches on the bed and returned to her own breakfast. When they'd left home yesterday, she'd bought cereal and milk for breakfast, but the aliens had eaten it all. This morning, it was simpler to buy extra sandwich fixings, since she didn't know if werewolves used spoons or if the fairy could even lift one.

Nikos filled two cups halfway with water and put them beside the plate. "Water," he said. "I'd give you a whole cup, but I'm afraid it would tip over on the bed."

The werewolf stuck a finger in the cup and said, "Cold."

"Was that coincidence?" Alexandria asked.

Ian beamed. "Nope. We've been teaching them words." He looked at the aliens and said, "Water. Drink water." He mimed drinking. "Food. Eat food." He mimed that, too. "Okay."

With a skeptical look, the werewolf picked up a sandwich. He muttered something to the fairy, then took a bite. After putting the rest of the sandwich back onto the plate, he licked his fingers and stared at the food as if it was a pot of gold.

The fairy watched him instead of the food.

Alexandria narrowed her eyes. "I think they're checking for poison. They think we'd poison them! They're the scary monsters, not us."

She stomped over and took a bite of the werewolf's sandwich, then grabbed a square of the fairy's and stuffed it into her mouth.

Once she could speak again, she said, "Okay, eat."

She threw herself back into the chair and bit her own sandwich. Just because she thought a pair of aliens might be perilous didn't mean she'd hurt them before they did anything. Good grief!

"Maybe they aren't sure if they can eat our food," Nikos suggested.

"They ate most of what we had during the night," she said. "If it didn't make them sick then, they'll be fine now."

On the bed, the werewolf shrugged and ate the sandwich. Obviously more reluctant, the fairy pulled apart her share and ate it one ingredient at a time. They drained their water cups and returned to watching the humans.

"Do you want more?" Ian asked. "More?" He mimed eating and drinking again. "Yes?" He held imaginary food and drink toward them. "No?" He shook his head and dropped the imaginary food.

"Yes," the werewolf said, eyes narrowed.

Nikos refilled the cups while Ian made two more sandwiches, which disappeared faster. Miknon accepted another cup of water but stopped eating, and Gil took another sandwich. While the boys took turns showering and dressing, Gil devoured six sandwiches and an apple before he said no to more, which was just as well since they were out of bread, meat, and cheese.

Great, they'd need another grocery stop today, as if they had enough time for that. The longer they spent on the road, the more hotels they'd have to pay for, and funds were already slim.

Mom checked her watch. "We need to pack and get going. We can drop them at the hospital on the way out."

"But he's my dog!" Ian wailed.

"No," Mom snapped, "he's a human being."

Alexandria raised an eyebrow, and Nikos chuckled.

Mom sighed. "Okay, not human, but still a person."

"Well, you still can't leave him in the middle of strangers," Ian protested.

"We *are* strangers," Alexandria argued.

Nikos rubbed his chin. "Do you still have the first contact protocol from Diplomacy Club?"

Their high school had started the club to deal with the excitement and panic caused by the odd behavior of the new asteroid discovered near Jupiter.

Ian chuckled. "I guess it was Alien Club after all."

On her way to her backpack, Alexandria thumped her brother on the head. "It was not."

Though now she had to wonder if NASA could see the spaceship on the moon and was hiding it from the public, or if the ship was simply too small for a good look. Either way, NASA had given no updates in the past month, and public interest had faded, based on dwindling comments online.

Still chuckling, Ian shrugged.

Alexandria found her notes. "Choose an ambassador and a linguist, because obviously they don't speak English; ask about greeting customs and forms of address; offer a tour of non-secret places; and ask about interests and goals."

She groaned. "What were we thinking? These are stupid plans. We aren't any kind of authority and can't do any tours or help with any goals. We can't ask or offer anything before we can speak to them. And none of this covers food, hygiene, clothing, or medical care. They're more like refugees than ambassadors."

She flopped back into the chair and stabbed at the list. Not just aliens, but injured monsters from legends. And last night, she'd thought Ian adopting a dog was the worst trouble they could have.

"Too much Hollywood," Nikos said. "We expected powerful beings, not, um, strays."

"If he's a stray, then I can keep him." Ian grinned from ear to ear.

Mom leaned down and bopped him on the nose. "Not. A. Dog."

"But seriously," Alexandria asked, "what should we do with them? If we tell the hospital they're aliens, they'll either believe us and lock them up, or not believe us and lock *us* up for being crazy."

"They'll believe us," Nikos said. "Miknon is too realistic to be a toy. Gil has blue eyes though his skin is as black as ink, and it's hard to tell with the tangles, but I think his hair is straight. Even without the claws and pointed ears, he can't pass as any normal human race."

Gil picked up the comb and started yanking it through his hair, without much success. Every time he grimaced, his too-sharp teeth flashed.

Alexandria rolled her eyes and leaned over to whisper in Ian's ear. "Still not your dog."

Gil tossed the comb onto the bed and yanked on his hair. He babbled something at Ian, slashing his hand across his tangled mess.

"He wants his hair cut," Ian guessed.

Alexandria dropped her pen onto the list. "The hospital will be almost impossible, but a broken leg is important. Why risk a barber seeing those ears just for a haircut?"

Her imagination provided the dramatic scene, followed by others. How could they possibly deal with two aliens? They weren't linguists or ambassadors or scientists, just three teenagers and their mother. All right, Mom was sort of a linguist, but she was trying to decipher Linear A, not Space Alienglish. Not that Alexandria wanted the aliens to be cut up by scientists, but there must be someone better equipped to take care of them.

They didn't have enough money to care for themselves, much less two strangers. Mom's job had paid for the divorce, barely, and they had less than two thousand dollars left from Alexandria's part-time job. It was supposed to pay for the trip *and* set them up in a new apartment, but it wouldn't last long if they kept having unexpected expenses. And even groceries would be a problem if the wolf ate that much every day. Nikos had some money, true, but he needed it for his college expenses. If he couldn't support himself, his student visa would be revoked.

Gil tugged on his hair again, his voice rising in complaint.

Hopping to his feet, Nikos dug through his pockets. "My pocket knife has tiny scissors, though the results won't be pretty." He unfolded the scissors and demonstrated how they worked on a paper plate, then touched the werewolf's hair. "Okay?"

"Okay."

"Um." Nikos ruffled his own black curls. "Short?" He pointed to Ian's floppy bangs. "Medium?" Pointing to Alexandria, he asked, "Long?"

Gil said, "Okay."

"Not helpful," Nikos muttered.

"Keep it a little longer to hide his ears," Alexandria suggested. "And don't worry about keeping it super neat with those tiny scissors; just cut where you can get through the tangles."

"Okay." Nikos sighed and approached his task seriously, attacking one lock of hair at a time and struggling through the knots with no attempt at style.

"Miknon want?" Ian asked.

"No!" Miknon covered her head with her arms.

Alexandria retrieved the comb from the bed and Miknon's clothes from by the hair dryer. "Okay?" She waved both items.

"Okay," Miknon said.

After stuffing the comb and clothing into her pockets, Alexandria held out her hands. With a highly suspicious look, Miknon climbed on, still wrapped in a hotel washcloth. Alexandria carried her to the bathroom and turned her back while the fairy dressed. Then she upended the hotel's ice bucket for a chair and set Miknon in front of the mirror.

She started at the bottom of Miknon's hair and gradually combed upward. Every time she hit a tangle, Miknon flinched, and Alexandria said, "Sorry."

Through the open door, she kept talking with her family. "Seriously, guys, what will we do with them? The hospital will want to know last names and social security numbers and what language they speak. And even if they're too distracted by the broken leg to notice their patient isn't human—"

"Ha," Nikos said.

"—who knows what will turn up in the x-rays."

"And if they notice their near-starvation," Mom said, "they might suspect us of torturing them."

"Oh, that's great," Alexandria said. "What the—"

"No swearing," Mom interrupted. "If the hospital tries to keep them prisoner, I guess we'll have to sneak them out. Alexandria can distract the bystanders, Nikos can carry Gil, Ian can open doors, and I'll try to head off any authorities."

Alexandria rolled her eyes. "We can't keep them." No way could they pull that off.

Nikos looked up from the last bit of hair-cutting and frowned. "If we don't get on the road pretty soon, we'll have to drive another day. And get another hotel room."

"Rooms," Mom corrected. "I realize this hotel was sold out, but next time we really need to get two rooms."

She'd been furious last night, though Nikos gave the king-size bed to the Fitches and slept on the floor in Ian's sleeping bag. And he'd been a perfect gentleman. He hadn't even snored, unlike Ian. But two rooms would use up their funds faster.

Nikos examined Gil's hair and shrugged. "I think that's it." He put away his pocketknife. "Not to be sexist, but if you ladies want to pack up the stuff in the bathroom, Ian and I will help Gil dress."

"Yes, please," Alexandria said. "He's been sitting around in that towel for long enough."

Mom joined her in the bathroom, brushing her teeth while Alexandria finished combing Miknon's hair. She braided a single plait down the fairy's back and fastened it with a tiny elastic.

"Sorry," she said. "That's the best I can do."

"Okay." Miknon patted her hand.

Alexandria smiled at her. At least the fairy wasn't fussing about a plainer hairstyle than what she had worn.

In the outer room, the boys yelled. Alexandria whirled, ready to use judo, werewolf or not. Mom crowded behind her, hairbrush in hand.

Ian and Nikos stood at opposite walls, as if they'd sprung backwards. A very large black dog — wolf — lay on the bed, head on the blanket and ears pressed to his head. He grinned a doggy grin and rolled his eyes at Ian.

Tiny hands pulled on Alexandria's shirt, and Miknon crawled up to her shoulder. She took one look and giggled.

"Sorry," she said. "Okay." She patted Alexandria's hair. "Gil okay."

"Um," Alexandria said. "I guess you don't have to dress him right now."

Ian straightened up. "I like him this way."

Mom, Alexandria, and Nikos chorused, "He's not your dog."

Ian stuck out his tongue and petted Gil's fur. The werewolf rubbed his head against Ian and licked his hand. Good grief, now Ian would really think he had a dog.

Mom helped Miknon use the toilet while Alexandria brushed her own teeth and hair. After that, they gave the boys a turn at the bathroom. Nikos rolled up the sleeping bag, and everyone packed their clothes. Mom emptied the tiny fridge back into the cooler, and Ian ran out for the food crate. Working together, they carried all the luggage and supplies to the truck in only one trip.

As Nikos picked up Gil again, Alexandria laughed.

"What's so funny?" Ian asked.

"We can take Gil to the vet now," she said, "instead of the hospital. At least there they won't ask for his last name, social security number, or language."

Nikos turned sideways to fit through the door with Gil. "But what will the x-rays show?"

Alexandria made a face and closed the door behind her. "Better hope his bones look like a dog's."

Because if the x-rays said "alien," her family would be lucky to escape without a ton of awkward questions.

The aliens would be lucky to escape at all.

CHAPTER 4

IN WHICH GIL VISITS A HEALER

GIL SQUINTED as the whole group exited the room into the blinding light outside. What kind of magic were they using to make so much light? And who was casting the spell? None of the aliens he was with seemed to be concentrating hard enough to be responsible. He tried searching for a mage in the area, but anything farther away than the length of a room in the spaceship was a blur.

Ian lowered the back of the wagon, which was brilliant blue, brighter than Miknon's wings. Nik slid Gil in, careful of his broken leg. Helen set Miknon beside him, and Alexandria added a pink bag with straps. She ran a flat rope through the straps and locked it in, then grabbed a little handle on the bag and pulled sideways, talking slowly. The bag tore open. She pulled the handle the other way, and the bag magically closed up again.

After repeating the actions several times, she opened the bag and indicated Miknon should get inside.

"No," Miknon said in the alien language.

"Wait a minute," Gil said. "I think this is a safety thing. She locked the bag to the wagon so it won't fall out. Look, the bag is made of cloth with lots of holes, so you can breathe through it and maybe see out, and she showed you how to open the bag again."

Miknon folded her arms.

"If they lock the bag, I'll cut you out," Gil promised.

"Fine." With a dirty look at Alexandria, Miknon climbed into the bag.

Alexandria slowly closed it most of the way, leaving a small gap. "Okay?"

Miknon stuck an arm through the gap and pushed the magic handle until the gap opened a little more. "Okay."

Nikos closed the end of the wagon, and the aliens climbed inside the belly of the magic beast. It rumbled to life and moved down the black road. Within moments, it was moving incredibly fast, and the air pushed against Gil's fur.

"I don't understand this world. Their magic is so different." He sighed. "I wish Grandsire was here to help me figure it out."

But Grandsire had died in an accident and would never see their new home. And Mother and his twin brother were still on the ship with the rest of the fae. He and Miknon were alone.

The wagon slowed, then stopped in front of another building. The aliens jumped out and gathered around the back of the wagon. Nik lifted out Gil, and Alexandria leaned close to the pink bag.

"Stae." She patted the wagon. "Stae, Miknon."

Then she closed the end of the wagon again. Nik headed toward the building, and Ian ran ahead to open the door.

"Don't let them take you away!" Miknon shouted. "What will they do to you?"

"If they come back without me," Gil called back, "go ahead and escape."

"That doesn't make me feel better!" his sister shrieked.

And then they were through the door. Helen smiled at an alien inside and chattered something while Nik sat on a bench and let Gil sprawl across his lap. Other aliens sat around the room, and most of them had animals with them. Small cats and dogs, or rodents, or birds.

One who sat alone responded to a call and rose to collect a sleeping cat from an alien emerging from a hallway.

Inhaling, Gil detected the scent of blood, with a tang that was probably some kind of medicine. Since the alien caressed the cat's fur lightly, he guessed they were in the office of a healer, not a torturer. So then, perhaps *his* aliens wanted to fix his leg. That would be nice.

Not long after, the alien who had brought out the cat motioned them down the hall. As Nik picked up Gil, the alien's eyes widened. Alexandria stepped close to Nik and chuckled, waving her hand, but her shoulders tensed. Around Gil, Nik's arms tightened a little. Ian and Helen also spoke, voices more strained than Alexandria's. Of course they were more afraid, not being a stonegazer like Alexandria, who was powerful enough to use her full name without fear. And yet they still defended Gil.

If only he could learn their language, they might be the allies he needed.

Something they said soothed the other alien, and he led them into a room with shiny surfaces and the pungent odor of many medicines. Nik gently settled Gil onto a cold table, and the healer gently prodded Gil's broken leg.

"Ow," Gil whined.

"Okay," the healer said, followed by a long string of babble. He brought out restraints and a muzzle and reached for Gil.

Ian jumped between them. "No," he said firmly.

"Yes," the healer said. "Babble babble babble."

"No." Ian hopped onto the table next to Gil. He lay on his back and put his arms over his head.

Alexandria said, "Stae."

Ian froze.

Alexandria said, "Okay," and Ian relaxed.

The two repeated the sequence, then Ian said, "Gil stae."

Gil rolled over to his back and put his hands over his head to match Ian.

Ian beamed and sat up. Gil rolled over, and Ian sighed. "No, Gil stae."

Returning to the lying position, Gil wiggled his ears.

Ian giggled. "Yes, Gil stae."

He hopped down from the table. The healer, eyebrows halfway up his forehead, arranged mysterious equipment for a few minutes. All five of the aliens left the room after a final "Stae."

Confused, Gil obeyed, though he hoped they hadn't left him behind. But they came back almost immediately.

"Okay, Gil." Ian rushed to the table.

Gil rolled over and licked his face, and Ian giggled again.

The healer shook his head. He lit up a picture of a bone and pointed to a spot, explaining something. Oh, it must be Gil's leg, and the healer had magically drawn the inside to show the injury! The healer kept talking, and Gil's aliens started frowning. Ian shook his head, and Helen kept repeating, "No."

The healer threw up his arms in frustration and made another suggestion in a voice full of sarcasm.

Helen nodded. "Okay."

The healer sighed explosively and reached for the restraints and muzzle again.

"No." Ian climbed onto the table and wrapped his arms around Gil. "Stae."

Since Gil couldn't roll over with Ian there, he assumed the boy merely meant him to hold still.

Alexandria stood next to them and closed Gil's mouth with two fingers. She leaned down and stared him straight in the eyes. "No." She pressed barely harder, and her eyes turned green.

Gil folded his ears in submission and lowered his gaze to avoid hers. He would hold still if she asked, as long as she didn't turn him into stone. Well, if she did, he supposed he would hold still then, too.

The healer shook his head but approached the table. After prodding at Gil's leg and staring at the magic picture, he tugged hard. Gil's bone snapped, and pain shot up to his hip. He whimpered, careful not to open his mouth or move, and Ian tightened his embrace. The healer made another adjustment, then let go of Gil's leg. Was that all? Where was the magic?

Gil rolled his eyes to look at Alexandria, who said, "Stae" again, so he held still. Arguing with stonegazers never went well.

The healer and Helen had another argument. Eventually, the healer wrapped two sticks to Gil's leg, one on either side. He muttered to himself the whole time, but he touched Gil gently. And still there was no magic.

Once he was finished, he pulled Helen to the far corner of the room and spoke softly but urgently to her. After only a moment, Helen's shoulders stiffened, and she motioned behind her back at the others.

Nik scooped up Gil, and Ian poked his head out the door before opening it all the way. They hurried down the hall, and when the alien at the front spoke to them, Alexandria smiled and chatted smoothly while the boys kept walking. Ian held the outside door open for Nik, then danced impatiently while Alexandria slowly backed up, still talking.

Once Alexandria was outside, she and Ian broke into a run. Even Nik walked faster. Alexandria lowered the back of the wagon and said something to Miknon while she waited for Nik. Quickly, they loaded Gil into the back and raised the end, then all three of them climbed into the belly. The magic rumble started, but the wagon didn't move.

"Are you well?" Miknon opened her bag a little more and stuck out her head to examine Gil.

"I'm fine," Gil said. "They were trying to fix my leg."

"Did it work?"

"I think it's straighter," he said. "They don't seem to be able to make it heal faster."

Unless they did but there was some hidden cost to it. Helen had certainly been arguing with the healer about something. He didn't tell Miknon it had hurt to straighten his leg. Of course it had, since his shifts had made it start healing already, crooked or not, but she would only worry they had hurt him on purpose.

In another minute, Helen emerged, nearly running. She jumped into the wagon, which promptly took off. Gil twisted his neck to watch the aliens inside. They waved their arms and talked excitedly, but their shoulders gradually relaxed.

The wagon drove for a while, then stopped at a building long enough for Helen to run in and return with a bag of something. Then they traveled again to a place with trees and green ground. The temperature was hotter than it had been during the sleep cycle, and Gil hung out his tongue to pant. Miknon wiped sweat from her forehead and flapped her skirt over her legs.

While Nik unloaded Gil and Ian grabbed the pink bag with Miknon, Alexandria pulled out the food and a bundle of cloth, and Helen brought the bag she had obtained. They walked to the closest table, and Nik put Gil on the ground with Miknon freed beside him.

The four aliens again assembled food, spreading brown and purple stuffs on the squishy slices. They gave Miknon two of the finished assemblies and laid an entire plateful in front of Gil. Tentatively, the siblings tasted the food. Surprisingly, it was not bad. Nutty and fruity, with the whiff of grains in the slices. Too sweet, but tolerable. Gil ate all of his and a quarter of Miknon's when she declared herself sated.

Once the food was gone, Nik carried Gil back to the wagon but opened the door to the belly and put him on a padded bench. Alexandria held Miknon while Ian approached Gil with the bundle of cloth. He unfolded it, revealing clothes much like he was wearing. He pointed to Gil, then the clothes, chattering the whole time, his forehead furrowed with effort and worry.

"I can't wear those like this." Gil hung out his tongue in amusement.

"Oh," Miknon said, "I bet that's why they fed us. They want you to shift back."

"What about my leg?" Gil twitched his splinted limb and wiggled his ears.

Slowly, Ian reached for the bandage. When Gil stayed still, he unwound it and removed the sticks.

"Hmm," Gil said. "I suppose the only way to find out their plan is to go along with it. After going to the trouble of fixing me, I don't suppose they're trying to hurt me now."

Miknon sighed. "One of these days, your trusting heart will get you in too much trouble."

Gil nodded at the aliens, and Ian beamed. Alexandria turned her back, and Gil took that as his cue to shift immediately. As soon as he was two-legged again, Ian pulled the short tunic over Gil's head. Then both boys helped him maneuver some sort of wide, white codpiece over his legs. After Gil pulled it up to where it belonged, they added loose, short hose like all the aliens wore.

"Okay," Nik said.

By then, Helen had finished cleaning up their meal site. While Alexandria held the sticks in place, Helen wrapped the bandage around everything. Then she put new magic sticky pads on his cut hand.

"See," Gil said to Miknon. "All fixed again."

Nik scooted Gil until he was sitting properly on the bench, then pulled out a strap connected to the side of the wagon. He stretched it over Gil while talking, then released it slowly. Ian climbed in the other door to sit next to Gil. He grabbed another strap and pulled it across himself, pushing down to somehow fasten it. After jerking forward into the strap, which somehow stopped him, he released it, then pulled it back and fastened it again.

"Oh," Gil said, "I think it's a safety harness." He nodded at Nik. "Okay."

"Okay." Nik started to pull out the harness again.

Gil stopped him. "What about Miknon?" How would they keep his sister safe?

Alexandria tapped on Nik's back, and they traded places. While Miknon sat on Gil's lap, the alien girl slipped Gil's arms through the pink bag until it rode on his chest. Then she opened the bag and set Miknon inside. After closing the bag most of the way, she threaded the safety harness through the bag straps and across his chest, and passed it to Ian to fasten on the other side.

"Are you okay?" Gil asked Miknon, peeking through the opening into the bag.

His sister nodded, but she clutched the pocket inside the bag as a lifeline.

Gently, Alexandria touched Gil's leg, testing how it hung to the floor. Apparently satisfied, she closed the door of the wagon. Helen took the last seat in the back, and Nik and Alexandria claimed the front.

Gil took a deep breath and tried to relax. The bright light stabbed at his eyes through the window until he had to cover them with his free hand.

From the front bench, Nik said something. Ian leaned forward, bumping Gil's arm, then sat back again.

"Heer." Ian tapped Gil.

Reluctantly, Gil opened his eyes enough to see what the boy wanted. Ian slipped something over Gil's face, settling it on his nose. The light suddenly dimmed, and Gil panicked again, flailing at his face.

Ian removed the thing and put it on his own face, pulling it on and off several times. "Okay?"

Gil surrendered. "Okay?"

Once the thing was back on his face, he realized it did nothing but shield his eyes from the bright light. It didn't even fasten in any way except balance.

Yet again, it seemed the aliens were only trying to help.

Did he have a hope of building an alliance with them, or would food and clothing be the limit of their care?

CHAPTER 5

SHOPPING

"THAT WAS COOL!" Ian bounced on the truck seat, then checked to make sure he hadn't scared Gil. But the alien was leaning against the truck door, either sleeping or looking out the window. With Nikos's sunglasses on, it was hard to tell.

"Cool?" Alexandria scowled at him from the front seat. "Which part? Trying to convince the vet we aren't torturing our new dog just because we don't want surgery or a cast? Or waiting to see if a werewolf bit off your face — or the vet's — or setting a bone without anesthetic because we don't know what drugs would do to an alien?"

"No," Ian said, "watching Gil change shapes, and the escape part. I don't know why the vet thought he had to keep him."

"He was only doing his job," Mom said. "If you had picked up a real wild wolf without knowing—"

"Instead of a werewolf," Alexandria muttered.

"—I'd definitely want to know about it," Mom continued. "Apparently, wolf hybrids are legal in Kansas, so he won't turn us in. He wanted me to be aware we didn't have the German shepherd we claimed, especially with the fragile bones the x-ray showed. But you all did a great job coordinating our exit. Very smooth."

"Well, he's still my dog." Ian folded his arms.

Mom sighed. "Stop calling him your dog. Please. He's neither yours nor a dog."

"Okay, he's my friend." The first friend he'd had since they moved to Colorado from Hawaii a year ago, and he was keeping him. Nikos didn't count, because he was a brother. "Are we heading out now? I thought we're in a hurry?"

Alexandria and Nikos exchanged glances with Mom, but Nikos didn't start the truck.

Mom cleared her throat. "It's time to discuss what to do next."

"Go to Pennsylvania," Ian said. "Nikos still has to sign up for classes and buy books and everything, right?"

School didn't start for another month or so, but the distraction was worth a try.

"I meant what we're doing with Gil and Miknon," Mom said. "With him in human form and dressed, we can drop them at a shelter or police station instead of the animal shelter."

"Please," Ian begged. "We should keep them. We don't need a hospital anymore, and turning them in to the police is cruel. We certainly can't kick them out and hope they survive. Gil's leg is still broken, and they only know a few words of English."

"Yes," Alexandria said. "How exactly are we supposed to deal with any of that? And if their bones are that fragile, we can't put Gil on crutches or he'll break his arms."

"We can feed them," Ian said. "We can dress them. Nikos can carry Gil until his leg heals."

In the rearview mirror, Nikos raised his eyebrows at Ian. Ian twitched his shoulders in a subtle shrug.

"I can teach them English," Ian promised. "And maybe learn their language. You know I'm good with that stuff."

And language skills were useful, no matter what Dad thought. Dad wasn't around anymore, thank goodness, or he'd probably want to blow up Gil and Miknon.

"What about the government?" Alexandria asked. "They must have immigration people or somebody who could deal with this."

"Immigration?" Nikos laughed. He sobered almost instantly. "Should we be asking if we *can* take care of them or if we *should*?"

Mom sighed. "Maybe the movies are wrong, but I still don't trust the government not to make them disappear, especially if they're the only two who landed on Earth." She looked out the window as if she could spot other aliens arriving. "I guess we'll keep them on a trial basis. Until we can solve the problems of caring for them, or until we think of a better idea."

"Mom, are you crazy?" Alexandria said.

Mom leveled a gaze at her. "Do you really want someone like your father dealing with them?"

"Heh, he'd shoot — Oh. Fine." Alexandria slumped in the seat. "For now, until we come up with a better idea."

"Yay," Ian said. "I can keep my—" He clamped his lips together, eyes wide. If he called Gil his dog again, Mom would probably change her mind. After clearing his throat, he finished. "My new friend."

Alexandria pulled out her notebook and clicked her pen. "More groceries. More clothes," she growled.

Ian pumped his fist.

Alexandria glared at him, eyes a worried green. "This doesn't mean we're keeping them forever, Ian."

Pretending a confidence he didn't feel, Ian smiled at his sister. "We'll figure it out."

"How will we even take them out in public?" Mom asked.

"Covid mask," Alexandria muttered. "I think I have one in my cedar chest." She read over her list silently. "Nikos, pull up the closest thrift store on your GPS."

After finding directions, Nik started the truck. Suddenly alert, Gil clutched at his seat belt.

Ian patted his knee. "It's okay. The truck won't hurt you."

He nodded at Nikos, who pulled away from the park and followed the directions on his phone.

Mom rubbed her head. "I don't know if we can do this."

"Of course we can," Ian said. "I bet Alexandria has a plan already." She always had a plan for everything.

His sister waved her notebook. "We're in a hurry, so we'll have to split up at the thrift store. Nikos will carry Gil. Mom, you look for a wheelchair or crutches, and a walking cast or splints or whatever you can find to deal with the leg. Ian and I will look for clothes."

Ian pursed his lips. "I'll go to the toy section for Miknon."

"Okay, good idea." Alexandria made a note.

A few minutes later, Nikos parked at the thrift store.

Ian dashed in without waiting for anyone else, shouting, "Don't bump his leg," over his shoulder.

He waved at the store clerk and headed straight for the children's book section. He would look for doll clothes, but he had another mission first. He had to prove he could handle the language issues, or Mom would eventually decide they had to turn the aliens over to somebody else.

Scanning the shelves as quickly as possible, he pulled every book that looked remotely helpful.

How much time did he have left? He poked his head into the aisle. Alexandria was still showing clothes to Gil. Ian separated the books by category, then compared them. Some were much too text-heavy. One of the picture dictionaries was alphabetical and wordy, but the other was mostly pictures and sorted by category. Perfect! No way Alexandria would let him buy all the books, so what would be most helpful? He grabbed two more, then backtracked for a box of crayons.

After checking on his family again, he raced to the toy section and hunted through the doll clothes for any shirt close to Miknon's size that might leave space for the fairy's wings. And two of the skirts might fit.

"Ian," Alexandria called.

"Coming!" He piled his loot in his arms and dashed for the checkout counter.

As the clerk rang up clothing, Nikos and Mom helped Gil, now in a wheelchair, don a medical boot. Ian dumped the books and stuff onto the counter, then stared at the clothing pile.

"Skirts?" He frowned at his sister. "I thought we were shopping for Gil."

She shrugged dramatically. "He wants skirts. And since they'll be easier to wear with his broken leg, we're going along with it." She scowled at Ian. "Right?"

"Right, right." He poked through the rest of it. Few of the bright colors coordinated with each other, but that wasn't important. Oh, good, sunglasses so Nikos could have his back, and a duffle bag, and two water bottles.

"Swim trunks?" he asked. "Can he swim with a broken leg?"

"Not yet," Nikos said, "but when he can, it's good physical therapy."

Ian grinned. Yep, Nikos was on his side, for whatever reason. Probably not because he wanted a dog, but it didn't matter.

The clerk bagged the last of the items, and Mom paid with only a slight wince. Ian grabbed the wheelchair handles and pushed Gil for the door while the other three took the bags. Once back at the truck, Nikos seated Gil with Miknon's bag on his lap, then tossed the wheelchair into the truck bed. Using the tailgate as a table, Alexandria and Mom folded the clothes and stuffed them into the duffle bag. The sunglasses and water bottles went to the werewolf, and Nikos took back his glasses.

Alexandria held up the books. "I must have been helping with Gil's boot when these were rung up. Ian, I thought we were only getting stuff for the aliens."

"Yeah," Ian said, "I thought it would help with language skills. I mean, think how much easier everything would be if we could actually talk to them."

He grabbed the books and cradled them to his chest. His plan depended on being able to communicate as quickly as possible.

"You mean like ask them what they're doing here and if anyone else is coming?" Alexandria's voice was very dry.

"Sure," he said, "soon, when we have enough vocabulary."

It probably wouldn't be "soon," but no way would he admit that. If his family thought this would be fast, they'd be more likely to give him a chance to exchange languages. And he could do it, he knew he could, if he had enough time.

His sister rubbed her forehead. "Then what's your plan, and can we discuss it while we drive? We need to get out of here."

Ian climbed into the truck and waited for everyone to join him. "I thought we could try to find common ground first." He opened the mythology book onto Gil's lap and turned to a story about werewolves. "Hey, Gil, is this like you?"

Gingerly, Gil turned the pages, squinting at the pictures. He looked at Ian, pointed to an image of a ravening werewolf in mid-change, and said something with a disgusted face. Miknon poked her head from the pink backpack and flinched at the picture. She and Gil talked for several minutes, then he covered the image with his hand.

"No," he said. "No Gil."

Ian shrugged. "Okay, no Gil. I have to admit I'm glad to hear that, though I don't know what he really is." He turned to a fairy picture. "Miknon?"

Gil laughed and held up the book so Miknon could see better, rattling off a long string of words. She snorted and dropped down into the backpack. Still chuckling, Gil slowly turned more pages, looking at all the pictures. In a while, he bumped Ian's elbow and pointed to a page.

"Alexandria?" Gil asked.

Ian turned the book for a better look and burst out laughing.

"What?" Alexandria asked. "I can't possibly be in that book."

Ian showed her the picture of a snake-haired woman staring at a statue. "He thinks you're a gorgon!"

Nikos chuckled.

Alexandria slugged his shoulder. "I do not have snakes for hair! Stupid boys!"

"Don't hit the driver," Nikos said, humor still lacing his voice.

Alexandria leaned backward and swiped at the book. "Give me that!"

Her hazel eyes turned green in her usual warning sign. Gil yelped and pointed at Alexandria, then stabbed the picture.

"Oh!" Ian said. "I get it. It's your eyes, Alexandria. When they turn green, he thinks it's magic."

His sister narrowed her eyes. "I have hazel eyes, twerp."

Ian nodded. "Yep, except when they turn green."

"They do not!" Alexandria protested.

"Yes, they do," Mom said.

Nikos nodded. "They're green when you're angry. Or afraid."

"Are not," she said.

Ian laughed. "Are so, and Gil thinks that makes you a gorgon."

"Gorgon," Gil repeated, pointing at Alexandria.

"No." Alexandria clamped her lips together and faced front, arms folded. "Crazy boys."

Nikos cleared his throat and pushed his sunglasses farther up his nose. Ian smothered his chuckles and gave the book back to Gil. He could start randomly teaching vocabulary, but Gil would remember better if the words were of interest to him.

For the next hour and a half, Gil worked through the mythology book, looking at the pictures at least twice. Most of them seemed to amuse him, though some made him frown. Finally, he turned to a page showing a wizard waving sparkles through the air. He nudged Ian and pointed to the sparkles, asking something.

"Magic?" Ian guessed at what word the alien wanted.

"Majik," Gil repeated. He lowered his voice and pointed discreetly to Alexandria. "Majik?"

Ian chuckled and shook his head. "No magic," he whispered.

He pulled out his notebook and the crayons from the thrift shop. Drawing two faces, he colored one set of eyes light brown and one green.

He pointed to the brown eyes with a smile beneath them and said, "Alexandria happy." He pointed to the green eyes and the frown and said, "Alexandria angry. No magic."

Gil tapped the sparkles again. "Magic?"

"Magic," Ian confirmed. "Alexandria no magic."

"Hmph." Gil pointed to everyone else in the truck, one at a time. "Magic, magic, magic?"

"No magic," Ian insisted. He opened the science book and found a picture of Earth. "Earth. No magic on Earth."

Squinting, Gil watched Ian for a long minute, disbelief clearly written on his face.

Oh, boy. How to explain stories? Ian turned to the werewolf story that Gil hadn't liked and tapped the picture. "No Gil?"

"No Gil," the werewolf confirmed.

"Pretend. Story." Ian turned to the fairy. "No Miknon?"

"No Miknon."

"Pretend. Story."

Ian turned to the gorgon. "No Alexandria. Pretend. Story." He turned to the wizard picture and laid it next to the science book. "No magic on Earth." He put a hand on the wizard. "Pretend. Story." He touched the picture of Earth, then waved to the scenery going by the truck. "Real Earth." He waved at Gil. "Real Gil." He pointed to Alexandria. "Real Alexandria." He touched the wizard again. "No real. Pretend. Story."

"Hmm," Gil said.

"Ian, do you really think this will work?" Alexandria asked. "Your language books assume you're starting with some language in common. You've got nothing to work with here."

"It's worth a try." Ian sat up straight and tried to look competent. "I can do this, really I can."

"I guess," Alexandria said. "I still think professionals would do better."

"Do you know of any professionals who speak werewolf?" Ian asked tartly.

"No," his sister said, "but I'm sure they have more practice in translating."

But then he'd have to give up his new friend. Not a chance.

"Is it lunchtime yet?" Ian asked.

She raised an eyebrow to mark the change in subject but checked the clock anyway. "We're out of bread again. Let's find a grocery store."

She grabbed Nikos's phone and tapped at the GPS for a minute. At the next exit, they pulled into Odessa, Missouri and parked. As soon as they opened the doors, the ninety-degree heat swept inside the truck. Almost immediately, Gil started panting.

"I'll get the wheelchair," Alexandria said, "while Nikos handles Gil. It's too hot to leave Miknon in the car, so make sure the backpack is zipped, okay, Ian?"

"Yes, boss." Ian stuck out his tongue.

She aimed a fake blow at his head, which he didn't bother to duck. Air rustled his hair, but she didn't even touch him. As he expected. His sister might be scary, but she wasn't mean.

All the humans hopped out of the car. After handing Gil his Covid mask, Ian made sure Miknon was secure in the mesh backpack and completely out of sight. Alexandria and Nikos settled Gil in the wheelchair and put the mask on him, then she turned back to the car.

"Ian, you ready?" she asked.

"Yeah," he said, "the zipper got stuck. Hang on."

Alexandria reached into the truck just as he fixed the zipper.

A scream split the air. Everyone jerked around. In the parking lot, a woman stood by her car, keys dangling from her hand and eyes wide. She was pointing at... Ian followed her finger.

Gil! The woman was pointing at Gil, who sat in his wheelchair, hair tucked behind his pointed ears, smiling at the lady with his sharp teeth showing. He panted, tongue hanging out, and his ears twitched, and the lady screamed again. Miknon forced the zipper open and threw herself out of the truck toward her brother, flapping hard but only slowing her fall.

The lady screamed louder. Other shoppers on their way to or from their cars pulled out their phones and pointed them toward the drama.

"Back in the car," Mom ordered. "Now."

Nikos picked up Gil while Ian lunged for Miknon. Mom hopped into the driver's seat, and Alexandria tossed the wheelchair into the truck bed. Nikos dropped Gil into the back seat and tossed the keys to Mom as he climbed in. Ian finally got his hands around Miknon and dashed for the other side of the truck. Alexandria boosted him into the back seat at double-speed and slammed the door behind him. As soon as she climbed into the front and closed the door, Mom stepped on the gas, and they squealed out of the parking lot, seatbelts still unbuckled.

"What the—" Alexandria started.

"No swearing," Mom said wearily. "Everyone buckle, please."

With Alexandria's help, she got her own belt fastened before they reached the freeway.

"Why wasn't he wearing his mask?" Alexandria hissed.

"He was," Nikos protested. "He must have taken it off because of the heat, I guess."

The backpack on Ian's lap punched him, and he unzipped the top so Miknon could see.

"If everyone will freak out at the mere sight of Gil," he asked, "how will we go shopping?"

Mom sighed. "We'll have to wait until we can leave them in a hotel room or our apartment. Or in the truck in cooler weather, with one of us to watch them."

"What about lunch?" Alexandria asked.

"I'll treat everyone to hamburgers," Nikos said. "We can do the drive-through and never get out."

"Thanks. That will make things easier." She peered into the back seat, biting her lip.

"What?" Ian asked. "Hamburgers will work."

"Yeah," Alexandria said, "but were those people in the parking lot calling 911 on their phones or taking pictures?"

Ian looked behind them, though the grocery store was completely out of sight. If photos of the aliens got out, would he still get to keep them?

CHAPTER 6

IN WHICH THEY LEARN SOME WORDS

DAY 2 AFTER LANDING, KI

MIKNON CLIMBED from the pink bag and struggled to Gil's lap. "What happened out there? I couldn't see why people were screaming."

Gil shrugged. "I don't know."

"Did the aliens do something?" she asked.

"No." He ran his fingers through his hair and twitched.

Miknon squinted at him. "What did you do?"

"Nothing. I smiled at her." His ears flattened. "Really. Will everyone scream when they see me?"

Using the shirt for leverage, Miknon climbed to his shoulder and anchored herself with a grip on his necklace. "She screamed at me, too."

Gil sighed, and Miknon leaned against his neck.

"I thought this would be easier," Gil said. "Fly down, talk to the natives, make a treaty to let us settle here. Simple."

Miknon patted his cheek and said nothing. They hadn't been imprisoned, or tortured, or killed, so they had already done better than *she* expected.

Soon, the magic wagon stopped again. Nikos talked to a building, then moved to a window where he collected a small bag that smelled delicious. After the aliens bowed their heads for a short magic spell, perhaps to make the food safe, Alexandria passed a wrapped package to everyone and two to Gil. Ian showed them how to unwrap and eat the food. Three boxes of some kind of food strips were shared out, and the water went into the new jugs for Miknon and Gil, since the Ki natives already had full jugs.

Once he'd eaten one of the food stacks, Gil paused and held up the other. "What is this called?"

"Hamburger," Ian said.

"Hambooger," Gil repeated.

Ian snickered, and Alexandria groaned. Ian didn't usually laugh at Gil's attempts, so Miknon wondered what terrible thing he had accidentally said.

"Hamburrrger," Ian emphasized.

He and Gil practiced a few times until the pronunciation was good enough, then Gil asked, "What is this made of?"

Ian thought for a minute, then held his fingers by his ears like horns and mooed.

"A cowman? We're eating a cowman?" Miknon gagged.

Gil stopped chewing and stared at Ian in horror. When Gil's face turned green, Ian grabbed his food and shoved the bag under his chin. Gil spit out his mouthful, then clutched his stomach.

Miknon tried to keep her own nausea under control. "Ask him if that's what he means."

The natives chattered in distress, and Nikos rolled down the window.

Gil grabbed the painted slate with pictures of fae and frantically flipped pages. He stopped on a picture of a cowman. "Moo?"

"Yes," Ian said, then his eyes grew wide. "No! No no no no no." He grabbed his backpack at his feet and hunted for a different painted slate, which he slid onto Gil's lap. These images showed fruits and vegetables.

"Food. Eat, yes." He revealed the cowman. "No food!"

Helen groaned and asked a question. Ian nodded, took a deep breath, and talked more to his family. Glancing from one to the other, Miknon wished she could understand.

Alexandria cringed, her face twisting in disgust. "Ew."

Slipping the fae slate away, Ian left the other with Gil. "Food," he repeated, tapping the pictures. He turned to a page of farm animals and pointed to the cow. "Moo. Cow. Hamburger."

Miknon and Gil examined the images carefully.

"Do they eat animals?" Miknon asked.

Gil swallowed hard. "I have to say yes."

"Do they eat intelligent animals?" Miknon's voice squeaked. "What about kelpies and gryphons and unicorns?"

"How am I supposed to know?" Gil turned back to the pictures of fruits and vegetables and tapped the book. "Eat, yes."

"Food," Ian agreed, then had a short conversation with his family that ended in a lot of sighs and grimaces.

Was it such a trouble to eat plants, then? If only they could talk properly, they could figure out the problem.

Starting at the beginning of the book, Gil and Miknon looked at every picture, trying to learn more about the new world before they got into trouble again. Ian left them alone except for hygiene stops when the wagon controllers switched seats.

Both she and Gil fell asleep, waking when Ian shook them. They got out at another green space, and the natives made more food, showing Gil and Miknon the tomatoes before cutting them to put between the now-familiar grain slices. The weather had cooled to very warm instead of boiling, and everyone lingered in the pleasant breeze.

Helen and the others glanced at their wrists or magic boxes and held a discussion with worried faces. Soon, they reached some kind of agreement and packed up the leftover food. Helen discreetly rubbed her hips and stretched her back, signaling a return to travel.

They reloaded the truck, and Gil and Miknon promptly went back to sleep. The next time they woke, the sky was dark and the wagon was parking in front of a large building. Nikos lifted Gil out, and Alexandria took Miknon. Then they headed for different doors.

"No," Miknon yelled, fighting to fly to Gil. "Don't take him away!" She twisted Alexandria's fingers and tried to bite her.

"Stop it, Miknon," Gil said. "I'm sure we're fine. The light magic turned off, so I think they want to sleep."

"But why are they separating us?" she wailed.

"I don't know," he said, "but we'll be fine. Miknon, stop it. We need to not antagonize our new friends, so stop biting Alexandria."

Miknon folded her arms. "Why doesn't anyone worry about antagonizing me?"

She glared at Alexandria but let the girl carry her off. Once in the room, she curled up on a pillow in the chair and frowned at the alien women until she fell asleep.

The sound of people moving and softly talking woke Miknon. Light once again came through the window. Helen and Alexandria scurried around, dressing and brushing their hair and putting stuff back into bags. When they noticed her awake, they smiled and offered her a new dress. Miknon glanced at the one she was already wearing. Was something wrong with it?

"No?" she said.

Alexandria shrugged and threw the dress into a bag. "Okay, lesgo."

She held out Miknon's pink carry bag while Helen grabbed the others. They hadn't harmed her yet, but if they didn't take her to Gil, she'd go back to biting. She hopped into the bag and let the alien carry her outside. To her relief, Gil was already there, waiting in the magic wagon. Nik and Alexandria threw the bags in the back and tied down the cover while Ian fastened the safety harness for Miknon and her brother. Helen climbed in the front and started the magic. As soon as the others fastened their harnesses, Helen turned the wheel, and the wagon started moving.

To Miknon's surprise, she found herself thinking of the aliens by name, despite the custom of avoiding names even in thought, lest a thought mage catch her at it. Was she so sure these aliens had no mind-touching? Or was she foolishly trusting them already? Gil's optimism must be infecting her.

Alexandria touched a dial, and music suddenly filled the compartment. They were casting a spell on her and Gil! She should never have trusted them.

Miknon yelled at the top of her voice. "Get us out of here!"

She stuck her arms through the opening of the bag and forced the magic fastener open. Gil yelled and scrabbled at the door. The safety harness held him in place, and when he found the handle, pulling on it didn't open the door. Once free, Miknon awkwardly flew to the window and pounded on the glass.

And then the music stopped. So did the wagon. Miknon stopped flapping and settled on Gil's lap. The aliens were all staring at them with various expressions of astonishment.

"Sorry," Alexandria said. "Okay?"

Was Miknon okay? She and Gil exchanged glances while they took inventory of themselves.

"I don't feel any different," Miknon said. "Was it not magic after all?"

Gil shook his head. "Neither do I. If they had been trying to enchant us, they wouldn't have turned it off, surely." Breathing hard, he settled back on the bench. "Okay."

With another look backwards, Helen started the wagon again. Alexandria didn't touch the music dial, and Miknon climbed back inside the bag held by the safety harness. Gil stuck a hand inside with her, and Miknon held on to him.

Helen said something, and most of them closed their eyes and bowed their heads while Ian talked for a minute. Once they opened their eyes, Nik passed food around. This time it was circular things, cut thinner for Miknon, and curved fruit that Ian showed how to peel. The fruit was creamy, and the rings were chewy and a little spiced, and both were delicious.

Without comment, the boys kept passing more of everything. They didn't care how much the siblings ate? Food wasn't rationed here? Or perhaps they were tallying the total for payment later. Could they trust these aliens or not? It was the most important question at the moment, and Miknon yearned for the answer.

Once finished, everyone cleaned their hands on a damp cloth. Ian pulled out his painted slates again. He chose one and opened it on Gil's lap, then opened Miknon's bag and folded down the front flap so she could also see.

The young alien turned to pictures of food. "Food, eat."

Miknon and Gil nodded. After the disaster with the cow, they remembered those.

Ian named fruits and vegetables, pointing to each picture as he went. Some of them were familiar, some not, but Miknon and Gil tried to memorize as many as they could.

"Plum." Ian pointed to a round purple fruit.

Miknon snickered. "Look, Gil, they have plums here."

"Lovely." Gil sighed. He hated plums and always slipped them to Miknon when he could.

"It is lovely," she repeated. "You know they're good for your bones."

Ian had been watching them talk, and now he tapped the picture again. "Plum. Plum yes? Plum no?"

"Yes," Miknon said at the same time Gil said, "No."

She poked her brother until he said, "Yes. Plum yes." But he grimaced as he said it.

"Yoodohntlykeplums?" Ian tried again. "Gil no eat plum?" He copied Gil's face. "Miknon eat plum?" He smiled and rubbed his belly.

"Yes," Miknon said. "But plums are good for both of us." She pointed to Gil and emphasized, "Plum *yes*." Plums would help their bones grow stronger.

Ian said something to Alexandria, who wrote on her empty slate. They returned to the vocabulary lesson, and after going over the produce words several times, they tried words for other foods. Since Gil and Miknon didn't recognize most of those images, the attempt was frustrating. What was the difference between the "doenut" in the picture and the "baygil" they ate earlier?

When they stopped for Helen to trade places with Alexandria, the aliens passed around a snack of "cheaz," which was delicious but mysterious. According to Ian, it had something to do with the creamy liquid Gil and Miknon had stolen the night they landed, though how the two were connected was unclear.

The vocabulary lessons moved to people, using the pictures and the aliens for definitions. Gil had been right about the gender of their new neighbors, despite the uniformity of their clothing.

With the help of the images, Ian explained the natives were called humans. He was a child, Helen was an adult, and Nik and Alexandria were in between.

Ian ran his finger from child to adult pictures and asked, "Gil? Miknon?"

Miknon and Gil both pointed to Alexandria and Nik. They were considered children themselves, but Ian seemed younger than anyone on their ship, so "teanayj" was their best guess, whatever that meant. Almost-adult, hopefully. Without knowing mutual numbers or units of time, it was the best they could do for now.

Then they moved to more people words, and it took Miknon and Gil a few minutes to figure out Ian was now talking about relationships and families. Helen was indeed Ian's mother, and also Alexandria's, who must look like her father. Helen also claimed Nik with an amused twist to her lips.

Gil leaned forward and smelled Helen, then sideways to Nik. "No," he said. "No mother."

Nik's eyebrows rose. "You smell family?" He sniffed to demonstrate.

"Yes." Gil waved between Helen and Nik. "No family."

Ian wrinkled his nose and blew out his cheeks. "Yes, family," he insisted.

Nik tilted his head sideways and furrowed his brow. He finally shrugged.

"Okay." Alexandria pulled out her slate and drew two families. One had one parent and two children, and the other had parents with only one child. Pointing to the first, she said, "Helen, Ian, Alexandria." She pointed to the others. "Nik, Mom, and Dad." She carefully ripped off the picture of Nik and moved his parents to the ledge at the front of the wagon. "Nik family far." She shaded her eyes and pretended to look far away then moved Nik's image next to theirs. "Helen uhdoptud Nik. Family."

"Oh." Miknon pointed to herself. "Uhdoptud." She patted Gil's hand. "Brother."

"Oh!" the aliens chorused, nodding and smiling.

"What?" Gil asked.

"They mean Nik is adopted, like I am," she said. "Except I think his parents are too far away, not dead like mine and your sire."

Gil's mother had taken in Miknon during the exodus from their old world. Miknon barely remembered her parents. Recently, they had found out their dead parents had been murdered, not killed in an accident like they had always thought. She wanted to find the murderers, but her quest had been interrupted when they fled the ship.

It was her fault. If she hadn't been caught spying, they could have stayed to continue the search.

Gil nodded. "That explains the scent difference."

After leaving the new pictures in the slate with the family words, he turned the page to the animals and asked Ian for the names. Miknon tried to remember them all, but the words swam into nonsense in her brain.

Eventually, the magic wagon stopped at another of the green spots for a hygiene break. This time, the aliens pulled out food and made a stack of "sandwich" for everyone. Despite the clouds, the air was hot, and sweat dampened Miknon's dress. She had never been so hot unless she was too close to a phoenix, but the aliens didn't seem to notice.

Nik took control of the wagon, and they were off again. Miknon watched carefully, but she couldn't tell how he started the magic besides turning a key and pushing a lever. The movement control seemed easier, just turning the wheel at the front. So far, all the aliens had taken turns except Ian. The magic must be too powerful for a child, but she was a little surprised the not-quite-adults were allowed to use it.

While they traveled, Ian and Gil discussed colors and feelings and ways to describe things. Miknon gave up and took a nap in the shady bottom of her bag. Gil could practice with her later.

She woke when the wagon stopped for another break. This time they were among many buildings, and Helen fed the magic beast inside the wagon while Alexandria snuck Miknon into one hygiene room and Nik carried Gil into another.

Once back on the road with Helen guiding the wagon, Gil pulled out the slate with magic and fae in it and started trading words with Ian again. How could he keep all those new words in his head? She let them drift around her without paying attention. What good was she on this world? She couldn't remember the language, she couldn't fly, and they didn't dare let her be seen. Useless. If she had died on the ship, at least Gil would still be with their family.

Out the window, the bright world flashed past. They must have left the dark side at some point, because she could see the sun shining much too brightly, even with a cloudy sky. The sun, not magic. Of course, Gil had thought they were landing near the edge between the dark side and the bright, so perhaps Miknon shouldn't be surprised they had already crossed the border.

But where were they going, and why was it taking so long? Maybe being here wasn't any safer than staying on the ship where the lords had tried to kill her for spying on them. Escaping to Ki had been Gil's idea to save her life, but here, people screamed at the mere sight of her and her brother.

And still Gil chatted with Ian as if they weren't in danger. As if the alien was nothing but another of Gil's endless parade of friends. He had more friends than anyone she knew, even among the highborn. The prince was one of his friends, somehow, as were the king's secretary — the other Nik — and the king's housekeeper, who ran everything on the ship together. But just because they had a name in common was no reason to trust this Nik. Gil trusted everyone until it was too late. If he had listened to her fears, she wouldn't have been on the last spying mission where she got caught.

Gil chuckled, and Ian giggled. Enough already! They had been talking about nothing important for hours. Miknon leaned out of her bag to obstruct her brother's view of the pictures.

"Stop playing around," Miknon told Gil. "We need to learn words that will actually help us."

Gil sighed and closed the slates. No, Ian had said it was called a "buke." Remembering the new words was hard, and Miknon already had a headache. Why did her brother think this was fun?

"What words do you want to know?" Gil asked.

Miknon threw her arms wide in frustration. "How about asking for sanctuary or finding out what they plan to do with us? Tell them where we come from. Tell them more of our people are on the way, and not all of them are friendly. You told the prince you wanted to come with me to make an alliance, remember?"

Gil raised his eyebrows. "You don't ask for much, do you?" He turned to Ian. "Buke?" He returned the one on his lap and held out his empty hands. "Buke?"

Ian offered both of the others, and Gil opened the one with a picture of the world on the front. He searched until he found an image of Ki and its neighbors.

Miknon peered over his shoulder. Oddly, the aliens had eight worlds in their picture, not seven, including the too-small worldlet next to the sun as if it were a proper world.

Gil touched the blue and brown world. "Ki."

"Urth," Ian corrected.

Retrieving the Ian-Alexandria-Helen image from the other book, Gil laid it over the world picture. "Urth?"

"Yes, Urth. Ian home." Ian turned to a new image of just the world and the rocky worldlet rotating around it. He touched the little neighbor and said, "Mune." Then he extended his hand toward Gil and Miknon and raised his eyebrows.

"We don't have any pictures of Kunisu or the ships," Miknon said.

Gil held out his hand. "Red, green, blue, brown."

Ian looked confused, but Nik dug through a bag and passed Gil the coloring sticks and the blank book.

Gil drew seven worlds around a red sun. He pointed to the middle world and said, "Kunisu. Home." Then he drew the ship that had carried them between the constellations. "*New Kunisu.*" Ripping out the ship image, he laid it on the picture of the "mune," then pushed it over to Ki. "Urth new home."

Nik and Alexandria talked to Ian for a minute, much too rapidly for Miknon to follow.

Ian nodded, then moved the image of *New Kunisu* back to their original world. "You go home?"

"Urth home," Gil repeated.

He slashed through the picture of Kunisu and its neighbors with the black color stick. The aliens conversed rapidly again, worried wrinkles on their foreheads. Miknon and Gil waited, but the aliens kept talking to each other.

"Will they not want to share their home with the fae?" Miknon asked Gil. "Will they fight to keep their own territory?"

If the aliens wouldn't talk about the fae moving to Ki, there would be no hope for either side. Not that Miknon believed it would work, but they had to try. The fae could not return to Kunisu.

Finally, the aliens stopped for a hygiene break. Once back in the wagon, Nik took the control seat. The other three spread food across their laps, making more sandwiches and passing around fruit. Apparently, they wouldn't stop to eat this time. But they were feeding everyone, so Miknon hoped they weren't too angry.

After the meal was over, Ian pulled out the empty book again. "Gil and Miknon on Earth." He set the image of *New Kunisu* on the moon. "Family on moon?"

"Yes," Miknon said.

Ian moved the ship to the world. "Family go to Earth?"

"Yes," Gil said.

"Houmenny family?" Ian held up one finger, then kept adding until all ten were raised. He wiggled his fingers, raising his eyebrows in a question.

"You'll have to teach them numbers first," Miknon said.

Gil took the coloring stick and drew a vertical line, then held up one finger. He drew another line and added a finger. After nine lines and nine fingers, he drew a horizontal line and added the last finger. Ten.

"Okay," Ian said.

Gil drew nine horizontal lines for tens, then added a circle for one hundred.

Ian wrinkled his forehead and said something to Helen, who leaned over to see the page. They talked for a minute, then looked at Gil and motioned for him to continue.

"Do you think they don't know how to count that high?" Miknon asked.

"What else can we try?" Gil drew nine plain circles — nine hundred — and then one with four rays. Thousand.

Ian and Helen exploded with excitement, tapping the page and gesturing while they talked.

"Do you think they want to know how many of us are already here or how many are coming?" Gil asked.

"The rest of the fleet won't get here for a long time," Miknon said. "Give us a chance to discover how they feel about us settling. If they will be an enemy to us, our true numbers are better kept a secret."

Gil grimaced but drew ten rayed circles for the passengers of *New Kunisu*, currently sitting on the moon around Urth.

Eventually, the aliens stopped talking and turned back to Gil and Miknon.

"Family." Miknon slipped the row of ten symbols to the picture of the moon.

Ian glanced at it, then stared and snatched the page. He showed it to Helen, whose eyes grew wide. Ian flopped against the back of the seat and rubbed his face.

Miknon exchanged a glance with Gil. Would the news now turn them into enemies?

CHAPTER 7

MYTHS

ALEXANDRIA WOKE before her alarm went off. After stopping at a hotel in Bethlehem, Pennsylvania at ten o'clock the night before, she'd slept fitfully, dreams full of ten thousand werewolves and fairies and who-knew-what-else wandering Earth. What if they weren't all as nice as Gil and Miknon? What if they were monsters?

What could Earth do against ten thousand monsters?

She mentally slapped herself. Way to look on the dark side. Maybe they weren't monsters.

But what would they do with ten thousand myths, either? Seriously, her family didn't know what to do with *two* of them. And even if they were friendly, if the rest of them had brittle space bones like Gil and Miknon, the problem got tougher. Now, if they were enemies, those brittle bones would be a blessing for Earth... Unless the aliens didn't have to land to blast everyone out of the way.

What had they gotten themselves into? Why had they ever agreed to keep Gil and Miknon, even for a few days?

Her conscience prodded her memory. Two days ago, they were just trying to help two injured and starving refugees, who, to be fair, hadn't tried to harm the humans in any way.

She desperately wanted to set up her telescope and get a look at the ship parked on the moon, but her telescope wasn't that good. Besides, if the ship were big enough for an amateur to see, someone would have spotted it by now.

Beep-beep-beep! Miknon sat up from the pillow on the chair and screamed, and Alexandria lunged for her phone. By the time she fumbled off the sound, Mom was also awake.

"Good morning," Alexandria chirped, faking cheerfulness as much as she could. "We'd better get dressed before the boys start pounding on our door. Once we find an apartment, we have to decide where to leave our guests."

Mom sighed and threw off the covers. "I'm so glad the traveling is over. And the late nights. I'm getting too old for this."

Gaze following both of them, Miknon shook out her skirt and slid to the floor. Step by careful step, she headed for the bathroom, shaking her head at Mom's offer of a lift.

While Mom helped Miknon use the bathroom, Alexandria dressed, then the three of them switched places. Alexandria dabbed a little concealer under her eyes and brushed her hair, then threw her toiletries into her duffle bag.

And just in time, since the exterior door suddenly echoed with banging, and the boys piled in noisily.

Mom shushed them. "Other guests are still sleeping."

"Okay, but Gil is hungry," Ian said. "And so am I."

Nikos's stomach rumbled audibly.

"Boys." Mom laughed. "Okay, we'll eat, but we need to plan the day while we do."

Ian grabbed the cereal while Nikos rummaged through the mini fridge for the milk. Alexandria tossed disposable bowls and spoons onto the small table. Trial and error had shown them Miknon did best with dry cereal she could eat with her hands, drinking the milk separately with the tiny straw from a juice box.

After the blessing on the food, Alexandria and Mom settled on the edge of a bed, leaving the chairs for the aliens. Instead of taking the other bed, the boys flopped onto the floor. Gil passed Alexandria her favorite cereal, and when she raised her eyebrows, he winked. Okay, that was odd. How closely had he been watching her, and why? But after the wink, he attacked his breakfast without a further glance at her.

"Okay, Nikos," Mom said, "what's the next step? Looking at apartments? Do we have time to do that before, um, other things?" She glanced quickly at Gil and Miknon.

"Actually, I already picked one," Nikos said. "We just need to sign the lease. I hope that's okay? It's three bedrooms, between the university and the high school. I planned for you ladies to share a room, and either Ian and I share and we have a study room, or we split up if he prefers."

"I'll share with Gil." Ian poured another bowl of cereal for the werewolf.

"Temporarily," Mom said. "Until we decide what to do with them."

Ian stuck out his lip but said nothing.

"We're already packed," Nikos said. "We can check out as soon as you're ready. Once we have the apartment, we can deal with other things."

"We're packed, too, so we can go as soon as breakfast is over." Alexandria drank the last of her milk and tossed the bowl into the garbage. "I win."

But after everyone else finished, Gil was still eating. The humans had plenty of time to load the luggage into the truck before he sighed and rubbed his belly. Nikos carried him to the truck, then headed to the office to check out while Alexandria dealt with seatbelts.

The sky was slightly cloudy, and Gil peered upward with a puzzled frown on his face. He pointed to the sun and asked Ian something in his own language.

"Magic," he added.

Grinning, Ian pulled out the reference books and started trying to decipher the werewolf's question. Miknon leaned over the edge of her backpack and chattered along, pointing to images.

By the time Nikos returned, Ian had a tentative interpretation. "I think they want to know who's doing the light magic."

"What magic?" Alexandria asked.

"Um, the sun?"

Alexandria twisted around to stare at him. "You can't tell me he doesn't know what the sun is."

Ian shrugged. "In the book, yeah, he recognizes the picture, though he says it should be red. But he keeps saying the world gets dark and then light, so who's doing the magic? And I'm not sure I have this part right, but I think he thinks the Earth has a dark side and a light side."

Nikos tapped on his phone's GPS and pulled out of the parking lot. "Do you think it's from being on the spaceship or something he learned about his old world?"

Alexandria snapped her fingers. "Tidally locked worlds have a dark and light side because they don't rotate."

"Thank you, Madame Astronomer." Ian flipped through his books, chanting, "Day, night, seasons, where are you? Okay, Gil, let me show you…"

The trip to the apartment building took only a few minutes. Nik parked by the office and ran in. Everyone else unbuckled their seatbelts to be comfortable while they waited, and Miknon hopped out of the backpack.

Ian finished his explanation and pulled off Gil's shirt. Before Alexandria or Mom could stop him, the werewolf had shifted to his dog form with his skirt still around his belly. The medical boot thunked to the floor of the cab. Ian cheerfully passed Gil a snack and stroked his fur.

Mom groaned. "Ian, he's not your dog."

"But, Mom, he's as much of a wolf as he is a person. Doesn't he deserve to be his whole self?" Ian beamed, gray eyes innocent and cheerful.

Alexandria smothered the urge to strangle him.

Mom groaned again. "We'll talk about this later," she promised.

Raising her eyebrows, Alexandria wiggled her finger between Ian and herself in a silent threat. They'd talk later, and she wouldn't be as nice as Mom.

Nikos returned with a strange man carrying a clipboard and opened the back door of the truck. "Okay, Helen, we just need your signature."

Miknon ducked behind the backpack on the floor and froze.

The man yanked back his clipboard. "Wait a minute. No dogs."

"We aren't keeping him," Alexandria said. "He'll only be with us for a few days."

"No pets. That's final." The apartment manager tucked the clipboard under his arm and left.

Alexandria covered her face and counted to ten.

Nikos closed his eyes and leaned against the truck. "No lease. Ian, why is Gil like that?"

"Sorry," Ian whispered. "He says it's good for his bones?"

"Can't it wait until we have the lease?"

"Yes, Nikos. Sorry. I'll feed him and have him change back." Ian climbed into the truck bed to rummage through the cooler.

"Now what?" Alexandria cast a dirty look through the back window at her brother.

Nikos tapped on his phone. "First, Gil has to stay a boy. Second, we look at other apartments. I still have a list."

Ian climbed back into the truck, arms full of snacks and fruit.

Nikos stopped tapping and looked up. "Do we look for pet apartments, or do we go back to hotels until our guests are gone?"

"What do you mean, gone?" Ian turned to Gil and held up the shirt. He stumbled through a few foreign words and threw the shirt over Gil's head as soon as the wolf shifted back. "Where are they going?"

Mom sighed. "Ian, if Gil is telling the truth and we understand him correctly, then there are ten thousand aliens on the moon, waiting to come to Earth. Someone needs to know about this."

"We know about it." Ian bent to put the boot back on Gil's leg, then sat up with his chin sticking out.

Alexandria glared at him. "And what can we do about it? We don't know what to do with two of them, much less ten thousand."

She helped Miknon back into her backpack and buckled both of the siblings.

"But we already talked about this," Ian whined. "You agreed we couldn't abandon them."

He pulled out new bandages for Gil's hand. Someone banged on the truck window, and everyone jumped. On the sidewalk, a woman bounced on her toes, holding a cell phone. Nikos rolled down the window, and she started talking immediately.

"What's the movie called? Can I be an extra? When is it coming out?" She waved the phone. "Can I take a selfie with you? I've never met a movie star before."

Nikos frowned. "What movie?"

"Oh, I saw the pictures online. The fairy and the vampire, right? Ooh, and there's the vampire. Hello!" She waved at Gil in the back seat. "Is it a romance or a horror film?"

Alexandria leaned over Nikos and smiled at the crazy lady. "Sorry, it's still top secret. I'm sure you understand. We can't let the script get out to the public." She tapped Nikos and lifted her finger slowly.

Nikos hit the window button as the woman protested, "Oh, but I won't tell anyone."

Still smiling and waving, Alexandria muttered, "Floor it, Nikos."

Obediently, he started the truck and pulled into the driving lane. Alexandria pulled out her phone and started searching for the mysterious new vampire movie while Nikos drove aimlessly through the city. It took a while, but eventually she found more than she expected. Fairly good pictures of Gil and Nikos's bright blue truck were posted, as well as a fortunately not-so-good photo of Miknon.

Nikos parked in the inconvenient parking behind a big store, and for the next hour, Alexandria read everything to the others. Some people were guessing about a film, true, but others were ranting about alien invasions and "that asteroid that crashed on the moon." Certain posts had degenerated into a fight between those voting for fake vampires and those sure of real aliens. Almost everyone wanted to find the people involved, either to rub against their fame or take them down.

And the viewer count was mounting rapidly. Depending on the social media channel, comments numbered in the hundreds or thousands already, with more every minute.

"And that," Mom said, "is only one reason we need help. We can't stay out of sight for much longer."

Ian folded his arms and slumped in his seat. "It's not fair."

"Lots of things aren't fair," Alexandria said. "Dad leaving us wasn't fair. Losing the apartment because you let Gil be a dog wasn't fair. Gil breaking his leg wasn't fair. Starving isn't fair. What made you think life would be *fair?*"

Ian stuck out his tongue at her.

"Ian, stop it," Mom said. "We must tell somebody official before the social media alarms the authorities and *they* start hunting us, too. Besides, they need to know there are actually aliens on the moon, not just an unmanned probe."

"Wouldn't they still lock us up?" Nikos said.

"Or them!" Ian protested.

Mom rubbed her forehead. "I think we have to take the chance."

"What, you want us to drive to the White House and ask to see the President?" Alexandria said.

Mom shook her head. "They'd never let us in."

"What about the U.N.?" Nikos asked. "They would at least have language experts."

Alexandria grinned at Ian. "The United Nations, not you."

Her fellow high school students had twisted his name because he knew four languages fluently and three more not-so-well. A total of eight now, if they counted the bits of Gil and Miknon's.

"What about NASA?" she asked. "They deal with space stuff."

"Well, NASA doesn't do much good *on* Earth," Ian complained. "They don't do anything with immigration."

"Immigration?" Alexandria blurted. "Aren't you being a little optimistic? I vote for NASA. It has a planetary defense plan."

"We don't need to defend against friends," Ian protested. "And what would they do — shoot down the moon?"

"Gil already said he's hiding from his people," Nikos said. "Are you sure they're friends?"

"Aren't you both being a little pessimistic?" Ian retorted. "Gil and Miknon have been perfectly friendly, and they said their people want a home here."

"A home," Alexandria asked, "or *our* home?"

Mom waved her hands. "Stop fighting, please. It isn't helping, and it's alarming our *friends*."

Every head swiveled toward Gil and Miknon. The werewolf had stopped eating and was staring with wide eyes. Miknon had climbed out of her backpack and now clung to her brother's necklace to keep her perch on his shoulder.

"Sorry," Alexandria said.

"Sorry," the boys echoed.

Mom rubbed her forehead. "Let's take this one step at a time. We don't have a hotel anymore, but we can't get an apartment until we only have tenants with us. That means another hotel, but we don't know where until we decide who can help us. How are we set for food, Alexandria?"

Alexandria glanced in the back seat at the wrappers and apple cores. "We should still have enough for lunch, but then we either need to go shopping or buy fast food."

"Then might I suggest we find a nice park and eat an early lunch while we have a calm discussion in the open air?" Mom raised her eyebrows.

Nikos tapped on his phone. "Lehigh Mountain Park looks out of the way."

"Great. Let's go."

While Nikos drove, Ian talked to Gil and Miknon in a mix of English and their language, frequently using the reference books to help with vocabulary. He was still talking while the others unloaded the food and made sandwiches.

The temperature had crept up to 86 degrees, and only a scattering of clouds kept them from sweltering. Gil panted, and Miknon fanned her wings.

"Okay," Ian finally said. "I asked what the ship is doing and when their people are planning to come to Earth. I don't know how long their days and weeks are, and they use a word I haven't cracked yet, but as far as I can tell, their people want to land within a few weeks. Some kind of 'soon,' anyway." He bit his lip, and his shoulders slumped. "You were right; we don't have enough time to solve this ourselves."

Alexandria wrapped him in a hug. "I'm sorry I'm right. Let's figure out what would be best for everyone, okay?"

In the blessing on the food, Mom included a request for clear thinking and a peaceful resolution.

"Amen," everyone chorused.

They passed around the food, and yet again, Gil made sure Alexandria got her favorites. In fact, he knew everyone's preferences and handed them to the right person. Was he being creepy or just thoughtful?

More calmly this time, the Fitches and Nikos rehashed the arguments for the President, the U.N., and NASA while they ate.

"But who can make the kinds of decisions involved?" Mom asked.

Alexandria pursed her lips. "I know who works with all those people. The military."

"No," Ian said. "They'll want to get rid of the problem with a bomb or something. You know what Dad is like."

"Not every soldier is like that," Mom said. "Why do you vote for the military, Alexandria?"

Nikos lay on the grass and threw his arm across his eyes. "I'm still listening."

Alexandria ticked off reasons. "They have access to the President and connections to almost everybody. If things go wrong, they can defend Earth. If things go right, they have a lot of people to devote to the problem. They have experience with refugee camps in war areas. They have language experts until the U.N. or somebody better comes along. They have airplanes. They're used to dealing with hard problems."

"By blowing them up," Ian muttered.

"Do you want to march onto base," Nikos asked, "and demand to talk to the commander?"

"Can't," Alexandria said. "We have to show ID, and Gil and Miknon don't have any. And that's assuming the military would let us — or at least them — march back out again."

"Then what's your plan?" Mom asked.

"Give me a while to research. You guys can take a nap or something." She picked up her phone and sprawled on the grass.

Within a few minutes, Ian, Gil, and Miknon were chattering together again. Nikos was snoring, and Mom made notes in Alexandria's notebook.

Alexandria browsed a list of military bases, then hopped onto social media. It took her a couple of hours of snooping around for connections to find what she needed. By then, everyone but Mom was asleep on the grass. Reaching over, Alexandria shook Nikos gently.

"Hey, everybody," she called. "I have a plan."

"Mmph," Nikos grunted. "Of course you do." He sat up, holding his head.

Mom nudged Ian with her toe, and they both turned to face Alexandria.

"Hanscom Air Force Base is the home of the Space Force's Strategic Warning and Surveillance," Alexandria said. "That means they can track the ship on the moon and will already have plans of some sort."

"I thought you said we couldn't go on base," Nikos said.

"We can't. But Major General Anthony walks his dog in a nearby park. His son posted a picture that still had geotags attached, tsk tsk. We'll take our *dog* for a walk in the same park and look for an accidental meeting." She spread her hands wide. "His watch showed in the photo, and between the time and the light, it was obviously early morning. It's only six hours away, so we can still make it there today and be ready to meet the general tomorrow."

Mom groaned. "Six hours? Okay, everybody, let's get moving."

"Yes, Mom." Ian hopped to his feet.

Nikos grinned. "Yes, Mama."

Smiling, Mom tapped his nose, then collected Miknon. Nikos bent to pick up Gil, and his sunglasses fell off. He flinched but collected the werewolf anyway.

Alexandria picked up his sunglasses and slid them back onto his nose. "What's wrong?" she whispered.

"Migraine," he said. "You and Helen will have to drive."

She nodded, not hiding her grimace. Driving wasn't nearly as much fun as she'd once thought it would be, but she had little choice. She opened the truck door for Nikos and helped him settle Gil.

"Mom," she said, "you and I are driving."

Ian climbed in the middle next to Gil, and Nikos took the other back window seat. Gil took a long look at Nikos and said something to Miknon, then pulled out the sweater she had been using as padding in the bottom of the backpack.

"Nik." Gil flopped the sweater over his head, then handed it to Nikos.

Nikos stared at it in bewilderment. Gil scrunched up his face and winced, shading his eyes, then mimed putting the sweater on his head again and fake-relaxing.

"Oh, to block the light!" Nikos threw the sweater over his head and leaned against the window.

Gil smiled at Alexandria. "Nik okay."

Silently confused, Alexandria shut the door. Why did the alien care about Nikos's headache?

"Are you sure we can't keep them?" Ian asked.

Alexandria took the front passenger seat and pulled up the GPS for Mom. "Ian, even if they're all friendly, if we can't get an apartment with two of them, what would we do with ten thousand?"

Please, oh, please, let the military have some good ideas. Without locking up anybody and throwing away the key.

CHAPTER 8

IN WHICH TALKING TO THEIR
LEADERS IS FINALLY POSSIBLE

DAYS 2-3 AFTER LANDING, KI

AS THE WORLD zipped by outside the wagon's window, Gil sighed. Would they never get out? He had enjoyed the time on the grass, but here they were, back to traveling. So much for his dreams of running across the new world. Of course, it was difficult to run with a broken leg, anyway. At least his vision was finally improving, and he could see into the distance now.

He would have to settle for a different kind of fun.

He bumped Ian's elbow. "Where are we going?"

Ian beamed and pulled out his books. Miknon poked her head out of her pink bag, and the language lesson entertained all of them for a while.

"Apparently, we're going somewhere to talk to some kind of leaders," Gil summed up. "Finally! I was beginning to worry we'd never have a chance to make a treaty with Ki."

"Urth," Miknon corrected.

Gil flipped through the book of "pretend" and found a picture of a man wearing a crown. At least, he assumed it was a crown, though it was considerably fancier than their king's circlet. He tapped the image.

Ian gave the word in his language.

Gil repeated it, then strung together his best Ki vocabulary. "Want king Gil talk Urth."

Ian squinted at him and mouthed the words several times before his eyes brightened. "Good," he said. "Good to talk to Urth."

He rattled off something to his family, faster than Gil could understand, and Helen and Alexandria made excited sounds.

Turning back to Gil, Ian offered the books. "What king want talk abowt?"

Gil turned to the picture of Urth. The page was still marked by the drawings of *New Kunisu* he had used to illustrate the fae position on the moon. "Want home."

Again, he moved the ship from the moon to Ki. They wouldn't move the actual ship, but for conversational purposes, this was much easier than drawing all the dragon barges.

"Yes." Ian bit his lip. "Talk abowt home? King talk abowt home? King talk here?"

Gil pulled his necklace out from under the colorful tunic they gave him and dangled the king's signet ring. Though the prince was hiding, presumed dead, he gave the ring to Gil as a sign of authority.

"Say king Gil talk about home," he explained.

"Oh! Gil talk for king." Ian's face lit up again, and he babbled to his family, who relaxed their tense shoulders a little.

Gil smiled at Miknon. "Apparently, we aren't the only ones worried about finding leaders for a conversation."

Not that he was actually any kind of leader, but he did have Shar's permission to negotiate a treaty. They had discussed possible terms in a general sort of way.

"Good," Miknon said. "I'd like to get an alliance settled before our people land."

A peace treaty would soothe several of Gil's fears, including nightmares of war. The old king's council was heavily interested in merely wiping Urth clean of the natives before settling the empty world. Gil had argued with Sharrukin over and over about friendship being a better option than the council's plan, but the prince hadn't seen a way to send an ambassador until Gil and Miknon decided to escape from the ship.

Now the two of them were the only hope for a treaty. If they could persuade the humans to agree to one.

The prince was willing to offer almost anything but death or slavery in return for territory, a way to support themselves, trade agreements, peace, and decent rights. The fae didn't have a lot to offer, but they could salvage the fleet or work for the humans. If the humans didn't have magic, like they said — which didn't explain the wonders Gil had seen — then the fae magic ought to be worth something.

Shar was willing to give up his crown if it would save his people. Gil hadn't told that to anyone, even Miknon. He certainly wouldn't add it to a treaty unless he had no other choice.

Unfortunately, he had no idea what the humans would want or be willing to offer, which made it difficult to prepare his arguments. Even if he knew the right words, which he didn't. He ran his fingers across the image of Ki — Urth, then gripped the book. How long would it take to learn all the words?

But he couldn't wait until then, because the passengers on *New Kunisu* were short on supplies and time. A series of accidents on the journey had ruined some of their stored food, and a leaking water tank reduced the amount of garden they could grow. After months on short rations, they were closer to starving than he liked to think, and the restrictions would only grow worse the longer they had to wait to land.

Gil had to succeed, or his people would be desperate enough to fight the humans for a place to live. How many would die on both sides? Too many. Maybe even his brother... But if he could convince the humans to make a treaty, everyone could live in peace.

If the council didn't discover the prince was still alive or Gil was on Earth. If he could find the right words to bargain. If the lords would honor any bargain he made.

If, if, if.

But what choice did he have?

As the humans drove their magic wagon on and on and on, their furrowed heads and tense gestures still spoke of worry. In an attempt to distract everyone, Gil tried to give a more precise explanation of his age and Miknon's. Now that Ian knew the fae numbers, maybe it would work.

He opened the book of words and found the people page. Tapping on the almost-adults and then himself, he said, "I'm one hundred and fifty-seven conjunctions."

Then he drew a circle, five horizontal lines, and seven vertical lines on the blank book. After drawing another circle, six horizontal lines, and five vertical ones, he pointed to Miknon.

Ian drew three shapes next to Gil's number and six by Miknon's, then showed the book to his mother in the front seat. She turned around to stare at Gil with puzzlement. Ian shrugged and handed the book back to Gil.

Gil tapped the numbers he drew, then the ones Ian wrote. "Are these your numbers? Why is Miknon's so long?" He squinted at the characters, trying to decipher the logic.

Ian peered over his shoulder, then laughed. "No, no." He pointed to the first set of characters and said, "Gil." For the second, he said, "Miknon."

"Yes," Gil said, "that's what I said. I'm one-hundred-fifty-seven conjunctions, and Miknon is one-hundred-sixty-five." He tapped his numbers again.

"No." Ian drew new characters, three by each of Gil's numbers, and tapped the almost-adults in the word book. "Age. Numbers."

"Then what's this?" Gil touched the other characters on the page.

"Gil. Miknon." Ian wrote more and touched each set of characters as he spoke. "Ian. Nikos. Helen. Alexandria."

The characters assigned to Alexandria were numerous, and Gil finally understood. Ian wasn't writing numbers, he was writing names.

"Look, Miknon," Gil said, "there's your name!" He touched the page with awe.

Miknon frowned at him. "Are they casting a spell?"

"Magic?" Gil asked Ian.

Ian shook his head.

"No," Gil said, "just showing us how they write. Ian wrote all their names, too."

She leaned from the bag and stared at the page. "Which one is mine? Can I write it?"

Handing his color stick to Miknon, Gil pointed to the appropriate spot. Using both hands, Miknon dragged the color stick across the page in a shaky copy of her name.

"Well. I wrote my name." She handed back the color stick and burst into tears.

Gil patted her head and wished for Mother.

Helen said something, and Ian nudged Nikos awake and talked at him until the older boy pulled a square of fabric from his pocket.

Very gently, Ian dabbed at Miknon's face. "Miknon okay?"

"Okay," Miknon sobbed. "I never thought I could learn magic."

"Magic?" Gil asked again.

"No." Ian pointed to his eyes, then the page. "No magic. Read." He scribbled the color stick on the page. "Write. All read and write. Gil and Miknon want read and write?" He handed the color stick to Gil.

Throat tight, Gil took it. "Yes."

Yes, they certainly did want to learn to read and write, even if the humans didn't think it was magic. They were wrong, of course. If he could read, he could discover what all the books said. He could learn *anything*!

The highborn fae kept reading for themselves, afraid that if the commoners knew their spells, they could find a way to defeat them. Either the humans were too powerful to care, or they didn't realize what an advantage reading could be. He tightened his grip on the color stick until it started to bend. If he could teach the reading to the rest of his people, it would be a huge step toward the equality of his mother's dreams.

Miknon wiped her face on the thin cloth and handed it back to Nikos. "Okay."

Gil shook his head and tapped on the numbers again. Focus on the original problem and worry about reading later.

"How do I explain conjunctions to you? Ah, yes." He flipped through the Earth book until he found the picture of the worlds lined up by the sun and drew an imaginary line from the farthest to the nearest. "Conjunction. One hundred and fifty-seven conjunctions."

"Yeers?" Ian scrunched up his nose. "So many yeers not teenager." He took another color stick and drew fae numbers next to each name on the page. According to him, he was thirteen "yeers," Alexandria was sixteen, Nikos was eighteen, and Helen was forty.

Now Gil and Miknon stared in puzzlement. Forty conjunctions old was almost a baby, and days or weeks were worse. Did the humans live and die as quickly as mice?

"Yeer?" Gil asked.

Ian tapped the image of Earth and swirled his hand around the picture of the sun. "Yeer?"

Gil shrugged, and Miknon bit her lip. What did the world's journey around the sun have to do with anything?

That started a confusing discussion among the humans, and Gil couldn't understand more than a few words. Either they didn't recognize a conjunction even with a picture, or he was missing some other bit of information. Or they were.

While the humans argued, Gil drew a different image of Kunisu and its neighboring worlds, out of alignment but with the same colors. He turned to his old picture with the worlds in conjunction, then tapped Ian.

He laid his hand on the old image. "This is Conjunction." He touched the new picture. "This is not Conjunction."

From the front of the wagon, Alexandria squinted at his drawings and held out her hands. "Mai eye see?"

Ian passed up the book, and his sister examined it, lips pursed. "Oh!" Her eyes lit up, and she chattered for a long time, waving her hands and pointing to his images.

"What?" Miknon asked.

Ian took a deep breath, then blew it out. He opened and closed his mouth several times, then shrugged.

"Alexandria likes conjunction," he said. "Alexandria likes…" He wrinkled his nose and spread his fingers across the book of worlds. "Syenz. But want know more about conjunctions."

The thought of trying to find the right words made Gil's head ache, and Miknon was already sagging to the bottom of the pink bag. He waved off Ian and went to sleep. They could try again later.

Nikos woke him later, when the light had dimmed to almost normal for Gil, and carried him into another room like the others they had used on the journey. The humans passed around crinkly-wrapped parcels of white-wrapped goo and showed him how to unwrap only the crinkly stuff. After Ian showed a picture of the plant that grew the contents, Gil and Miknon gobbled down the hot, spicy bundles.

Once again, the group split by gender for sleeping. Gil took off his clothes and leg brace and shifted to wolf. He was nearly asleep on top of the blankets when he scented Ian crawling into bed next to him.

In the morning, everyone combined in one room for a meal. The humans turned on the big magic box and watched the images move, commenting much too rapidly for the fae to understand. After a few minutes, the picture showed a lot of humans running. And they kept running all through the meal and packing. They were still running when Helen turned off the magic and the image disappeared.

"Where are they going?" Gil asked Ian.

Figuring out how to discuss that question took longer than loading the wagon, and they were far down the road by the time Ian managed to explain about "meruthonz." Gil and Miknon listened open-mouthed to descriptions of humans running for *hours*, not because they needed to get somewhere or escape something, but *for the fun of it*. And many humans did this! They didn't need a healer after, and they didn't hibernate for weeks to recover.

"Trolls," Miknon uttered. "Are humans indestructible?"

"They had better not be," Gil said, "in case our negotiations go badly. Few of the fae can match that kind of stamina."

"Maybe we outnumber them." Miknon snorted at her own comment.

They both knew the number of lights that had shown in the scrying bowl.

Gil pulled out the blank book and pushed it at Ian. "How many humans are on Earth?"

Once he calculated the question, Ian grimaced. "I don't know your numbers enough." He drew nine rayed circles and tapped the blank space after them. "What next?"

Gil shrugged. Maybe the highborn knew the next symbol, but he didn't.

Ian pushed his floppy hair out of his eyes and bit his lip. "Okay." He drew a vertical line on the left side of the page and another on the right. "One."

Gil nodded.

Ian continued drawing lines on the left and symbols on the right until he reached nine. Then he drew a horizontal line on the left and a vertical line and circle on the right. "Ten."

"Okay," Gil said.

Ian drew a circle on the left and a vertical line and two circles on the right. "Hundred."

"Okay." Gil saw the pattern; every time the fae switched to a new symbol for ten of the prior symbols, the humans added a circle. It was odd but compact.

Ian drew a rayed circle on the left and added a third circle on the right. "Thousand."

Then he added a line with four circles, and a line with five circles, though without symbols for the equivalent fae numbers. If Gil hadn't lost track, five was how many circles he would need to use to report the number of fae in the entire fleet. Ian continued with a line and six circles.

Gil pressed his hand to his forehead. The human counting system was versatile, but the implications made his head ache. They used very large numbers, too large for his imagination.

"That's how we would have counted the fae on Kunisu and its neighboring worlds," Miknon said. "Three or four of those."

"How do you know that?" Gil asked.

"I heard the secretary talking to the king, and I'm not stupid."

"No, of course you aren't." But Gil's head still hurt.

Ian tapped higher on the page where he had counted to ten, then copied his character for "eight" and added six circles. "Humans on Earth."

"All seven of our worlds had fewer people than their one," Miknon said numbly. "And we could only evacuate a fraction of our people. We aren't just outnumbered, we are facing potential enemies of twenty to one. Or something like that."

"Or twenty new friends for each of us," Gil said. "We can ask Nik when we see him again."

"Twenty to one," Miknon repeated. "*If* we see Nik again." Her lip quivered, and she blinked rapidly.

Despite a little private worry, Gil smiled. "Then we had better make peace, hadn't we?"

Miknon frowned at the page. "I know the prince said you can negotiate, but do you really think you can handle this?"

"I have to." Gil rubbed his forehead. "If we don't, who will? When the council lands, they will want conquest."

Chapter 9

General

"Do you see him yet?" Ian whispered from the side of his mouth as he passed the park bench.

Gil hopped beside him on three legs, and Ian kept his pace to an infuriating crawl so the wolf wouldn't hurt himself. Fortunately, Gil seemed happy to ignore the dogs running around the park, though the little yappy ones seemed to amuse him. Ian didn't know if Earth wolves could chuckle, but Gil's bouncy wheeze was obviously a laugh.

"No." Mom didn't look up from her book. "Be patient." The backpack next to her squirmed, and Mom casually touched her elbow to it. "Okay."

Inside the bag, Miknon must have settled again, because the pack returned to looking like an ordinary inanimate object. Everyone had agreed that until they knew how the general and his dog would react, Miknon must stay safely out of sight. The last thing they needed was Miknon becoming a chew toy for a startled dog.

Under the cloud cover, the weather was cool for summer, but not cool enough to wear a jacket. Not far away, Alexandria laughed and dove for the frisbee, rolling across the grass in a failed attempt to catch Nikos's long throw. The two older teens used their mobility to watch in all directions for the approach of their target.

Gil sat on his haunches and sniffed the air, tongue lolling from his mouth. They looked like a normal family out for a day in the park. They'd better look normal, or their plan was ruined from the start.

"Hey, watch out," Alexandria protested.

But when Ian glanced to see the problem in the frisbee game, she tilted her head sideways and raised her eyebrows. A man and a German shepherd were getting out of a car. The man matched the picture Alexandria had found for Major General James Anthony. Ian's heart raced, and he tapped Gil on the head. It was time.

The wolf rose a little creakily to his feet and took his place at Ian's side. They'd tried their best to explain the whole plan to the aliens, but with the language barrier, it was hard to be sure how much of it they understood. Hopefully, it would be enough.

With Gil heeling like a well-trained dog, Ian wandered toward the man with the German shepherd. He was tall, with a soldier's physique despite his graying hair. His shirt was ironed crisply, but he wore jeans and hiking boots.

"Good morning," Ian said. "Nice dog."

The German shepherd and Gil sniffed each other. Gil wolf-grinned, and the other dog flinched.

"Morning," the major general said. "Hey, Sarge, what's wrong?" He bent to caress his dog.

Gil smiled at the general, too.

"That's a big dog you've got," the general said as his dog leaned into his side. "Is he a shepherd, husky, or a mix?"

"Um, yeah," Ian said, "he's big, but he's friendly. Gil, come say hi."

Anthony reached slowly toward Gil, then stroked his fur. "Hey, fella. How you doing, huh?"

Gil grinned harder, then licked the general's face. Ian bit down hard on the giggle that threatened to escape. Wait until Alexandria heard about this!

"Look, Sarge," the general crooned, "nothing to worry about. Just a big softie, huh?" He ran his hands over Gil's side and frowned. "Are you starving your dog? And why is he limping?" He patted Gil again, then rose to his feet. "Have you been abusing him, mister?"

"We only got him a few days ago," Ian protested. "We've been feeding him, but there's only so fast he can gain weight." He nudged Gil into a walk and subtly headed for the nearby bushes. "And the leg was an accident."

Still scowling, Anthony followed. "I'm glad to hear this isn't your fault. I hate to see a good dog mistreated."

"We would never do that," Ian said. "He's my buddy."

The general let Sarge off the leash. The German shepherd detoured around Gil to run into the park.

"That's odd," Anthony said. "I've never seen Sarge afraid of another dog before."

"Well, Gil is no ordinary dog," Ian said.

They were almost to the bushes that would shield them from other eyes. And then their plan would either work or explode in their faces.

"I thought you said you just got him," the general said. "You don't even know what breed he is, right?"

Ian avoided the question. "We know a few things, and he's not ordinary."

"What do you mean?"

"Well, Major General Anthony," Ian said, "that's what we wanted to talk to you about."

"What?" Anthony's gaze sharpened, and he reached for the gun that wasn't on his belt. "How do you know who I am?"

"Please don't panic," Ian said. "We don't want to hurt you."

"Hurt me?" The general stopped and raised his fists. "What's going on?"

But now they were behind the bushes. "Now, Gil!"

Ian's family rose and headed his way, but the general didn't notice. His attention was fastened on Gil, who had almost instantly turned into a naked young man.

"Please, General, listen to us," Ian said.

"Us? Who? What?" Anthony's voice croaked, but he stood firm.

Gil smiled at the general, revealing his sharp teeth. Anthony slapped again for his absent gun. Alexandria and Nikos rounded the bushes from one direction, and Mom came from the other, carrying the backpack in one hand and a skirt in the other.

Mom dropped the skirt into Gil's lap. "Don't worry; we just want to talk. We have something important to tell you."

"Where'd the dog go?" Anthony asked. "Who's that?"

"I'm sure you've seen that spaceship parked on the moon," Alexandria said. "The castle. We have a message from there for you."

"How did you—" The general took a deep breath. "I don't know what you're talking about."

"Sure you do," Ian said. "The castle on the moon that everyone thought was an asteroid until it was close enough to actually see. I'm sure they showed you the photos."

Anthony looked at Gil, still struggling into his skirt, then at the rest of them. "If that were true — and I'm admitting nothing — how would you know about it? I'm sure anything like that would be top secret, and no amateur telescope is good enough to see much detail on the moon."

Mom reached into the backpack and passed a single page to the general without a word.

Anthony examined the crayon drawing of a castle on the moon, then pulled out his phone to compare something to the drawing.

"Where did you get this?" he demanded.

Everyone pointed to Gil, who had finally managed to get the skirt in place.

Gil waved cheerfully. "Okay."

"We found some, um, people from the spaceship," Ian said, "and they want to make a treaty with us. I told you, we need to talk."

"Is his leg really broken, or was that a ploy of yours?" The general scowled harder. "You'd better not have broken it as part of your strategy."

"Really broken," Ian said. "But it was an accident!"

Major General Anthony relaxed his fists and ran his fingers through his hair. "If I wasn't seeing this myself, I wouldn't believe it."

"Maybe we should sit." Mom pointed toward the bench.

Nikos picked up Gil, and Ian waved his arm to indicate the general should go first. Anthony sat on one end of the bench. Nikos settled Gil on the other, then reached under the bench for the medical boot.

The others sat on the grass, watching the general watch Gil get his leg re-splinted and his hand cleaned and bandaged.

"So, General," Mom said, "about that treaty?"

"Impossible," Anthony said.

Ian smiled at him. "Do you need to see Gil turn back into a wolf again?"

"Wolf? Not dog?"

"Sure." Ian shrugged. "Gil's a werewolf."

The general stretched out his legs and glared. "There are no were-wolves, and that's not how werewolves work, anyway. I don't have time for stupid pranks."

Alexandria laughed. "Apparently, it is how werewolves work. I mean, have you ever met a real werewolf before now?"

"No," the general barked, "because werewolves aren't real!"

Nikos pulled a bag full of sandwiches from the backpack and passed it to Gil. "I understand how you feel, but they are real, and Gil is one. Myths and legends are coming to Earth. Gil has authority from his king to negotiate for homes, but their people are coming whether we like it or not. And they have magic."

"There's no such thing as magic." The general's face was straight, but his voice seemed stunned.

Alexandria shrugged. "Okay, they have science so advanced that we don't understand it, that will look like magic to us. And werewolves are just the start of it. They have fairies and gorgons and who knows what else!"

"I don't like threats," Anthony said.

Ian shook his head vigorously. "He hasn't threatened us. He's just telling us how it is. His people *are* coming, and they *do* have magic. If we're smart, we'll benefit from it."

"There is no—"

"Science so advanced it allows them to change shape," Nikos amended.

Anthony grimaced. "How does he do that? Was it an illusion?"

"Nope." Ian grinned at him. "And we don't know how. But you touched him as a wolf, remember?"

The general reached out and touched Gil's arm. Flinching a little, the werewolf stuffed the last of his third sandwich into his mouth with his clawed fingers.

The general swallowed and let go. "We could fight them when they land."

"Sure," Nikos said, "but are we sure we can win? There are ten thousand of them on the moon."

The general crossed his arms. "There are eight billion humans."

"How many have magic?" Ian asked. "If we start a war, can Earth win against legends with magic? Excuse me — advanced science. This is our chance for peace. We can make a treaty now, or they can thrash our butts and take our planet."

Mom winced and rubbed her nose at his word choice, but she didn't say anything.

"We could nuke them off the moon before the rest of them land," Anthony said.

Ian turned to Gil. "What if—" He pretend-exploded with his hands and puffed cheeks. "Ship on moon."

Gil tilted his head to one side and held both hands in front of him as if blocking something. "Magic."

"Against a nuke?" Anthony scoffed.

Ian raised his eyebrows. "Gil, how much magic?" He mimicked the blocking gesture.

Gil took the notebook and drew a sun with long rays stretching to a crayoned Earth. "Okay." He drew a new, larger sun that engulfed his Earth. "No."

"General," Alexandria squeaked, "in case you aren't familiar with relative power outputs, a solar flare large enough to actually reach Earth is many times more powerful than a nuke. If they can block that, a nuke would make no difference to them, though Earth might be hit with the fallout."

"I still think it would work," Anthony said.

"Maybe," Alexandria said, "but if you fail, you will have declared war. We have an opportunity to make friends. Are you sure you want enemies instead? Think what amazing things we could do with a little magic on our side."

"I've got to think about this," the general said.

"Of course," Mom said.

"Why don't you come sit on the base while I talk to people?" Anthony asked.

Alexandria snorted. "No way. You can call us when you're ready to meet at a neutral location."

"Are you on the side of these werewolves?" Anthony asked. "Don't you want what's best for Earth?"

"What's best for Earth is peace," Ian said.

"Well, how do I know this isn't some scheme?" the general asked. "Your so-called werewolf hasn't been talking, just eating."

"He doesn't speak much English," Ian said.

"A handy excuse," Anthony said. "What do you feed him, anyway? Raw roast beef?"

"Those are peanut butter and jam," Mom said mildly. "He doesn't like meat. We haven't decided if he's actually a vegetarian or if he's afraid we eat people."

The general opened his mouth, then closed it with a puzzled look. Finally, he shook his head. "How do I know their leader will agree with anything, no matter what we say?"

Ian turned to his friend. "Gil talk for king?"

"Talk Gil for king," the werewolf agreed.

"What king want?"

"Want king home."

The general stared at the drawing of the castle on the moon one more time, then shoved it at Mom. "I'm still looking for the trick here. Maybe I'll walk away and your little friend will start spouting Russian."

Nikos raised his hand. "Do you have a recorder on your phone?"

"Yes, why?"

"Make a recording." Nikos shrugged. "You will see it's not Russian."

Anthony pulled out his phone and tapped it for a minute. "Okay, I'm ready."

In his best alien vocabulary, which wasn't very good, Ian told Gil to talk to the man about the king, in his own language.

Gil sat up straight, looked the general in the eyes, and chattered for several minutes. He spoke quickly enough that Ian couldn't understand much, but not so fast that individual words disappeared. One word came up several times, and Mom choked every time. Finally, Gil shrugged and stopped.

"Okay, sir," Ian said, "take that to your linguistics department and see if they can identify it. If they can't, consider we might be telling the truth and you have a chance to end a war before it begins."

Major General Anthony slipped his phone back into his pocket and whistled for his dog. "If I discover this is a prank, I'll do my best to bring you up on charges."

"And when you decide it isn't," Mom said, "I hope you take advantage of the opportunity before it's too late. My name is Helen... Ellison, and here's my phone number." She recited the digits while Anthony entered them into his contacts.

Ellison. Ian hunched his shoulders. With the divorce final, Mom had changed her name back and no longer sounded like part of the family. But she had stayed with Ian and Alexandria, and Dad hadn't, though he still shared their name. Ian would get used to Ellison, eventually.

Sarge ran up, and the general stood. Despite his broken leg, Gil struggled to stand on one leg, bowing to Anthony. The general stared at the young man, skepticism clearly written on his face. Finally, he bowed in return. Gil grinned wide enough to expose his sharp teeth. Anthony grunted, nodded at the humans, and left with his dog.

Everyone watched him go until he got in his car and drove away.

"Well," Mom said, "I hope it works."

Ian bounced on his toes. "Then I have two questions."

Tucking the frisbee under her arm, Alexandria raised her eyebrows. "And what's that, squirt?"

"First, Mom, why did you keep jerking when Gil was talking?"

Mom sighed and scratched her nose. "It's probably a coincidence, but it sounded like Gil was saying 'dupure.'"

"Dupure," Gil agreed. He put his hands around his head like a crown.

"So?" Ian said. "It's the werewolf word for 'king,' I guess. Or some kind of noble, anyway."

Mom choked again. "It's the Minoan word for 'lord.'"

Ian felt like someone had hit him across the back of the head with a baseball bat. "How does a werewolf know Minoan?"

"It might be coincidence," Nikos said.

Alexandria took a deep breath. "Or did the Minoans know werewolf?"

Ian puffed out his cheeks. How could any civilization on Earth have learned a language from space myths? The implications were fascinating.

"Minoan werewolves." Mom leaned forward and rested her head on her knees. "I can't do this," she muttered.

"Please tell me your second question is less alarming," Alexandria said.

"Definitely," Ian assured her. "I wondered what we ought to do while we wait for the general to think?"

"We can't get a hotel until tonight," Alexandria said, "so how about a little sightseeing?"

"Like what?" Nikos asked.

"A planetarium," Alexandria suggested. "We could try to learn more about Gil and Miknon's world."

"A zoo," Ian said. "Gil likes animals."

Mom sighed and climbed to her feet. "We can research both and see what options we have."

"It doesn't matter," Nikos said. "We just need to stay busy while the general decides if he believes us."

Ian ran ahead to open the truck doors. If the general didn't believe, Earth might be invaded by myths.

CHAPTER 10

IN WHICH THEY DISCOVER
A HOLE IN THEIR PLAN

Day 3 after landing, Ki

ONCE SETTLED IN THE WAGON, Miknon glared at her younger brother from the pink bag on his chest. "I suppose you think it will be easy now."

Gil shrugged. "No, but at least we're getting closer."

"Are we?" Miknon asked. "The man didn't stay to talk to us. You revealed yourself to a stranger, and for what?"

"But the humans asked me to," Gil argued. "We have to trust their plan."

Miknon folded her arms. "I don't think we do."

"We can't do this alone," Gil said.

Then Miknon would have to think of a way to make sure the humans couldn't betray them.

In the front seat of the wagon, Alexandria tapped her magic box. She smiled excitedly, then frowned and tapped again. Several times, she repeated the same cycle. Her magic box didn't seem to work the way she wanted, judging by her heavy sigh. Finally, she turned to Ian and asked a question.

Ian opened the book of word pictures to the page of animals. "Want see animals?"

"Yes," Gil said.

Miknon nodded. Though she didn't like animals as much as Gil did, she wanted to learn more about this world.

Alexandria tapped her magic box again and read something aloud. Helen nodded. Nik turned the key of the wagon and started the magic.

In preparation, Ian, Miknon, and Gil practiced the words for animals. The drive took long enough that even Miknon could remember most of the vocabulary by the time they stopped again.

A gray building sat in the middle of grass and trees — hundreds of trees.

"Ash would love this," Gil murmured.

His dryad friend frequently climbed the trees on the ship, leaves sprouting from his hair.

As Nik lifted Gil from the wagon, Alexandria unfolded the wheeled chair, and Ian took the pink bag with Miknon in it. Once Gil was settled, Ian returned Miknon to his lap.

"Stay," he whispered, closing the bag most of the way.

Hmph. Miknon never got to be *out*. But as she complained to herself, Helen fit the mask across Gil's mouth and nose again, checked that his dark eye coverings were secure on his nose, and fluffed his hair over his ears. Then the humans surrounded the chair and started forward.

On the way to the door, two stone bears guarded the path.

"What happened to them?" Gil asked. "Stonegazer?"

"Pretend," Ian said.

Inside the building, they gave paper to another human and left out another door.

"Where are the animals?" Miknon asked.

They emerged into the bright sunshine, and Miknon moved a little inside the bag to stay in the darkest, coolest corner. Poor Gil, stuck in the blinding light and stifling heat.

Thanks to the loose, holey weave of the bag, she could see through it as well as breathe. A stream ran around in a circle, surrounded by more trees, more grass, and a few buildings. Across from the building they had exited, birds paddled in the water or flew lazily. One tall bird waded on very long legs.

After a short conversation, Nik pushed the chair left, and they crossed a bridge over the stream. Gil waved at the other humans, and Alexandria stopped the procession long enough to tell him "No" and tuck his hands under his legs. Gil sighed, and his shoulders slumped.

"Don't draw attention to us," Miknon said.

"I'm being friendly," he protested.

"Well, don't."

He grumbled something she didn't catch. Probably better that way.

The path was lined with a barrier of logs on either side. Beyond that were more barriers of wood and metal, then large spaces of grass.

Ian pointed to the animals grazing. "Deer."

Gil and Miknon watched for a few minutes, but they saw no signs of intelligence. Either they were only animals, they were hiding their intelligence from the humans, or they were completely distracted by eating.

A little farther on, Alexandria pointed to a large, curly-haired cow. It, too, seemed interested only in grazing.

"So if the man comes back to talk to us," Miknon asked, "what is our plan?"

"I'll tell him we want somewhere to live. We would prefer to spread out, but if the humans want us to stay together, we'll make it work." Gil's nose wrinkled under the mask. "Blech, living with the highborn. Oh, well. Anyway, we won't fight if the humans don't fight. We'll want to trade somehow, but we can work out the details."

The next animal was a cat with almost no tail. Ian assured them it was uninjured, born that way. Across the path from that cat was a smaller one, and as they watched it play, a human joined it and talked to the crowd gathering on the path.

Ian crouched by Gil. "He talk about cat."

The boy tried to translate what the human said, but often he didn't know the right words. The cat played with the human, obviously used to the interaction. It seemed smarter than the deer but not truly intelligent.

When the human went away, they continued down the path to

another cat. This one was much larger, at least as big as a human, and when it caught Gil's scent in the air, it hissed.

Gil leaned close to Ian and whispered, "Eat cat?"

"No," Ian whispered.

Nik pushed the chair toward a covered bridge.

"Even if the humans agree to a treaty," Miknon said, "how will you tell the prince about it from here? And once you do, somehow, the council and most of the fae will think we betrayed them to the enemy. How will you keep the council from starting a war despite the treaty? If the fae land and try to fight, we can't win."

"We'll hurt a lot of humans, though," Gil said morosely.

"Yes," she agreed, "many will die on both sides. How will you prevent that?"

Once they crossed the bridge, more animals were visible. One side of the path held a cow and a large pig, while the other had horses. Unlike the green and black kelpies, these horses were mostly brown.

"Moo?" Gil asked.

"Yes, cow," Ian said.

Gil narrowed his eyes. "Hamburger?"

"Yes." The boy's shoulders slumped.

Gil pointed to the log barrier in front of the cow. "Stay."

"Okay." Nik stopped the chair as requested.

Leaning forward, Gil watched the cow intently. Miknon examined the beast through the pink mesh of her bag. It ate grass, like the other animals, with no signs of interest in anything else.

After a glance around for eavesdroppers, Gil started talking to the cow. He tried standard fae, then he tried every beast language he knew, most of which were pure gibberish to Miknon.

The cow didn't twitch an ear.

Finally, Gil leaned back. "I don't think it understands me."

"Wrong language?" Miknon asked.

"I — don't think it speaks, actually." Gil ordered Nik to push him across the path to the horses, and he tried again.

The horses didn't respond, either.

"I think they are only animals," Gil said.

"So it's okay to eat them?"

Gil twitched his shoulders. "Yes?"

He motioned for Nik to continue onward. After a brief stop at the pig, they watched human children play for a while. Gil took a turn banging on the giant musical instrument.

"We obviously need the council out of the way," Gil said. "Or locked up."

"We don't have enough warriors on our side," Miknon said, "but what if we sent the council on a mission?"

"What would they consider more important than conquering Ki?"

"Nothing," Miknon said triumphantly, "and that's how we trick them. We send them back for the rest of the fleet, while only a few of the fae land for now."

"It took us a dozen conjunctions to get to Ki from where we left the fleet," Gil said. "It would take twice as long to return with the fleet. Our people don't have that long before they starve."

While they thought, Nik pushed them past the horses and cow again to get to the next animals. The path crossed behind the territories of two of the cats for a second view.

"What if they take only one barge?" Miknon suggested. "Its smaller size would be easier to push than the whole ship. Fill it with food and water, one navigator, a pilot or two, a water mage, and minimum staff. They wouldn't even need a dragon. Traveling faster, they would have enough food to make the trip."

"*They* would," Gil said, "but what about those left behind?"

"Oh, the council won't care about them," she said, "but while the council is gone, we simply use the dragons and the other barges to bring the rest down to Ki."

"Huh."

While Gil thought, they looked at a small canine and several birds-of-prey. The "kiyotee" barked at Gil until Nik pushed them onward.

"But how would we tell the prince about the plan?" Gil asked. "Neither of us have any mind touching."

"I know," Miknon said. "And we don't have enough air and cool spells left to get us both back to the ship, even if we can find the dragon again."

"Poor Azidaka," Gil said. "He must be so frightened."

"We can't leave the humans, anyway," Miknon said. "We have to keep an eye on them."

"Oh, they'll be fine," Gil said. "Look, are those selkies?"

He leaned forward until his head pressed against the window separating them from the pool. Striped shadows fell across the rock in the middle of the water, and in the depths, such as they were, hoops and balls floated. Dark, sleek shadows zipped through a hoop and chased a ball. Gil called out to them, but they didn't turn their heads.

"Seel," Ian said.

"Do you think they aren't really selkies?" Gil asked. "It's hard to tell which might be fae and which just have a resemblance."

"I assume none of them are fae," Miknon said dryly.

And she didn't share Gil's trust of the humans. No, one of them had to go talk to the prince, and the other had to stay here to make sure the humans followed the plan. If they sent the dragonet alone, he wouldn't understand the plan or the need for secrecy. And neither Gil nor Miknon could write, even if they dared risk a message being found by someone else.

Miknon wasn't nearly as good at the human language as Gil was, but she was smaller and used less air. The remnant of the spell would be enough for her, though it would not support her brother. She would have to be the one to go back.

Back to the ship where the powerful, magic-wielding lords wanted to kill her for being a spy. And they knew she had blue wings. Though it wasn't a unique trait, it was obvious. If they saw her, she would have no chance of survival.

But Gil couldn't go, and she was the only other possibility. It was the only way to make the plan work.

But how could she convince her brother to let her go into danger? He had escaped to Ki with her rather than send her alone.

Nik stopped the chair by a small table, and he and Alexandria sat with Gil while Ian and Helen went inside another building. Mother and son emerged a few minutes later, hands full of delicious-smelling packages.

"Oh, good," Gil said. "I'm hungry."

"You're always hungry," Miknon teased.

Her own stomach growled, and Gil laughed. The humans did the head-bowed talking, then passed around sandwiches. Miknon finished eating before presenting her idea to her brother.

"I need to go back to the ship," she said. "I'll tell the prince about our plan."

Gil dropped his last sandwich onto the table and stared at her in horror. "But you're under a death sentence!"

"There isn't enough air for you," she said, "and you're better at talking to the humans. You set it up so it looked like the dragon escaped accidentally, so everyone will think it finally made its way back to the ship. I'll stay out of sight in the maintenance tunnels, I promise. Everyone thinks I'm dead, so as long as nobody sees me, I'll be safe." She poked his belly through the side of the bag. "Eat your food. What would you do, hmm? Everyone thinks you're dead, too, and you don't fit in the tunnels. As soon as anyone saw you, our whole escape would be ruined."

"But we ran away to save you." Gil chomped on the sandwich like it was an enemy.

"Gil, your leg is broken," she reminded him. "You can't move around, and you certainly can't run. And even if you persuaded them that the dragon saved you among the stars, how would you explain your short hair?"

"Ready?" Ian asked.

Gil shoved the rest of his last sandwich into his mouth and glared into the bag at Miknon.

Nik pushed the chair to a third building. After pointing to writing on the door, all the humans put on masks. Inside, the air was damp and much hotter. Windows showed birds and fish and frogs and snakes.

The chatter of humans echoed from the walls, and Gil put his hands over his ears. Well, that would give him time to think, then, because Miknon couldn't listen to him argue in this noise.

Sadly, it gave her time to think, too. If anything went wrong with their plan, she would be back on the ship, but Gil would be abandoned on Ki with no way to get home. And how would she explain that to their mother?

But there was no safety anywhere, on the ship or on Ki. Not even their old world was safe, which was why they had left Kunisu. With danger everywhere, what difference did it make?

Her heart didn't believe her own arguments.

They left the building and saw a bundle of red fur high in a tree, which slept too soundly for them to tell what it was supposed to be.

Though Gil's mouth was covered by the mask, she could read his frown in his deeply scowling eyebrows. He didn't say anything, so maybe he was considering her arguments.

He ought to, because she was right. They had no other choice.

The next animal was huge, as large as a roc, but with a nose so long it reached the ground. And it used its nose to bang on a metal pipe in a simple rhythm. A human was with it, giving another of the explanations too complicated for Ian to interpret, though he tried his best. Near the end of the lecture, the "elufunt" reached out with its nose and poked the human in her belly.

Across from the animal's territory was a miniature of it in stone or metal, obviously not real from the difference in size.

"Fine," Gil said, "you can go back."

"Oh, thank you for your permission, *younger* brother."

Gil scowled harder. "And how would you tell the humans you need to find the dragon, hmm?"

They stopped near a tiny antelope, then a black bear behind large glass walls, then otters playing in the water. Gil took off his mask and leaned against the glass, making faces at the otters.

Helen checked her magic box, and talked to Ian, who crouched beside Gil.

"You want listen—"

Someone screamed. Miknon flattened herself on the bottom of the bag, peering up through the slit at her brother's face.

Ian slipped the mask back on Gil and jumped to his feet. Nik pushed the chair rapidly down the path and over another covered bridge. They all ran back to the building they had first come through and out to the wagon.

Working together, the humans got Gil and Miknon loaded before the other humans appeared to wave their magic boxes at the wagon. Nik drove away, winding down streets for a while.

Helen's magic box rang like the shift bells on the ship. She tapped at it, shoulders stiff, then held it to her ear and spoke.

Heartbeat too loud in her own ears to hear anything else, Miknon waited. Finally, Helen put down the box and spoke to her children. Nik nodded and turned the wagon around. Alexandria took a deep breath, and Ian rubbed his face.

"Talk about home now," Ian explained to Gil.

Miknon climbed from the bag and took her customary perch on Gil's shoulder. One hand on his necklace for balance, she leaned against his cheek.

"You can do this," she said.

But how could they make peace when the mere sight of them made some humans scream?

Chapter 11

Talks

THE DRIVE back to Bedford took an hour and a half, plenty long enough to let Alexandria fret.

Mom had completely rejected the general's idea to meet on base, insisting on neutral, public territory. She diplomatically didn't mention they were avoiding any traps. Instead, she explained that Gil didn't have any kind of ID, so he'd never be allowed on base in the first place.

The general said in public was too obvious, especially if soldiers were guarding it. Mom allowed a closed door for privacy, but forbade soldiers or guns. They didn't have weapons, so nobody else got weapons. Besides, if they were there to talk about peace, why would they start out in a hostile environment? The general could bring one of his soldiers, preferably someone useful to the conversation, and invite a couple of government officials who could make decisions.

As for the location, they settled on the local library. And Mom's voice stayed calm, without so much as a hint of worry. Mom was a wonder, that was all Alexandria could say.

But how would a fairy and a werewolf convince the United States military to facilitate a treaty with aliens? Mythical aliens, at that. They didn't even speak English!

Alexandria leaned toward the back seat. "Ian, are you sure you can translate everything?"

Her little brother grimaced. "I've had three days to learn! Of course I can't translate everything. Got a better idea?"

"No." She flopped against the seat and drummed her fingers on the door, thinking words that would get her mouth washed out with soap if she said them aloud.

Behind her, Ian, Gil, and Miknon practiced vocabulary again. Mom patted her shoulder with slightly shaking fingers. Maybe her calm was only a pose. Somehow, that made Alexandria feel a little better.

"We will make it work," Nikos murmured, sparing a glance away from the road.

Nodding, Alexandria reached for her notebook to make a list of their reasons and proofs. They'd better make it work. Somehow. Or everyone would be in trouble, not just them.

Three lists later, Nikos parked at the library. Alexandria hopped out to retrieve the wheelchair while Nikos lifted Gil from the truck. Mom slipped Miknon's backpack onto her chest, and Ian grabbed his books.

"Are we ready?" Mom asked.

"Okay?" Ian asked Gil.

The werewolf smiled before donning his mask. "Okay."

With Nikos pushing the wheelchair, the group wound through the library to the study room the general had designated. A burly man in a suit and dark glasses stood in front of the doorway.

"Hello," Alexandria said. "Excuse us, please."

"No kids allowed," the man grunted. "Private meeting."

Alexandria leaned sideways to see into the room, and the man squared his shoulders to fill the whole doorway.

"Beat it, kid."

Alexandria and the others retreated a few steps, and she waved through the room's small window at Anthony.

Major General Anthony jumped to his feet, nudged aside the hulk, and motioned the Fitches into the room.

"I'm sorry," Anthony said. "There seems to have been a misunderstanding."

"They're a bunch of kids," the hulk protested.

Mom blew him a kiss as she entered the room. "I appreciate the
compliment."

Nikos chuckled, and Alexandria rolled her eyes.

Inside the room, four more people sat around a long table. One
woman was dressed casually, and one wore a nice business skirt. Both
men wore suits and ties, and the older one jumped to his feet.

"What is this, General?" he protested. "We were told this concerns —
A bunch of kids don't belong in a top secret meeting."

What idiots. What difference did their age make if they were the
ones who had the information? Forget diplomacy, and if they didn't
want to talk privately, forget secrecy, too.

"You mean the peace talks between Earth and the spaceship that
landed on the moon?" Alexandria said.

The man in the suit glared at General Anthony, who quietly closed
the door with the hulk on the outside.

"I didn't leak anything," Anthony said. "They came to me. I've seen
proof of part of their story with my own eyes." He pulled out a chair for
Mom. "Mrs. Ellison, would you like to introduce the rest of your party?"

"Ms.," Mom corrected gently. "These are my children, Nikos, Alexandria, and Ian, and our guests, Gil and Miknon." She unzipped the backpack to reveal Miknon's blue head.

"This is ridiculous," the older suited man sputtered.

"Emil Compton is from the State Department," the general said
calmly, as if the government official wasn't acting like a child. "His
secretary is Allan Riggs."

Ah, then Compton was the one they had to convince.

After a glance at Anthony, the younger man stood and shook hands
with Mom, then with everyone but Miknon. Gil touched the man like
his hands were hot, jerking back after only a second. When Riggs shook
hands with Alexandria, his palms were cool and slightly damp, and his
smile wavered nervously. She smiled back, and his ears turned pink. She
hid her amusement and turned to the next person.

"My linguistic specialist, Raquel Maxwell," Anthony continued.

That was the woman in jeans and a pretty pink t-shirt, and her handshake was firm. Her grip on Gil lasted no longer than the others, but she turned his hand slightly to see his fingers better, and peered into his blue eyes.

"And Therese Ortiz from NASA."

"The Minor Planet Center," Ms. Ortiz corrected in a faint French accent, also shaking hands, "though we send information to NASA."

Compton might be the decision-maker, but if Alexandria could convince Ortiz they were telling the truth, the science arm might be a powerful ally.

Anthony sat, and Alexandria and Ian copied him on either side of Gil. Nikos remained standing behind Gil's wheelchair. Gil wiped his hands on his skirt. Maybe they should have asked him about greeting customs, after all.

Ian started to translate the introductions for Gil.

Mr. State-Department-Compton cleared his throat. "I don't think that's necessary when the meeting will be over in a few minutes."

He sank into his chair, with his secretary beside him. Major General Anthony sat on Compton's other side, followed by Maxwell and Ortiz.

"I don't believe in aliens. Can you prove your story?" Compton smirked, already sure of the answer.

With malicious glee, Alexandria reached for Gil's notebook in the stack of books. "I know you haven't released any photos of the spaceship, but we have a picture of it."

Ms. Ortiz-the-astronomer gasped. "You can't have a photo. All the professional telescopes are now classified, and no backyard telescope is strong enough to see anything."

Major General Anthony grinned.

"That's classified information," Compton complained. "We confirm nothing."

"Who said anything about a photo?" Alexandria flipped open the notebook to Gil's drawing and dropped it onto the table, turning it to face the inquisition. "Here."

Mr. Compton grunted. "That's not a spaceship, it's a castle. A kid's drawing."

But Ms. Ortiz grabbed the notebook. "Where did you get this?" Her hands shook, and her face paled.

"Gil drew it," Ian said. "It's where he came from."

Ms. Ortiz leaned down and pulled a photo from her briefcase. As soon as she slid it to Mr. Compton, his face turned red.

"General, arrest these people!" he bellowed.

Alexandria's heart rate rocketed, and she rehearsed judo moves in her head. Beside her, Nikos closed his hands around the wheelchair handles.

Mom remained sitting. "General, you gave your word we'd be safe."

Ms. Ortiz compared the drawing and the photo again. "I'm not blaming you, but did someone send this to you? Do you know who it was?"

Alexandria leaned over and removed Gil's medical mask. The werewolf's cheerful smile revealed his pointy teeth.

"Oh." Ms. Ortiz blinked. "He doesn't look quite human, does he?"

Mr. Secretary-Riggs flinched, and the military linguist squinted.

Mr. Compton flushed. "It could be a horrible birth defect."

"He has claws, too," Ms. Maxwell said, "instead of fingernails."

Linguist she might be, but her military training was showing. They all tried to look, but Gil's hands were currently in his lap, under the table.

"Birth defects, plural," Mr. Compton protested.

"And blue eyes," Maxwell said, "despite his black skin."

"Unusual," Ms. Ortiz said, "but you can't count that as a birth defect."

"Whatever." Compton waved his hand. "Got anything better?"

Ian turned to Miknon, who had barely moved so far. "Miknon magic?" he requested.

Slowly, Miknon began to glow. At first, the light in the room masked it, but the blue radiance increased a little at a time until it was bright enough to color the table blue.

"Nice toy you have," Mr. Compton said.

Good grief. Alexandria clenched her fist and smothered the urge to punch him in the face. "General, did you show that recording to your linguists?"

"Sure did." Anthony leaned back. "They don't know what language it is."

Maxwell leaned forward eagerly. "It might have bits of ancient Greek, or Babylonian, maybe Akkadian or Sumerian or something. But it isn't actually any of them. We don't understand what he said. Did he memorize a bunch of old words and then mispronounce them?"

Alexandria flipped through the notebook again until she found Gil's drawing of his original solar system. Um, planetary system, since his sun wasn't Sol. "Ian, please ask Gil to describe his home world, in his own language."

Fingers twitching, Ms. Ortiz stretched her neck to examine the picture. She slipped a small notebook from her skirt pocket and scribbled notes.

Ian sighed and rubbed his forehead, then stumbled through a mix of English and Alienglish.

Gil asked a few questions, then nodded. Pointing to different parts of the image, he talked and talked and talked. Maxwell-the-linguist blatantly recorded it on her phone, also taking notes of where Gil pointed and when.

Ms. Ortiz hummed. "Can you send me a copy?" she whispered.

Ms. Maxwell nodded and held a finger to her lips.

When Gil finally finished, he winked at the ladies and started over. This time, he spoke one word at a time. "Harmakis." He pointed to the innermost planet. "Hot." That was in English.

The second planet, Nirgul, was also labeled hot. After the third, Semud, he paused and opened the science book. A whispered consultation with Ian eventually settled on "rock."

"He might be talking about mining," Ian said, "but I'm not sure."

Fourth was Kunisu. "Home," Gil said in English. Madim was called "water," and the last two, Kayamanu and Chandri, were labeled "cold."

"Can I—" Ms. Ortiz's hands shook as she reached for the drawing. "May I have a copy of that?"

"Sure," Alexandria said. "Nikos, please go ask a librarian to make a few copies of the picture."

Mr. Compton sat bolt upright in his seat and adjusted his lapels. "My secretary can make the copies. Allan, make copies."

Folding her arms, Alexandria stared him down. "I'm afraid you haven't proven yourself trustworthy yet, *sir*. Nikos will make the copies."

Mr. Compton pressed his lips together and glared at Nikos. "I order you to let Mr. Riggs copy the paper."

Nikos took the drawing from Alexandria. "Sorry, sir, I've got my own chain of command."

He left the room with a soft remark to the hulk at the door, then disappeared into the library.

"Are you satisfied of the accuracy of their claims?" Major General Anthony asked.

"I have to admit," Ms. Ortiz said, "I don't know how they could have gotten an image of the spaceship."

"I need to analyze the language further," Ms. Maxwell said, "but I haven't caught an inconsistency yet."

"Ha," Mr. Compton said.

"But — what *is* he?" Mr. Riggs blurted. "Besides an alien, I mean."

"He's not an alien," Mr. Compton ground out. "It's a stupid prank by a bunch of kids."

Alexandria ignored Compton and grinned at the poor secretary who had to put up with the jerk. "He's a werewolf."

That turned every gaze to Gil in disbelief.

"Oh, you can't prove that," Mr. Compton complained.

"Sure we could," Alexandria said, "but this study room has a window. You want the library patrons to see a werewolf?"

"I saw him change," Anthony said, "with my own eyes this morning."

"You were tricked," Compton insisted. "Incompetent fool."

Major General Anthony glared at him, and a muscle in his jaw twitched.

Ms. Ortiz cleared her throat. "Perhaps you have other proof?"

"We already showed you Miknon's magic," Alexandria said, "their language, their spaceship, and their world. What more do you want?"

"The magic is nothing but a trick." Mr. Compton sneered. "Your little toy has wings, too, but can it fly?"

"Not at present," Mom said calmly. "She's still getting accustomed to Earth's gravity."

"That makes sense," Ortiz muttered, making another note.

"I don't believe in werewolves or — or fairies," Compton stated flatly. "They aren't real. And if they were real, we could win against them anyway. Wolves can't survive against a hail of bullets."

"Shouldn't we at least ask how many guns the aliens have?" Maxwell said dryly. "If we're determined to fight instead of let them land peacefully?"

While Ian tried to find the vocabulary to ask Gil the question, Nikos returned and passed around the photocopies. Finally, Ian pulled out his phone and found a photo of guns.

Gil shook his head. "No gun." He stared at the picture in puzzlement. "What is gun?"

"Ha!" Compton said. "Then why should we be afraid of them?"

"Who asked you to be afraid?" Alexandria said. "We're asking if they can immigrate peacefully. You know, cultural exchange and all that. Think what we could learn from them. Of course, if you don't believe them, they can go to the media and tell their story there. It will probably be a PR nightmare for the government. Wouldn't it be better to control the narrative from the start?"

Anthony nodded. "Much better."

Compton glared at her. "If you contact the media with wild stories, I'll have you thrown in jail."

"There are only ten thousand of them on the moon," Mom said. "Earth is big enough for us all."

"Earth isn't interested in them," Compton said.

Maxwell cleared her throat loudly.

"They have magic," Alexandria said. "If the United States won't ally with them, what about China, or Russia, or Iran? Do you want to risk them becoming our enemies? Isn't it better to see what they can offer us?"

"We'll shoot them from the sky before they can land," Compton said.

Mr. Riggs winced. "If you do that in a foreign territory," he whispered, "it would be an act of war."

"Then we'll tell the country there's a danger and let *them* shoot it down," Compton said. "They have no guns, no physical prowess, and *no magic*. I'm not worried, and dirty refugees don't have anything we want." He folded his arms again and leaned back in triumph, smirking. "No alliance. No landing. No aliens on Earth. Go away, stupid kids."

Stalling for time, Alexandria thumbed through her pages of lists. Had they failed, then? Was there no way to change his mind? Was a treaty doomed before they began?

CHAPTER 12

IN WHICH THEY BREAK
THE REST OF THE NEWS

DAY 3 AFTER LANDING, KI

GIL EXAMINED the grumpy man across from him. His crossed arms said he had made up his mind, and his smirk said the answer was no.

Ian's family had slumped shoulders and bowed heads. They saw the same thing.

No treaty with Ki. No peace for the fae.

Gil had failed. Tears burned at the back of his eyes, but he refused to let them fall. Once they left this useless meeting, he would find a way to get Miknon back to the dragon. She would tell Shar there was no hope, and the prince would let the council lead their armies against this world. Many thousands would die on both sides. His chest ached for family, friends, and failed allies.

The dark-haired lady raised her hand and asked a question.

"Why can't you go somewhere else?" Ian translated.

"We don't have enough supplies and don't know anywhere else to go," Gil said.

"If you know another world that is habitable, and give us a map and supplies, we'll leave," Miknon offered.

Gil flashed her a scowl, and she twitched her shoulders. She was right, though; like it or not, leaving was an option if there was somewhere else to go.

The lady glanced at the grumpy man, then licked her lips and spoke.

"I can give you a list of worlds that are moderately close and similar to Earth," Ian translated.

Alexandria leaned close and whispered in a hodgepodge mix of fae and human, "No. Worlds maybe good by star, but don't *know* if *good*." She grimaced. "I mean..."

Gil nodded. "Like red world here."

She relaxed and nodded. "Yes. Maybe good, maybe bad."

He faced the other humans. "No. We stay here. This our home now." They had nowhere else to go.

"It's *our* home," Grumpy said. "We don't need refyoojeez from spayse."

Not understanding the last words, Gil looked at Ian.

Ian flipped through a book and showed Gil and Miknon a photo of stars. "Spayse, between the stars." He pursed his lips and thought for a minute. "Refyoojeez leave their old home because it bad, and go to new place without home yet."

Gil nodded. "Refyoojeez from space, yes."

"We have enough refyoojeez already," Grumpy said. "Why should we take more? What can you offer?"

Alexandria lifted her gaze from her book and squared her chin. "Ian, ask Gil about magic."

Ha, he understood every word! And then the meaning sank in. Why did she want to know about magic?

Grumpy snorted and said something in a tone dripping with skepticism and derision.

"I don't think he believes in magic," Miknon said.

"That's stupid." Gil reached for the stack of books and pulled out the one about words. Whatever Alexandria had in mind, if it could convince the man to listen, he would tell them whatever they wanted to know.

Ian offered him the book with the pretend stories instead and opened it to show the page with sparkling magic. "Magic?"

"Yes," Miknon said. "Our people have magic."

Of course they did. Many of them, anyway, though some had more than others. Gil could only shift, and she could glow like all the pixies. Her light was useful, but it wasn't the pixies the humans should worry about. Not every fae cared if their magic was turned to the good.

Gil turned to the page with natural disasters and pointed to a flood. "Water mages can reroute a river or lake to irrigate crops or drown you." He mimed the drowning, then waited for Ian to decide what he meant and translate. "Earth mages can make flat ground for cities or crack the ground to swallow you." He pointed to a picture of an earthquake and clapped his hands together.

Grumpy still looked unimpressed, and Gil was tired of trying to appease him. The man ought to appreciate the warning instead of disregarding it. The book had no image of air, of course, but Gil pointed to a wind storm.

"Air mages can take away your air until you suffocate," he said. That took a little longer for Ian to decipher. "Fire mages can burn an entire forest." Easy with the pictures.

Grumpy stirred but kept his arms crossed. Something had caught his interest.

Gil continued, answering questions from Ian after every sentence until the boy nodded and translated. "We have mages who can read the secrets in your mind. Some can take over your body and turn your weapons against your neighbors."

True, not many had that much power, and they needed a name and a touch first, but all it took was one in the wrong place at the wrong time. And if Alexandria was trying to impress the man, pointing out the limitations wouldn't help. Considering how casually they touched each other and used their names, even in greeting, they couldn't have thought mages.

"Stonegazers can turn you to rock with a single look." He winked at Alexandria, who rolled her eyes. "Giants can squish two of you with every step." They only had one on *New Kunisu*, but once the rest of the fleet arrived, there would be more. "Shapeshifters come in many varieties, so you would never know if the animals you saw were one of us."

Alexandria opened the book of myths and stabbed her finger at various images, staring Grumpy in the eyes as she talked too fast for Gil to understand anything.

"She says you know most of these," Ian translated.

"None… real," Grumpy insisted, only some of his words recognizable. "Magic is not real."

"Stories. Magic pretend," Ian translated.

"Guns real, blah blah blah." Grumpy leaned forward and slammed his hands on the table, half-yelling a single sentence.

Ian rubbed his forehead and thought for a minute. "You say you give us wawr?" The last word was in his own language.

"What is 'wawr'?" Gil asked.

"War is fight." Alexandria punched her fists together. "Peace is not fight." She raised her eyebrows and jerked her chin in a tiny nod.

Most of the humans smelled of fear, and he finally understood. The humans feared the fae, feared their magic, lied about "real."

He still had a chance at peace.

"We don't want war," Gil said. "We want a home. There's no need to fight."

He had landed on Ki to save his sister and his people. As inadequate as he was to the task of making a treaty between the two worlds, he was the only one available. The responsibility weighed more than the constant downward pull of Ki.

Ian translated, a hopeful look on his young face.

"You go away." Grumpy spread his hands. "No war."

"We stay," Gil said. "We stay in peace or we stay in war. You say."

Leaving was not an option. Now was not the time to mention the council's plans for conquering or destroying Ki. If he could convince Ki — Earth — to seek peace, he would worry about the council later. With a treaty in hand, the prince would help him convince the rest of the fae.

"We stay," Gil repeated.

He held his breath and hoped for the right answer.

The man with the dog leaned over and whispered to Grumpy for several long minutes.

Miknon climbed to Gil's shoulder. Once at her customary perch with a grip on his necklace, she leaned against his cheek.

"You tried," she whispered. "Whatever happens, you tried."

Keeping his smile mild though his heart raced, Gil waited.

Grumpy frowned as he listened to the man with the dog. He shook his head, then shrugged, and finally nodded, though his frown continued.

The man with the dog sat back and raised an eyebrow at the woman in the pink shirt. She nodded once. The other woman looked from one face to another but said nothing. The youngest man watched Grumpy, sweat beading at his temples. He stank of fear, and Gil almost asked him if he needed help.

Finally, Grumpy smiled. It was not a nice smile. He said more words, then leaned back in triumph.

"He says he talk to king about peace," Ian translated.

"King not here," Gil said. "I here."

Ian rubbed his forehead. "Yes. But he says no peace without king."

Ah. It was a trick to avoid a treaty. Gil reached down the front of his shirt and removed his necklace. He slid aside his family emblem with a quiet pang and let the chain dangle from the king's signet ring. Tilting it to show the crest on the ring, he spoke in human so everyone would understand and wouldn't blame Ian for bad translation. "Say king *I* say. Talk peace, yes, or say I war."

The room erupted into loud conversation. The broad man outside the door peeked inside, then shut the door again at a motion from Grumpy.

Again, the man with the dog argued with Grumpy, but this time the other strangers joined in. Their body language said they opposed Grumpy, though the youngest man winced every time he spoke. Ian started to translate, but after the first word, the man with the dog waved him down. Ian grimaced at Gil and shrugged.

Gil shrugged off the silent apology. If the humans wanted to talk privately, he would let them. He could understand a few words without Ian's help, anyway, and the humans wouldn't realize how much he was picking up. "Peace" and "war" and "magic" were frequently mentioned.

Miknon gripped Gil's ear until he had to tap her foot to make her stop pinching him.

From behind the wheeled chair, Nik laid a gentle hand on Gil's shoulder.

Shifting to a more comfortable position, Gil waited. Across the table, the reek of fear increased until his nose burned.

Helen said something about "go," waving toward the door. The man with the dog shook his head, and Helen leaned back in her chair.

And still the humans argued. Gil smothered a yawn and resettled his broken leg. He had shifted often enough in the past three days that his leg had healed enough to start itching. Fortunately, he could remove the boot occasionally to scratch, but it wouldn't be diplomatic to do so now. As if to emphasize his helplessness, the itch intensified. Worse, the skin on his face, arms, and legs was tight and prickly. Even a gentle touch made it sting. If this was some magical torture from Grumpy to give a bargaining advantage, Gil dared not reveal its effectiveness. To keep his mind off his various discomforts, Gil tried to read the body language of his new friends.

Alexandria turned to a blank page and scribbled. Still planning, as always. Ian bit his lip and flipped through his books as if looking for something, but the answer wouldn't be there. Helen hummed almost inaudibly, sounding calm though her scent was spiked with anxiety. Nik transferred his weight from one leg to the other and back again. All of them were nervous, but none smelled panicked. Gil would wait, then, and see if Alexandria's plan worked.

Ian raised his hand and asked a question. The man with the dog raised his eyebrows and nodded. When Grumpy protested, the man with the dog nodded harder.

Turning to Gil, Ian whispered, "I say names and how people work, okay?"

He grimaced and rolled his eyes, then continued despite his obvious dissatisfaction with his vocabulary. Discreetly, he pointed to each human across the table and gave their names, then added a description.

Gil was surprised to be gifted the names. Did that mean the humans trusted him, or merely that they were so powerful they were unafraid of anything he might do? Or they had discovered he didn't have the magic to do anything with their names and were taunting him with his help-lessness?

Com-tun was called a lord, with a hand wiggle Gil interpreted to mean the term wasn't accurate but was the closest Ian knew. Gil had already identified him as the one to convince of the benefits of a treaty, unfortunately, since he seemed set against the fae. The younger man, Rigz, was some sort of helper to the not-quite-a-lord, which explained why he was afraid to contradict Grumpy.

Anthunee, the man with the dog, was a war man — warrior, Gil corrected, unsure if he meant a special warrior like the Companions who protected the king personally, and Ian wrote it down — though he was speaking sternly for peace. Mak-swill was a speaker for the warrior, and Ian motioned between himself and Gil, then between the woman and the warrior. Some sort of interpreter, then, and she was listening intently to Ian's explanation.

The other woman, Ohrteez, had something to do with the stars and spayse. A navigator, perhaps, or a contriver? If Gil's shipmates landed safely, he would see if Zak could discover a better explanation. Maybe with the help of Alexandria, who seemed to love that sort of thing.

Whatever their exact jobs, it seemed the warrior Anthunee had gath-ered a varied group to address their problem. That was a good sign. Com-tun's continued scowl was not. If the warrior was willing to consider peace, why wasn't the lord? Was he as arrogant as the old king's council members, sure of their power and right to rule?

Considering he didn't believe in magic when Miknon demonstrated it before his eyes, maybe he was stupid. But was he too stupid to want peace?

Ian finished talking and scanned his list of words again, mouthing them silently. The other interpreter asked him a question, and Ian nodded and handed his book to Nik, who took it outside the room. In a few minutes, Nik returned and gave pages to Mak-swill.

Anthunee thumped his fist on the table, startling everyone. Com-tun stopped talking, though his face turned red. Meeting the gaze of everyone in turn, Anthunee asked them each a question.

"Peace?"

"Yes," Mak-swill said.

Ohrteez bit her lip. "Yes."

"Yes," Rigz squeaked, moving slightly farther from Com-tun.

"Yes." Anthunee glared at Com-tun.

Com-tun folded his arms and glared back. "Not up to you." He turned to Gil and spoke sharply for a minute.

Ian translated the speech into three words. "What you want?"

Did they still have a chance, then? Gil reached up to touch Miknon softly, meeting the gaze of the angry man with all the hope in his heart.

"Home," Gil said. "Food, clothes, place, work. Peace."

With a nasty grin, Com-tun spoke. Ian turned the page in the word book to show a picture of endless sand. "Give home here?"

"Okay," Gil said, "and more."

Some of the fae would like the sand, but not all of them. They still needed a place for a garden, and some preferred water or ice. Com-tun snorted and bit out another question.

"How much land do you need?" Ian translated.

"You have to tell them about the fleet now," Miknon murmured in his ear.

But would the news improve their chances or ruin them? If they didn't appreciate the fae on the moon, they would like the rest of the fleet even less.

"Tell them," Miknon urged. "You're so sure you can make allies, and they have to know our needs."

Gil took a deep breath and reached for the empty book and the one with images of the stars. "One ship on moon."

"Yes," Ian agreed, then repeated it in human.

"Ten thousand on ship."

"Yes."

"More ships in stones." Gil flipped to the page with Ki and its neighbors lined up and moved the ship drawing to the first ring of stones between the worlds.

Alexandria peered over his shoulder and helped Ian interpret.

Ohrteez pressed her hands against the table and wheezed. Com-tun would have glared, but his eyes were too wide.

The warrior asked a question, and Ian translated. "How many people in all?"

Gil took a color stick and drew on a blank page. For ease in counting, he put ten rayed circles in a row, then moved to a new row. While he drew, Ian and Helen grabbed their own paper and explained how to count in fae. By the time he reached the bottom of the page, he didn't have quite enough room, so he ran two rows of ten up the side.

The humans silently watched, craning their necks in a vain attempt to see the paper. He double-checked his figures, then slid the paper to the middle of the table.

Anthunee counted across one row, then counted rows out loud. "Three hundred." He glanced at Helen. "Three hundred... thousand?"

The room was silent as everyone stared at Helen.

"Ye–yes," she said.

"Three hundred thousand," Mak-swill repeated. "With magic."

Ohrteez squeaked a question.

"They all come here? To Earth?" Ian translated.

"Yes, coming here to Ki." Gil held his breath and hoped.

CHAPTER 13

TREATY

IAN STARED at Gil in shock. Three hundred thousand aliens were coming to Earth?

"Oh, crap," Mom said.

Ian gasped. Mom never swore and never let them say bad words.

Alexandria blurted, "Mom, no swearing!" She bit her lip, but her eyes crinkled with humor.

"Okay, okay, I'm sorry." Mom waved her hand. "But three hundred thousand?"

"With magic," Ian added.

Alexandria turned to face Mr. Compton. "I think the State Department had better agree to a treaty, or you'll have to deal with an invasion instead of an easy little annihilation. Never mind ten thousand pixies — what about three hundred thousand werewolves? Or vampires or monsters. Maybe there's a Gil-galad among the elves!" She slammed open the myth book. "How many of these legends are real? How many do you really think we can win against if there are three hundred thousand of them?"

"Yeah," Ian said lamely.

Gil and Miknon were fine, but what if the other myths were like the horror stories?

Nikos snorted half a chuckle. "Do we need to add another war on Earth?"

Mom shook her head. "Don't forget the other side of the equation. Think about what they might be able to offer us. Whether you call it technology or magic, they clearly have abilities we don't. The opportunities for trade and learning might be endless."

Mr. Compton rubbed a shaking hand over his pale face. "I must talk to the President first."

Major General Anthony rose to his feet. "Then we will meet again. On Monday?" He looked from person to person, and everyone nodded. "Thank you for coming." He shook hands with each human as they exited.

Ms. Maxwell pulled Ian aside. "Thank you for the copy of your vocabulary list. Are you sure you have these spelled correctly? Frankly, I'm surprised to see they use Latin characters, though of course that would be easier for you."

Ian laughed. "Neither Gil nor Miknon knows how to read in any language, so I wrote them phonetically."

"Oh." Ms. Maxwell blinked. "They can't read at all?"

"That's what they said."

"Ian," Mom called.

Ian shrugged. "Sorry, I've gotta go."

"Right." Ms. Maxwell scanned the papers in her hand. "We'll talk later."

"Sure, as soon as the treaty is settled."

The military linguist groaned. "Right."

Mom called again, and Ian dashed off.

After everyone was loaded into the truck, Nikos twisted to look at Mom. "I guess we stay in Massachusetts for a few more days. Now what?"

"We need groceries," Alexandria said.

"And clean laundry," Mom added. "Pick a hotel, Nikos."

He nodded and pulled out his phone.

"By the time we get a room," Alexandria said, "we won't have time to shop, cook dinner, and do laundry before the Sabbath."

"We can skip laundry," Ian offered. "I don't mind wearing the same clothes."

Alexandria stuck out her tongue at him, and Nikos wrinkled his nose.

"Divide and conquer," Mom said, ignoring Ian's offer. "I'll stay at the hotel with Gil and Miknon to do laundry, and you kids can go shopping. When you get back, we'll eat dinner and fold the clean clothes."

"I hate folding," Ian groaned.

Mom rolled her eyes. "Well, lucky for you, you only have a few outfits in your bag, so it won't take you long. Keep up the attitude and I'll make you fold Gil's clothes, too."

"Yes, Mom."

Nikos started the truck and followed the GPS directions while Alexandria reviewed her shopping list. Ian explained the new plan to Gil and Miknon, who didn't raise any objections though they frowned and stared out the window. Gil rubbed his arms over and over and scrubbed at his face.

Finally, Mom leaned over Ian and took Gil's hand. She stretched his arm toward her and peered at his skin. "Oh my goodness, Gil! What happened to you?"

Small bumps were rising on Gil's arm. Ian checked the werewolf's cheek and neck. "There's more here. Is he allergic to something?"

"We have antihistamines in the first aid kit." Alexandria grimaced. "Do we dare give them to him?"

"Is he breathing well?" Nikos asked.

"Yes," Ian said after checking.

"Then we should wait until we get the room and can look better." Nikos glanced at his phone and sped up a little.

Fortunately, the rest of the trip to a motel didn't take long, and Nikos carried Gil inside for Mom to examine, then returned to help with the luggage.

Ian threw his duffel bag and Gil's into the corner. "Is he okay?"

Mom sat back with a sigh. "I think it's sunburn. These look like blisters rather than an allergic reaction." She stopped Gil from rubbing his arm again. "When you go shopping, please get aloe gel and sunscreen."

"He's got black skin," Alexandria protested, even as she amended her shopping list. "How can he sunburn?"

"How am I supposed to know?" Mom snapped. "Maybe the black isn't melanin, or maybe it's because a spaceship probably doesn't have sunlight. And humans with black skin can sunburn with enough exposure. Just get me the lotions, please." She grabbed Gil's hand again. "Ian, come tell him not to rub."

"I'll get ice." Nikos grabbed the ice bucket from the bathroom and disappeared down the hall.

The basic instruction wasn't too hard to interpret, but trying to explain how sunlight could burn from so far away was considerably more difficult. Gil kept asking about magic, and when Nikos returned with ice, Ian gave up.

Mom showed Gil how to gently rub the ice across his skin, and the boy's heartfelt sigh made Ian's stomach twist with guilt. How long had Gil been in pain? Why hadn't he said anything earlier?

"I'm ready," Alexandria said. "We can go as soon as you boys pull out your dirty clothes."

Ian dumped his entire bag, and Nikos pulled out a stack of folded clothes.

"You fold your dirty laundry?" Ian asked.

"In my suitcase, yes." Nikos ruffled Ian's hair and jingled his keys. "Ready?"

Snatching the keys, Ian raced outside. He managed to get in the truck before his sister or unofficially adopted brother, and stretched forward to lock them out.

Alexandria yanked the door open and watched the lock button descend. "Nice try, twerp."

She unlocked the doors so Nikos could enter, and Ian passed over the keys.

"Same food as always," Alexandria said, "but twice as much, plus the aloe and sunscreen. If you boys will get the food, I'll find the lotions."

"Deal," Nikos said.

Since their sister was on the other side of the store, Ian and Nikos picked a couple of treats not on the approved list, and had them paid for and opened by the time Alexandria arrived with the medical supplies.

Mouth full of delicious junk food, Ian grinned at her.

"Gross," she hissed. "Close your mouth. Honestly, can't I trust you two to behave yourselves for ten minutes?"

She rang up the lotions and grabbed a bag of groceries on her way out of the store. Shoulders shaking with amusement, the boys collected the rest of the food and followed her.

Her lecture on nutrition and budget lasted all the way back to the hotel and through Gil's treatment with the aloe gel. When the wolf asked for a translation, Ian giggled and shortened it to the minimum.

"She mad we not do what she say."

Gil looked at Miknon and laughed so hard Alexandria had to stop applying gel to his face.

"Sisters," Gil suggested in English.

"Argh!" Alexandria glared at Ian, but her fingers dabbed gently at Gil.

With everyone working together, they got a tall stack of sandwiches ready for dinner before Mom returned with the pile of laundry. She dumped it onto the empty bed and flopped into a chair.

"Thank goodness for multiple machines in the laundry room," she said. "Good work, everyone. Ian, say the blessing, please."

And then food occupied everyone. Gil grimaced every time he accidentally licked his fingers, but he didn't stop eating. The sandwiches vanished, and Alexandria threw a treat to everyone without tattling to Mom about the unauthorized buy.

Under the circumstances, Ian didn't dare complain about folding the clean laundry. They repacked their bags, and the ladies disappeared to their own room. Gil shifted to wolf and curled up on Ian's bed, and Nikos locked the door.

Early in the morning, Ian dug out the nicest clothing he had available, since his actual church clothes were packed in Alexandria's cedar chest. He chuckled. If he couldn't reach his good clothes, then Mom couldn't be mad at him for not wearing them.

That plan lasted only until the ladies arrived for breakfast. Alexandria, already in a skirt, passed him long pants and a blue button-up shirt.

"Best I could find in a hurry," she said.

"Ah, nuts," Ian grumbled. But at Mom's raised eyebrow, he changed without further comment.

Alexandria waved her phone. "I've been doing research. Lowell is only twenty minutes from here, and it has LDS and Greek Orthodox churches on the same street, that meet at about the same time. We can still make it if we hurry. Nikos, is that good enough, or do I need to look for a specific church?"

"Fine with me." The over-achieving Greek not only wore a nice shirt, he'd put something on his hair to make his curls stay in place.

Ian brushed his long bangs out of his eyes. He'd combed his hair; that was good enough.

Neither alien had church clothes, of course. Miknon would be inside the bag, and if anyone saw her, they'd have much bigger problems than what she wore. Gil's skirt and t-shirt matched for once. Mom showed him how to rub sunscreen on his skin, and Ian tried to explain it would protect him from the sun. Without magic. Really.

Gil insisted on calling it magic-in-a-bottle.

Once the werewolf was covered in bottled magic, it was time to go. They left their baggage in the hotel, since they'd be there at least until tomorrow.

As soon as they left the room, Gil shivered and wrapped his arms around himself. "Cold."

Ian glanced upward. The sky was cloudy, but it was only cool, not cold. The werewolf kept shivering, and Miknon squeaked inside the backpack.

"We can fix this." Nikos dropped Gil into the back seat of the truck, then hopped into the bed and rummaged through a previously untouched suitcase.

In a minute, he was back with a jacket and a pair of thin gloves. The jacket hung on Gil's near-starved frame, but too big was better than too small. Miknon shoved her legs into the fingers of one glove and wrapped the other around her back before sticking her arms down the fingers. Ian waited to grin until she was back inside her hideaway.

With everyone buckled, the truck headed out.

"Who's taking the aliens?" Nikos asked.

"I think we'd better," Mom said. "Miknon can't handle a human-sized bathroom by herself, and the siblings won't split up. Besides, there's more of us."

"I am badly outnumbered, yes," Nikos teased.

Nikos dropped everyone else at the LDS church, lifting Gil into his wheelchair. "I'll be back by eleven."

"We'll be fine," Alexandria said.

Ian grabbed the wheelchair and spun it in a circle before heading for the front door. Gil's laughter rolled across the parking lot, and Alexandria hurried ahead to hold open the door.

After church, Nikos was already waiting in the lobby. The trip back to the hotel was uneventful, and lunch was yet again sandwiches.

Mom sighed. "I will be so happy to finally have a stove again."

"Yeah, well, we don't have an apartment yet," Alexandria complained. At Nikos's hurt look, she patted his knee. "Not your fault. We'll get there. Sorry for being grouchy."

"I don't know how long we'll have to stay here," Mom fretted.

"Now that we have someone working on the problem," Ian said, "make them go to Pennsylvania to talk to Gil. Then we can find a place to live."

"We don't have a treaty yet," Nikos said. "Will they do that?"

Alexandria squinted her suddenly green eyes. "Tough, that's their problem. We need to find an apartment before school starts or we run out of money, and I assure you, we'll run out of money first."

"Any of those treats left?" Ian asked.

His scary sister could handle the military, the State Department, and just about anyone else, which left him free for more important matters, like wrestling Nikos for the last junk food.

MONDAY WAS sunny and warm again, but not hot. Gil slathered on the bottled magic but skipped the jacket.

Ian's head ached with an oncoming migraine, and though he took his meds and wore sunglasses, it was hard to think. Sadly, they had yet to find a medication that really worked for him, unlike Nikos. Not the best condition for translating, but he couldn't afford to stay in the hotel and curl up under the blankets.

When their group arrived at the library, the rest of the contingent was larger.

"This is Tricia Stafford, refugee specialist," Major General Anthony said, "and Clyde Farrell from the Office of International Affairs."

Ms. Stafford was not much taller than Ian and as cheerful as Gil, in contrast to serious Mr. Farrell, who barely fit between the arms of his chair. Both of them examined the Fitches and their friends with poorly hidden surprise, especially when Miknon climbed out of the backpack to sit on Gil's lap. Eyes wide, they looked at the general until he nodded.

Ian managed to explain "refugee specialist" to Gil and Miknon but got stuck on "International Affairs." They seemed to think he meant interracial or other species, and Ian couldn't get his brain to cooperate to explain separate countries. When he finally gave up, the general nodded at Mr. Compton.

Mr. Compton folded his hands on the table. "I talked to the President. He has agreed to a *temporary, provisional* treaty until the actual leaders land and we have enough language in common to discuss further terms."

Ian translated. Gil made a face and touched the lump under his shirt that was the king's ring, but he didn't argue.

"So," Mr. Compton continued, "we need to discuss your early needs."

"Home." Gil opened the picture dictionary to the farm pages. "Food home."

"He means they want farmland instead of desert," Ian said. "They weren't impressed by your last offer."

The newcomers squinted at Mr. Compton, whose cheeks turned pink.

"Farmland seems perfectly reasonable," Ms. Stafford said. "If they can grow their own food, they'll be less of a drain on other resources."

"Farmland," Mr. Compton agreed with a choked voice.

"Okay," Ian told Gil. "What else?"

"Want people free."

Mr. Compton winced a little. "Laws are laws, but we'll try not to add anything unreasonable."

After that was translated, Gil frowned. Miknon whispered something, and Gil smiled. "Talk to king."

"I suppose a maybe is as good as we get," Anthony said. "What else?"

"Want Earth magic," Gil said.

"What?" everyone chorused.

"Hang on," Ian said. "I'll try to see what he means."

He grabbed the picture dictionary and his vocabulary list and took a deep breath. Earth didn't have magic, so what was Gil talking about?

Fifteen minutes later, Ian laughed. "He means technology and reading, that's all."

"We won't give aliens our weapons technology," the major general said.

"Oh, no," Ian agreed. "He means microwaves and fridges and electricity and sunscreen and stuff."

The adults stared at him.

"Magic, huh?" Ms. Ortiz, the astronomer, said.

Ian shrugged. "I guess they look like magic to them."

"And reading?" Ms. Maxwell asked. The military linguist looked at her copy of Ian's vocabulary notes. "Why reading?"

Ian asked Gil and Miknon and relayed their answer. "Books trap thoughts. Reading lets us see the minds of others and learn what they know."

Mom chuckled. "I'm sure any librarians would agree. Really, how can you disagree with literacy?"

Ms. Stafford nodded. "Reading is a good idea. I would have suggested it eventually, anyway."

"How will we teach that many aliens to read?" Mr. Riggs said. The timid secretary clutched his pen like a lifeline.

"And how to live on Earth and speak English," Ms. Stafford said. "The sooner refugees are integrated into their new society, the fewer problems we hope to have."

"Just English?" Mr. Farrell asked. "They aren't all going to the U.S., are they?"

"Of course they aren't." Relief shone on Mr. Compton's face. "They can spread across the world."

Ms. Stafford groaned. "You just made everything harder."

"Only at first," Mr. Farrell said. "Eventually, having them in lots of different countries will spread the load, so to speak." He raised an eyebrow. "It's only harder until then."

Gil tugged Ian's elbow, and he turned aside to translate as much of the conversation as he could, shading his eyes from the bright library lights. The adults waited, more or less patiently.

When he finished, Alexandria raised her hand. "What about training the early ones as ambassadors? Then when the rest of them land, there will be lots of teachers and interpreters and so forth." She wrote "Alien Club" on her notebook and underlined it heavily. "I mean, only some of them are on the moon, right? It will take a while for the ones in the asteroid belt to get here. We might as well get some of their own people ready to handle stuff."

Ian smothered a giggle at her note. Who knew the ridiculous school club would actually come in handy?

"What about a school?" he asked. "I mean, if we need to teach them to speak and read and everything else, what about sending the kids to school? Gil, want children learn soon? Before all ships come? Send adults for other ships?"

"Okay," Gil agreed. "Children eat here, yes?"

"Yes," Ian agreed.

Mr. Compton grimaced. "You can't expect little kids to be ambassadors."

"How old are your people?" Ian asked Gil and Miknon. Oh, yeah, they only knew age in conjunctions, which wasn't yet translatable. He winced and tried to think of another way to put it. Stupid headache, anyway. "Um, how many much-little children?"

Gil laughed. "I most young. No little children, no."

"In all people?" Ian clarified. "All ships."

"Yes. No new children on ships."

Ian shrugged. "He says he's the youngest of them all."

Ms. Stafford tapped her lips with a pencil. "Then we could limit our efforts to high school. Save college for a few years until they speak an Earth language. That's much more manageable, especially since we'd only have the teenagers from the one ship at first."

"I'm sure one high school in Pennsylvania wouldn't be that hard," Ian said.

"We'll choose the location," Mr. Compton corrected.

"Pennsylvania," Alexandria said. "Nikos is going to college in Bethlehem, and our family is staying together. If you want our help, the school needs to be in Pennsylvania."

"Yeah," Ian said.

"Of course," Mom said.

Nikos grinned. "Family together."

"Oh, we don't need your help," Mr. Compton said.

Ms. Maxwell cleared her throat loudly, and Ms. Stafford winced.

"You want to lose our best translator?" Maxwell asked.

"And separate refugees from their only familiar faces?" Stafford said. "I don't advise it." She flipped to a clean page in her notebook. "Please ask them how many will be coming at first. I wonder why they're willing to send their children?"

Ian asked in several different ways and got several different answers. "Um, I think there are only two or three hundred teenagers, but the... wagons... or whatever they use for transport can hold more than that, maybe, so Miknon thinks maybe several hundred would come at first, then regular landings until the ship on the moon is empty." He spread his hands. "Or something like that. Sorry; I'll ask again when we have more vocabulary in common." And less of a headache.

Ms. Ortiz eyed Gil's wheelchair. "And they'll all need physical therapy, I assume, after years in space."

Ms. Stafford groaned and made another note. "This will take a lot of planning. How long do we have to get this done? A year?"

Ian translated for Gil, though he had to give the time in days.

"Oh, no," Gil said. "Must come soon or have no food. Children eat here, yes?"

Miknon rubbed her stomach for emphasis.

So that was why he had agreed. They were all starving, and Gil wanted to save the children. Ian shouldn't be surprised, considering the way their ribs could be easily traced, but he had foolishly assumed it was just the two of them in difficulties, not the entire shipload of aliens.

When Ian translated for the adults, everyone froze.

"How soon is soon?" Mr. Riggs whispered.

After consulting with the aliens, Ian said, "They aren't sure, but they guess between ten and fifty days before they have to start landing. If they translated the times correctly."

Ms. Stafford pressed hard enough on her pencil that the tip snapped. Wordlessly, Ms. Maxwell passed her another one.

"If we only have weeks before they attack," General Anthony said, "how do we get the news to their people that we'd prefer peace?"

"How tell king want peace?" Ian asked Gil.

Miknon stood straight, though she didn't reach Gil's chin. "I tell king," she shouted.

"How will you get to ship?" Ian translated for the astronomer.

Miknon shrugged and said a word he didn't recognize. He reached for the picture dictionary, but Gil pulled out the book of myths and flipped the pages to an image of a dragon.

"Dragon!" Ian said. "You have a dragon?"

Was it true or just a misunderstanding?

CHAPTER 14

IN WHICH THEY MUST FIND THE DRAGON

DAY 7 AFTER LANDING, KI

MIKNON LISTENED TO IAN CAREFULLY, trying to understand his instructions about the strange talk contrivance. Raydeeoh, according to the contriver who had brought it and taught Ian how to use the magic that would let her talk to the humans when she went back to the ship.

"No touch." Ian pointed to one of the wheels on the strange black box. "No, no, no."

She nodded. Never touch that wheel. The unrelenting gaze of the stranger in the room made her wings itch, and she stopped to glare at him. Helen and Anthunee-the-warrior spoke softly to the contriver, taking his attention off her, and Alexandria and Nik leaned forward to block the man's view.

Miknon focused on Ian again. She didn't know what might happen if she did touch the wheel, but it didn't matter. She had spent enough time with Zak, the youngest ship navigator, to know contrivance magic was picky. Maybe that wheel would blow off her fingers, or maybe it would only break. She had no room for error, so no touching.

"On." Ian twisted his fingers above the other wheel, which he had labeled with a single vertical line. First step.

Using her full arm strength, Miknon twisted the wheel.

"Talk." Ian pushed the bump on the side, now labeled with two vertical lines, and held the box near his mouth.

Too weak to lift a box half her size, Miknon left it on the table. But when she pushed the bump, the entire box slid away.

The stranger spoke with a mixture of derision and amazement in his tone. Ian didn't translate, so Miknon was sure the comment hadn't been kind or useful. The man in the green-splotched clothes hadn't stopped staring at Miknon since she emerged from the pink bag. He tried to touch her in the beginning, though Anthunee had jumped to stop him.

Obviously reluctant but obedient to Anthunee, the man in green had taught Ian how to use the black box, and Ian was now showing Miknon, though his instructions were much shorter than the stranger's. She was in favor of simple. Something in all this ought to be simple, and nothing else was.

"What if—" Gil started, but Miknon raised a hand.

"I can do it." She knelt on the opposite side of the box and reached across, pulling the bump toward her until it clicked into the box. "Talk."

"Good," Ian said.

The contriver argued with him, but Ian shook his head.

"Good, Miknon," Ian repeated.

He turned the marked wheel of the black box the opposite direction and slipped it into the bottom of Miknon's bag. The man in green examined Gil and Miknon again, as if they were a fungus on his grain, then left. Anthunee put three pictures on the table. Instead of being floppy like the book pages, these were stiff and slick.

Ian translated. "Land here, in night."

The first picture showed a lot of Ki and had an area circled. The next image showed the circled area but bigger, with another circle. The third showed a more detailed picture, as if the person drawing the image had been diving on the back of a dragon, closer and closer to the surface. Good, then she could match up their path as they traveled. But even the closest picture didn't show a landing dock.

"This isn't close enough," Miknon said. "Where exactly do we land?" She looked in vain for another image.

Ian conferred with Anthunee. Finally, he winced. "Not know where. Will say when you come."

Not a great plan so far, but she had to admit her end wasn't great, either. Fly back to the ship on the dragon, and hope Zak could let it back into the ship without being caught. Find her way through the ship without being seen. Tell the prince they had a treaty — sort of — and convince him to send all the children to a strange world without the army to protect them. Wait to send a message until the last minute, and make it hard for anyone but Gil to understand, because Ian said it could be overheard by others on Earth, and nobody knew if any of the fae could hear it.

Compared to those problems, not having a landing place sounded almost as easy as using the talk box.

They had all discussed the plan as much as possible with the language barrier. On the dragon, Miknon would take three Earth days to return to the ship. The air and cooling spells would hopefully still be with the dragon — or their plan had already failed — but she needed more food and water as well as the maps and speech contrivance. Once back on *New Kunisu*, she would plan the return trip with the prince and those of his advisors that knew he was still alive.

Ian tucked the pictures into her pink bag with the black talking box, and Nik opened the door. It was time to go. Miknon slid off the table into her pink bag on Gil's lap, and her brother curled one arm around her. Ian's family left the building and emerged under a cloudy sky.

No other humans were in sight, so Miknon opened the bag and folded down the top. The air was pleasantly warm, and she lifted her face to the breeze.

"I still think this is a bad idea," Gil muttered. "It should be me."

"I promise to be careful," Miknon said.

He sighed. "I know you will. You're always careful."

She patted his hand and closed her eyes to enjoy the fresh air before she was shut in a sealed box. If the council caught her sneaking around the ship, she might never feel this air again.

Instead of loading them into the wagon, the humans stood around talking. Nik held up four fingers. Anthunee frowned and argued. Nik shrugged, and Alexandria scowled. Helen spoke in a soothing voice.

Ian crouched by Gil's wheeled chair. "We talk about how to go to dragon."

Gil patted the vivid blue wagon.

Ian shrugged. "Anthunee not like four days."

The warrior pulled out yet another magic box and spoke into it for several minutes. Finally, he smiled and returned it to his pocket.

Ian translated. "He say friend help. Two days."

"How?" Miknon asked. "Will we fly?" She flapped her wings to demonstrate.

"Yes." Ian grinned and stood as Nik reached for Gil.

Within minutes, they were loaded into the wagon and leaving Anthunee behind. As Helen drove, Ian bounced on the seat and hung out his window.

"We know they don't have a dragon," Miknon said to Gil, "so are you guessing a roc or a phoenix or what?"

Gil leaned out his window and peered into the sky. "I don't know, but I'm excited to find out. What if they have a completely new beast?"

Eyes shining, he flashed his old grin, the one that said every day was exciting. Despite her continued worries, Miknon smiled. That was the brother she knew and loved, not the worried critic he had been lately. She settled back and let him crane his neck out the window.

No large birds appeared in the sky, but they soon saw flying barges. Unlike the fae vessels, these had nothing pulling them, though they had wings of their own.

"Amazing," Gil said. "Flying contrivances! Make sure you tell Zak about them."

"Maybe that should wait until after we land," she said, "or he'll want to spend time figuring out how to make his own."

"Oh, Zak knows what's important." Gil snickered. "But you can save them for a surprise."

This whole world was a surprise. A sun that rose and set, many new contrivances, talking boxes, and bottled magic that blocked the sun. And everyone could read and write. Mother would cry with happiness.

Helen stopped the wagon in the middle of a large complex of roads. Ian climbed into the back and stuffed some clothing, food, and water into a bag, then grabbed Nik's jacket. Once he hopped down, Helen hugged everyone, including Miknon and Gil, and Alexandria patted them on head or shoulder. Ian dropped the jacket inside Miknon's bag to pad the black box under her. Nik scooped Gil into his arms.

Ian threw the supply bag over his shoulder and gently held Miknon's in front of him. "Okay, we go."

To Miknon's surprise, the boys left Helen and Alexandria behind, heading for one of the smallest flying contrivances.

"What about family?" Miknon asked Ian, peering through the holey fabric of her carry bag. "And chair?"

"Family and chair stay," Ian said.

"I don't think there's room for them," Gil said. "That's a pretty small barge."

All four of them stared at the flying barge, which wasn't much larger than Nik's blue wagon. The red-striped wings extended straight, but the tail slanted up on each side, and three stiff feathers stuck out around the nose.

A female hopped from the barge and approached, smiling. She and Nik spoke, and though her eyebrows rose almost to her hair, she soon boosted Ian onto the wing and into the flying barge, bag and all. Nik lifted Gil onto the wing and let him carefully hop in by himself.

Four seats faced each other in the back. Nik helped Gil with his safety harness while Ian buckled Miknon's bag into another seat. The woman asked a question and waved toward the spot where the supply bag now sat. Ian answered in a breezy but squeaky voice, one hand clutching Miknon's bag. The woman shrugged and headed for the front seat, and Ian bounced next to Miknon and clicked his own harness.

The boys put big disks over their ears, and after a furtive look at the pilot, Ian unzipped Miknon's bag and tugged on the jacket. He mimed covering his ears, and Miknon nodded. Apparently, the disks were to protect their ears, but they didn't come in her size. Nothing on this world came in her size. She sighed and rearranged the jacket to pad her seat *and* cover her ears.

The need for ear protection soon became evident. The flying barge roared to life, accompanied by squeals and beeps and crackling speech. Then it moved forward, shaking and rumbling under Miknon, worse than the dragon. The noise and shaking continued, then the barge tilted and slowly rose. They were off. Through the giant sleeves pressed to her ears, Miknon could hear Gil's delighted laugh.

How could he be so carefree when everything could still go so very wrong? The dragon might get lost and wander around until Miknon starved. The prince might tell her the temporary treaty wasn't good enough. The council might see her or the prince and execute them for spying, or find the prince and kill him for being the heir. Someone might *tell* the council about the escape. Or maybe everything would go well to that point, but the council would botch the retrieval of the fleet or decide to invade anyway.

In a while, the temperature dropped, and Miknon burrowed under a layer of the jacket to keep herself warm. The noise and the pilot in the front seat kept her from talking to the boys, and boredom and the constant vibration soon put her to sleep.

A high-pitched squeal and a bump jolted her awake. Had they crashed? Been attacked? Only Gil's laughter kept her from panic. After more bouncing and squealing, the barge stopped and became silent. Nik hopped out first and helped Gil exit, then Ian carried Miknon's bag, leaving the supplies behind.

That must mean their trip wasn't over. Miknon subtly stretched, careful not to move the fabric and reveal that Ian had a hidden passenger. The air was boiling hot until the boys entered a nearby building.

Once inside a hygiene room, Ian froze. "Um, Nikos, we need Alexandria."

At the inns, everyone had used the same hygiene room. Were rules different here? Miknon couldn't go by herself, both because she would be seen and because she was too small to use the facilities by herself. But she didn't want Nik's or Ian's help, either.

"Gil," she begged, heat rising in her cheeks. Her brother was the least embarrassing option she had.

"Give me." Gil tugged until Ian let go, then stuck his arms through the straps to hang the bag on his chest.

Nik carried both of them into a tiny room inside the room and carefully set Gil standing on his good leg.

"Say okay," he instructed, then he left and closed the door.

From her position, Miknon couldn't see anything embarrassing while Gil took care of his needs. When it was her turn, Gil rather ostentatiously stared at the door while he kept her from falling into the water. Miknon ignored his smothered chuckles and hurried as fast as possible.

"Okay," she whispered.

"Okay," Gil repeated loudly.

Nik returned in a moment and took them to wash their hands.

Outside the hygiene room, Ian passed around snacks and water, then the four hurried back to the flying barge, which was ending its own meal.

Miknon slept through the next section of the trip, too, since it was easier to ignore the cold, noise, and vibration that way. This time, voices woke her instead of the thump of landing.

"Look," Gil shouted over the noise of the barge. "Trees and water. Good place—" He grunted and stopped talking.

Good place for a small dragon to hide, Miknon finished silently.

They kept flying for a little longer. When the barge landed again, Miknon held still and kept quiet to avoid detection.

When the prince negotiated a final treaty, she wouldn't have to hide anymore. Then she could see out her own window and feel the sun and fresh air always on her face.

If she was still alive by then.

This time, the boys took both bags with them, so it must be the end of the trip, but there were no trees or pond near them. Yet again, they were in the middle of roads and buildings, and the air was hot. Inside the nearest building, the four of them took another hygiene break and ate, then the boys talked to someone at a high table for several minutes.

Nik accepted a key and led the way to a wagon. With Ian and Miknon in the back and Gil in the front, Nik followed his magic box's directions to another road. He drove for a short time, then turned and drove again toward an empty field. Within a few minutes, trees appeared on either side of the road.

"There," Gil said. "I can smell the water. I doubt Azidaka would fly far away, not when shelter and water are so close. Poor little dragon; he's probably terrified."

Nik stopped the wagon, and everyone got out. Miknon climbed to Gil's shoulder and flapped her wings to work out the kinks of long inactivity.

Gil took off his shirt and sent Ian to leave it closer to the pond. All of them sat on the ground to wait for the dragon to catch his scent.

"What if the dragon did leave?" Miknon asked.

"Then we'll try again tomorrow," Gil said.

The sun sank closer to the horizon, and Miknon watched it with dread fascination. Ian had said the sun disappeared every night and came back each morning, but how did he know it would return tomorrow? A proper sun never moved in the sky.

Ian emptied the bag of supplies and counted the water bottles and food. He passed around one more snack to Gil and Miknon, though he and Nik took none. The light slowly dimmed, and still they waited. The dragonet might not emerge until it was truly dark.

"Are you ready?" Gil asked Miknon.

"Yes," she lied.

In truth, she wasn't ready. Not ready to hide from the council. Not ready to ignore her parents' murderers running free on board. Not ready to make the prince and his advisors believe the treaty was secure. And not ready to sneak two hundred children off the ship without getting caught.

Gil rubbed a hand through his raggedly cropped hair. "I think you'll have to kidnap Ram so he doesn't tell the council."

"Okay," Miknon said.

And how was she supposed to do that? Gil's twin brother was of course the same size as Gil, and stronger.

"Make sure you bring all the dragons," Gil continued, "so the council can't follow you."

"Okay." Which meant she needed to convince at least two dragon drivers to come.

"Shar, Nik, and Shalla will help you make plans and choose who to come."

"Of course," she repeated.

She hoped they would take over the plans entirely. Being a messenger was enough excitement for her. Ram was the one who wanted to be a hero. All she wanted was to survive and return safely.

"Meep."

Gil smiled. "Azidaka, there you are."

In the half-darkness, the baby dragon was a large shadow that gleamed when stray light struck it. Its eyes glowed as it crept closer.

"Um." Ian gulped. "Is dragon safe?"

"We hope the trees gave him enough cover to protect him," Gil said, mostly in his own language.

Miknon didn't know the right words, either.

After a minute of thinking, Ian squeaked. "No, is dragon safe for people? Dragon eat people?"

"Why would he eat people?" Gil asked. "No."

"What dragon eat?" Nik asked.

"Sun."

The humans said nothing for a long minute.

"Eat all sun?" Nik asked slowly.

"Sun in sky?" Ian said.

Miknon and Gil burst into laughter and couldn't stop. Imagine eating the whole sun! That would only make one meal, and what would the dragons do then? Holding her aching belly, Miknon shook her head.

"Eat sun come down." Gil spread his arms to indicate the sunlight that no longer shone in the "night."

The glowing eyes were now only a stone's throw away.

"Come on, Azidaka," Gil crooned. "Don't move, Nik, Ian. You are scary."

"Meep."

"*We* scary?" Ian whispered. But he and Nik froze, barely breathing.

With one eye watching the humans, the baby dragon crept to Gil and flopped to the ground, head in his lap. Its eyes closed, and a loud sigh blew Miknon's hair straight behind her.

"What's on its back?" Ian asked.

"Message box," Miknon said. "Where we escape."

"You *traveled* in that coffun?" Ian squeaked. "All the way from the moon?"

"What is coffun?" Gil asked.

"Um, never mind," Ian muttered. "Is dragon ready, then?"

Miknon closed her eyes and took a slow breath. Was *she* ready? Whether she was or not, it was time.

Gil patted the dragonet's head, then gently pushed it off his lap. "Up, Nik."

Once Nik helped him to his feet, he stepped on the dragon's knee with his good leg and carefully boosted himself to the top. He unlatched the message capsule and dropped his knife and Miknon's baby blanket to Ian, replacing them with the food, water, maps, and black talking box. He refolded the one remaining blanket to be more Miknon's size.

"Ready," Gil said.

The boys passed Miknon to her brother, and he paused for a hug. His arms were warm, but a suspicious dampness trickled down his cheek.

"May the stars light your path home." Gil's voice cracked on the last word.

"I love you," Miknon said.

Her chances of returning to her brother were smaller than she liked, but if she got the message to the prince, that would be good enough. She might even get to see Mother again before the lords killed her.

Slowly, Gil tucked her into the blanket-nest and lowered the lid. The reek of their prior trip had mostly faded, and Miknon took a deep breath to inhale the last bit of her brother's scent. It was almost like having him with her.

No, not at all like being with him. Sudden loneliness tore at her heart, and she pressed her hands to her chest.

The click of the lock echoed. She tapped the air spell to activate it. It gleamed lower than the halfway mark, but it didn't matter. Without Gil, it would last long enough.

The dragonet rose to its feet, and only the straps around Miknon kept her from sliding to the other end of the box. Then it ran, and Miknon bounced in her nest. She clutched the straps and concentrated on breathing slowly. Don't panic. She had done this before, and surely it would be easier for the dragon to return to the ship than it had been to land on a strange world.

Bounce, bounce, jerk. The dragon launched into the air, and with every flap of its wings, Miknon was pressed against the floor. Soon, the sense of too much weight returned. Her rib cage squished, and her lungs struggled to expand. Her limbs stuck to the floor like they were glued there. She concentrated on shallow breaths. In, out, in, out.

The temperature rose, and she tapped on the cold spell while they crossed the world barrier. In a few more minutes, weight and heat vanished, and only the straps kept her in place. The dragon had passed beyond the pull of Ki and was traveling to the moon.

Now all that was left was to report the treaty and convince her people to send their children to Ki. Earth, not Ki. The natives called it Earth, and courtesy demanded the correct usage.

And what of Gil, left behind in the hands of very tentative allies? If the prince didn't accept the treaty, Gil would be abandoned on Earth. If the council discovered he had landed on Earth without permission, they would declare him a traitor, to be killed on sight.

He could be the first casualty in the war if Miknon failed to prevent one.

Chapter 15

Science

June 23-24, 2023, Allentown and Reading, Pennsylvania

Alexandria waved her arm from the still-moving truck at the three boys huddled under the airport pickup awning. Nikos and Ian still wore the same shorts and t-shirts from the day before, but Gil was bundled in Nikos's jacket. The werewolf watched the pounding rain with an expression of awe.

"Roll up the window before we get wet," Mom said. "I'm sure they see us."

"Yeah, because this truck is as bright as a peacock," Alexandria joked. "With the sun behind the clouds, we're the brightest thing out here."

When Mom stopped at the curb of the Lehigh Valley International Airport, Alexandria shouted, "Hurry, slow pokes."

"You're a slow poke," Ian said. "We've been waiting for you for twenty minutes!"

He opened the back door for Nikos, whose arms were occupied with Gil, and all three were loaded in under a minute. Despite their hurry, they were rain-soaked and shivering.

"We left the hotel as soon as you called." Alexandria turned on the heat and pointed the vents toward the back. "Not our fault we had to drive instead of fly."

"Hello, Gil." Mom pulled back into the driving lane. "Nikos, Ian, did you eat lunch on the plane?"

"Just a snack when we refueled," Ian complained. "It was warmer in Columbus."

"It was hot in Columbus," Nikos corrected. "Gil almost melted."

Alexandria passed granola bars and pudding cups to the back seat, which two of the boys immediately pounced on. Instead of his usual smile, Gil's mouth was turned down, and for the first time since she'd met him, he didn't take any food. He rolled down the window and stared up at the gibbous moon peeking between the clouds, though no dragon could be seen. Poor guy must be worried sick about his sister.

"How was your flight?" Mom asked, taking the Thruway.

"It was the GOAT," Ian said. "Can I be a pilot?"

Mom exchanged a grin with Alexandria. "When you grow up, I don't care."

"But that's so long," Ian whined.

Nikos ruffled his hair. "It goes fast."

"Never mind the plane," Alexandria said, "tell me about the dragon!"

Ian shrugged. "It was too dark to see much."

"It was barely smaller than the truck," Nikos said, "but its wings were very large when it took off."

"And its eyes glowed in the dark," Ian said.

Nikos frowned. "I thought Gil and Miknon traveled in a cabin or something, but it was just a box on the dragon's back. I'm not sure how Gil fit in it."

Gil glanced briefly at them, then returned to his examination of the sky.

"Yeah," Ian whispered, "it was like a coffin."

Nikos elbowed him. "Yeah, and you *told* him that. Very diplomatic, considering his sister is traveling in it."

Ian stuck out his tongue. "What? It was! I didn't tell him what the word meant."

"All right, boys," Mom said. "That's enough."

"So," Alexandria said, "we've got good news and bad news."

"Bad besides the rain?" Ian asked.

"What's the good news?" Nikos asked.

"I found a judo class that starts next month," Alexandria said, "and Mom got a job."

"It's just stocking in a grocery store," Mom said, "but it will do while I look for something better. Once we get an apartment, I hope to find something in Bethlehem, anyway."

"Great," Nikos said. "Now as soon as I get a job—"

"And me," Alexandria interrupted.

"—we will be fine," Nikos finished.

"But until then," Mom continued, "I'm afraid we don't have enough money for two hotel rooms if we want to have enough for a rental deposit. We got the cheapest pet-friendly room, which is in Allentown." She bit her lip and looked at the boys in the rear-view mirror.

Ian shrugged. "So? Nikos is part of the family now. We can change clothes in the bathroom, and Gil usually sleeps as a wolf."

Alexandria and Nikos raised eyebrows at each other. Though they were siblings now, it wasn't the same as if they'd been reared together. To say nothing of the addition of Gil, who wasn't any kind of family. But Ian was right, even if he didn't recognize the awkwardness. Hopefully the business with the aliens would be settled soon so they could get an apartment with proper bedrooms.

"Are you sure that tiny radio will signal all the way from the moon?" Nikos asked, clearly changing the subject.

"Yes," Alexandria said, "I told you, the receiver will do the work."

He wrinkled his nose.

"Look, I promise," she said. "That handset has more power than some of the stuff they used in the Apollo missions. It's almost as powerful as Voyager's radio, and we pick that up even farther away."

Nikos raised his hands in surrender. "Okay, okay, you're the scientist. What are we doing next, besides waiting for the signal?"

"Dinner tonight," Alexandria said, "then a planetarium tomorrow. Therese Ortiz, the lady from the Minor Planet Center, really wants more information about Gil's home planet. Since we don't have a common vocabulary for that, I suggested we take him to the planetarium."

Ian rolled his eyes. "I shouldn't be surprised you found some excuse."

"Listen—" Alexandria started.

"No, no." Ian raised a hand. "In this case, I agree with you. I'm just not surprised, that's all."

"Hmph." Alexandria folded her arms and listened to the rain pound on the windows.

In the back seat, the boys talked about how cool the plane ride had been. And she hadn't gotten to go. Boring her, looking for jobs and hotel rooms. Well, somebody had to do it.

But she remained grumpy through dinner and bedtime.

THE NEXT DAY was still cloudy, but the rain had stopped and the temperature was warm enough that Gil didn't fuss about short sleeves or a liberal application of sunscreen. The planetarium show they wanted to see was in late afternoon, so they spent the morning searching online for jobs for Alexandria but finding nothing. Nikos was limited to on-campus jobs during the semester to avoid the hassle of a permit.

After lunch, they dropped Mom at her new job and restocked groceries. Gil's eyes grew wide over his mask as they walked the rows of the store.

"Much food," he croaked.

He grabbed random items, none of which were on the list, and explaining a budget to him was impossible. Apparently, he didn't have to pay for anything on the ship, though he also didn't get to choose what to eat.

When his ears drooped, Alexandria let him choose *one* snack not on the list, and he carried it on his lap to the checkout lines. Sadly, without proper cooking facilities, they were still mostly limited to sandwiches and cereal. To battle the craving for a hot meal, Alexandria started a list of recipes they could cook as soon as they got a kitchen again. Ian and Nikos enthusiastically suggested ideas in Greek and English.

Next on her task list was making more of the endless sandwiches for dinner after the planetarium. Once the food was stashed in the cooler, she and the boys drove an hour to Reading, Pennsylvania. They parked between the museum and the planetarium, then unloaded Gil and his wheelchair. Nikos pushed, Ian opened doors, and Alexandria bought tickets. The cost was almost as much as groceries, and her fingers shook as she handed it over. She'd better find a job soon, or her new judo class wouldn't be the only thing cut from the budget.

The rest of their party was already waiting for them amid the crowd. Today, Ms. Ortiz was dressed in slacks instead of business dress, though her sober navy blouse had fancy puffed sleeves with cuffs and her dark hair was impeccably brushed. Beside her, Ms. Maxwell yet again wore jeans and a plain t-shirt, this time in purple.

While they waited, the women chatted with the teens about the weather and the tiny deer in the area, and reintroduced themselves to Gil now that there were fewer names to remember.

"It's Mrs., not Ms.," the astronomer corrected. "Old-fashioned, I know, but I like it that way."

"Please call me Raquel," the military linguist said. "I get enough of Maxwell at work."

"So can we communicate any science words yet?" Mrs. Ortiz clenched her fingers on her black notebook.

Ian reviewed his list of vocabulary and the science picture book for a few minutes before the movie started.

The screen took them from the European Southern Observatory's Very Large Telescope (a name which made Ian snicker at its obviousness) to look at the stars, before virtually traveling through the solar system with a soundtrack representing each visual. Alexandria battled the compulsion to compare it to Peter and the Wolf, and won only because explaining it to Gil would give her a headache. Especially the parts about eating the duck and tying up the wolf.

Since the movie ended right before closing time, the group headed to a nearby park to talk more. Mrs. Ortiz opened her notebook and showed copies of Gil's drawings, laminated into a flip chart.

"I'm trying to decide where he came from," she said. "Ask him which direction."

With Ian's help to translate, Gil opened the science book and pointed to Jupiter.

"Okay, yes, but before that?" Mrs. Ortiz said.

Gil shrugged. "Not know."

"Not helpful," Mrs. Ortiz muttered. "How long did they travel? And how fast?"

"One hundred fifty-seven conjunctions," Gil said through Ian. "And not know."

Mrs. Ortiz took a deep breath. "He means a conjunction with planets lining up? They have them often enough to use them as a measurement of time? How often?"

"Yes, yes, and we don't know," Alexandria said.

Ian tried again to get more information.

Gil took back the laminated copy of his drawing of the worlds. He put his finger on the innermost planet and drew an imaginary line around that sun. "Harmakis up," he said. "Day."

"Days by the rising of a planet?" Raquel said. "Not the sun? That's odd."

"I already asked him," Alexandria said. "He thought it was strange our sun rose and set, and didn't recognize seasons in the book, and no, it wasn't because he was raised on a spaceship. I'm pretty sure his planet was tidally locked."

"Um—" Raquel said.

"Doesn't rotate," Alexandria explained. "Same side always faces the sun."

Mrs. Ortiz made a frantic note. "So they can't count years because there's no way to mark them. But then how do they tell time?" She dropped her pencil and rubbed her face.

Gil had watched her carefully, and now he tapped her shoulder and pointed to his image again. "Harmakis up. Day one." He tapped on the planet again, then a picture of a phoenix in the myth book. "Harmakis up, Nirgul up. Day two." An image of a singer, and a grimace that indicated an inadequate explanation.

For the third day, he tapped a gorgon and winked at Alexandria. Despite herself, she laughed. No, she was not a gorgon, thank you very much.

"I think he's giving us the days of the week," she said.

"Named after mythical beasts?" Raquel asked.

"Why not?" Mrs. Ortiz sighed. "Ours are named after mythical gods, mostly."

"The bigger question is why we have mythical beasts in common," Nikos murmured.

The women gasped, but Gil started talking again. The fourth day had three planets risen and was matched with a yeti. The fifth day was called a dragon, the sixth a giant, the seventh a griffin, the eighth a hydra, and the ninth a kraken. The sixth and ninth days also had three planets up, but not the same three. Every day was marked by the rise of Harmakis.

Gil then repeated the first eight days, but on the ninth, he said, "Conjunction."

"Okay, then, a week with nine days, and every two weeks is a conjunction." Mrs. Ortiz reviewed her notes, lips pursed. "How long is a day?"

Ian chatted with Gil for a minute before replying. "If I understand correctly, their day is forty-eight hours long."

"How long is an hour?" Raquel asked.

After translation, Gil shrugged. "Magic picture one hour, maybe?"

"The movie lasted forty-five minutes," Alexandria said. "Obviously, we shouldn't take that too strictly until we have more proof, but as a ballpark, we can guess our hours are roughly equivalent."

"That's still a pretty big margin of error," Mrs. Ortiz protested. "We could be off thirty-five percent."

"Or more." Raquel sighed.

"Any better ideas?" Alexandria asked tartly.

The poor werewolf was doing the best he could. She patted him on the shoulder and glared at the astronomer.

"No." Mrs. Ortiz made another note and tapped rapidly on her calculator. "Forty-eight hours in a day and nine days in a week gives thirty-six Earth days between conjunctions, times one hundred and fifty. They traveled about fifteen years, give or take a year or two, if we haven't completely miscalculated somewhere."

"Fifteen?" Alexandria narrowed her eyes to remember. "He told us he was one hundred and fifty-seven conjunctions old and guessed he's about my age. I think that's probably confirmation we aren't thirty-five percent off. Interesting that he's the same age as the journey took. I didn't realize he was born on the ship. Or maybe right before?"

"That also means they mature at about our rate," Raquel said. "Or at least some of them do, for at least a while. So the students going to high school should look about the same age, maybe."

Nikos grinned. "I think the human students might have other things on their minds than how old their roommates look."

"Like, are gorgons real?" Alexandria grinned. "Gil thinks they are."

Raquel widened her eyes. "Wow, I have so many questions."

"Since faster-than-light travel is impossible," Mrs. Ortiz muttered, "the formula for relative time gives us the maximum distance they could travel. With margin for error. I hate error." Her pencil zipped across the page. "I really want to learn where they came from."

"That might be useful," Raquel agreed.

"In many ways," Nikos murmured.

"Gil thinks our sun is very bright," Alexandria said, "If that helps."

"Okay, I'll start with dimmer stars." Mrs. Ortiz chewed on her pencil. "Wait a minute. Are these all planets in his drawing? None of them are moons? I assumed some were moons, but if they're all in a conjunction—?"

"He didn't know what our moon was," Ian said.

"Seven planets, then. Dimmer star. Fast orbit, since Harmakis rises every day. Seven planets. I wonder—" She rose and wandered toward her car. "But then their speed would have to be — There must be another option. Excuse me, goodbye."

"Goodbye." Alexandria waved to the woman's retreating back.

Raquel put a hand over her mouth and giggled. "Got something on her mind, apparently."

Gil's stomach rumbled loudly.

Alexandria didn't bother to hide her own laugh. "I think that's the signal to leave. I'm sure we'll talk to you again."

"I can practically guarantee it," Raquel said.

Once back in the truck, Alexandria passed around the sandwiches to eat on the way back to the hotel. They crossed back over a million bridges and hills, arriving in Allentown in time to pick up Mom from work. Ian scooted over next to Gil, who had fallen asleep on the way. Mom climbed into the back seat and took the sandwich Alexandria had saved for her despite the greedy boys.

Alexandria opened her lists and started planning the next day. Work for Mom, fortunately. Job hunting. Make a list of apartments to check out? Or was it wasted effort until Gil and Miknon had somewhere else to live?

Nikos parked the truck and pulled down the wheelchair. Mom and Ian got out, and Alexandria scribbled another note. Can't move in until Gil and Miknon move out. When would that be, anyway? Argh, why couldn't they get a home!

"Mama," Nikos said, "something's wrong with Gil."

"What?" Alexandria slammed her notebook closed. "Isn't he just sleeping?"

Ignoring the wheelchair, Nikos carried Gil inside and laid him on the bed. Ian pushed the empty wheelchair into the corner, and everyone crowded around the werewolf.

Helen touched his forehead. "He's burning up."

"What can we do?" Alexandria asked. "We don't know what human medicines might do to him, and we can't go to a hospital."

"Vet again?" Ian asked.

"He isn't a wolf right now," she said, "and I don't know if he's capable of shifting like this."

Alexandria stared at Gil, who thrashed weakly on the ugly hotel bedspread. What if he died? Worse, what would happen to the treaty if they couldn't save him?

CHAPTER 16

IN WHICH GIL IS SICK

DAYS 9-10 AFTER LANDING, KI

HOT, so hot. Gil pulled off his clothes.

Someone gasped and threw fabric over him.

No, too hot.

His whole body ached, and he was too tired to move. Too tired to open his eyes. Uselessly, he pushed at the blanket. Too hot. His stomach cramped and roiled with nausea.

His skin itched worse than it had from the sunlight blisters, but when he tried to scratch, someone held down his hands. He was no more effective at freeing himself from them than he had been at escaping the blanket.

Cold air hit him, and he shivered.

"Turn down the cold spell," he mumbled.

The cold froze his bones, especially his broken leg. He pulled off the boot and shifted to wolf. Someone pulled the blanket over him.

Too hot. He rolled away from the blanket and dropped his aching head on his paws. The mattress under him was soft and much too big and smelled peculiar. Had he accidentally crawled into a troll's bed?

He tried to get out, but his legs refused to obey him.

Shifting had been a bad idea. Now his stomach growled with hunger before twisting into a knot.

"Merodach, help," he called, but his voice was only a whisper. Where was his favorite healer? Or any healer. "Mother." Why wasn't anyone helping him?

He panted, and someone stroked his head. The scent of water hit his nose, so close. He moved barely enough to lap at the bowl touching his paws. The water cooled him, but his stomach protested, and he gagged.

The water disappeared, replaced by an empty bowl. Why were they tormenting him, keeping him from food and water?

The soft hand kept stroking his head and ears, and a quiet voice murmured something he couldn't understand.

"Mother," Gil cried.

He panted, and the water reappeared. Two swallows went down before he gagged again and the water was removed.

His fur itched. His ears itched. He scratched at his neck, then let his heavy paw fall.

Too cold. He shivered, and someone pulled the edge of a blanket over him.

His stomach cramped again. Had he been poisoned? Was it the contaminated grain or the council out to get the prince? Better tell Merodach and the prince's guards. But his throat croaked silently, and no one came. Where were they?

Where was he? The voices around him spoke nonsense, and he didn't hear Mother.

The water slid under his nose. He lapped once, then gave up. Too tired, and water only made his nausea worse.

Itchy. He rubbed his head on his paw only once. Too many fleas to fight. Let them eat him.

The light faded. Who had turned off the magic? Were they hiding an assassin? Was Miknon safely in the tunnels? He forced his eyes open, but the dim room swam in his vision.

"Miknon," he tried, but no sound emerged. "Mother."

Too hot. He pawed at the blanket, unable to move the leaden weight.

The voices kept talking in strange words. Magic spells? Useless to resist with no magic of his own.

The room grew bright and dim and hot and cold, and he could never get the right blankets. His body ached, and his head pounded, and his guts twisted with stabbing nausea. He shifted from wolf to boy and back again several times, desperate to ease his pains, but nothing worked. Water came and went, but no food despite his growing starvation. The room spun if he dared open his eyes, but his vision was too blurry to see anything anyway.

And always, the strange voices babbled around him. Where was his family, his people? Where was he?

He slid into unconsciousness.

In his dreams, monsters stalked him. He ran and ran, sides aching with breathlessness, panting and straining. His paws burned from thorns and sharp pebbles, and his stomach clenched with fear.

The monsters veered closer on the left, and he spun to the right, digging in his claws for an extra burst of speed. Just as he thought he would get away, a monster rose from the ground directly in front of him. It reared to full height, five times his size, and smashed him flat.

He died slowly, air and blood leaking from his body until he dissolved into the ground.

He reformed under the dirt. Clawing his way free, he found the monsters already waiting. This time, they held Miknon, Mother, and Ram in their terrible hands. Leering, the one that held Miknon flattened his hands together until her screams squeaked to silence.

Gil lunged at the one holding Mother. The monster turned aside, and another stabbed a spear through Gil's belly. Pinned to the ground, life dripping from him, he watched helplessly as the monsters ran off, with his mother and brother screaming his name.

Once dead, he came alive again, this time to face an entire army of beasts with talons or venomous tails or enormous teeth. And he was the only one on his side of the battlefield.

After he died, hacked to pieces, he rose again to face new horrors, again and again.

An eternity later, Gil opened his eyes to pale sunlight. His body ached like he had died a dozen times, stabbed or flattened, twisted or torn to a dozen pieces, poisoned or slowly starved. Had he finally escaped the monsters? Where was his family?

No, the ugly white walls of the Ki inn surrounded him. He was no longer on the ship. He was a boy again, naked under the blankets. The light streaming through the window was dim enough to be either early morning or late evening. Had he been trapped in evil dreams for a full day or only overnight?

It had felt like a dozen conjunctions. Or eternity.

Next to him on the bed, Ian slept on top of the blankets, one arm thrown over Gil.

Gil raised his head slowly to examine the room, and something rustled in the corner.

"Gil?" a voice said. "Okay?"

Nik. That was Nik. The human Nik, not the king's secretary.

"Okay," Gil whispered. "Ow." He gently lowered his head before it could fall off.

Nik sighed gustily and moved toward the other bed. "Helen, Alexandria. Gil is awake."

"Mmph," Alexandria said. "Goway."

"Wake up," Nik insisted.

The blanket on the other bed flipped back, and Helen swung out her feet and yawned. "I'm awake," she whispered. "What happened?"

Beside Gil, Ian stirred. "Gil?"

"Ow," Gil repeated. "Water?"

Alexandria shot upright in bed. "Gil?"

She bolted from bed, and all four humans stared at Gil.

Helen touched his forehead. "How do you feel?"

"I'll get water," Ian said.

"Are you hungry?" Alexandria asked. "Want food?"

"Yes," Gil said. His stomach churned. "No!"

He gagged, and Nik immediately held a bowl next to him. Just in time, for Gil's empty stomach rebelled. Acid burned his throat on the way out, and his belly cramped worse than ever. When he stopped vomiting, Nik removed the almost-empty bowl, and Ian pulled the blanket to his shoulders.

Gil pressed one hand to his head and the other to his stomach and groaned.

"How we help?" Helen asked.

"We need to take him to a dokter," Ian said. "Dokter helps sick person," he explained to Gil.

"Healer." Gil croaked the word in his own language. He shivered, and Alexandria added another blanket over him.

"We can't." Alexandria threw her hands into the air.

"How healer help you?" Helen asked.

"Magic," Gil said. How the healers took the illness out of blood was a mystery, but it always worked.

"Um." Ian winced. "Dokters not magic."

That started an argument Gil couldn't follow, especially with his aching head. Helen and Ian seemed to be on the side of taking Gil to a dokter anyway, while Alexandria and Nik seemed to think it was a bad idea. Dangerous, maybe? Not surprising. Gil didn't want to give any of his blood to people he didn't trust. Any number of terrible magics could be worked with a bit of blood. Maybe the "kwarunteen" Alexandria kept mentioning was one of those spells.

While they argued, Nik helped Gil sit, and Helen and Ian piled pillows. Once he could recline, Gil sipped cool water, eyes closed, and tried to decide what hurt most. He was still debating when the humans stopped talking.

"No dokter." Helen sighed.

"Not want go," Gil mumbled. "Stay with you."

Once again too hot, Gil pushed the blanket to his waist, stopping when Alexandria's cheeks turned red.

Ian pointed to Gil's chest and frowned. "Need eat more."

Weakly, Gil touched his sides. Every rib stood out. Too much shifting without eating. But food sounded horrible, and his stomach churned. "No food."

Helen touched his forehead again. "He still feels hot. What is nawr-muhl for him?"

Gil turned his head a trifle to look at Ian.

"Nawrmuhl is good, right, same all time," the boy explained.

"Oh. I am hot," Gil agreed.

He didn't know the words to tell them how hot, even if he could detect it himself.

Helen snorted. "Yes, but how hot? Sad hot or die hot?"

Gil shrugged. Even that little movement hurt.

"What meduhsin healers give you?" Nik asked.

That took Ian a long time to try to explain, and Gil still wasn't sure he understood at the end. The healers sometimes gave plants or drinks to the sick, but it was different every time, just a base for their healing power.

"Magic, not meduhsin," he repeated.

Alexandria said a word that Ian refused to translate. Helen scolded her, but Gil was now too cold to care. He pulled the blankets to his chin and shivered.

"Water," he begged.

Ian handed him the glass, and Gil managed to drink half of it before his stomach rebelled. Fortunately, Nik had kept the empty bowl nearby.

When Gil finished vomiting the water, he repeated, "No food."

He closed his eyes and huddled under the blankets. Food! Had he been poisoned after all?

He opened his eyes and grabbed Ian's arm. "Food bad?"

Ian frowned. "I don't think so. We ate the same food, and we're okay."

"He's eaten that stuff before," Alexandria said, "and not had a problem."

"No," Helen said, "food good. Gil sick."

"Blech." He'd never been sick longer than an hour before. It was no fun at all.

Gil threw his arm over his eyes to block the increasing light. It was morning, then, and he had only slept a few hours. He started to scratch his arms, and Ian grabbed his hands.

In desperation, Gil shifted to wolf again. At least his fur protected his skin a little.

But now he was too hot. He nosed the covers downward and fell back to an uneasy sleep.

He woke again to the sound of the door closing. Apparently, he had shifted again in his sleep, since he was yet again a boy. The covers were pushed down to his waist, and he was still hot.

Alexandria dropped several bags onto the table and removed the mask from her nose and mouth. "I think I got everything."

Helen immediately sorted through the bags, ordering her children to get water and put things in the magic heat box. Too dizzy to follow the conversation, Gil closed his eyes and concentrated on breathing.

In a few minutes, Alexandria tapped his shoulder. She stacked pillows again and helped him sit, then gave him a cup of something that smelled fresh and zingy.

"Drink," she said. "Slow."

He placed a hand on his stomach and grimaced.

"Yes." She shoved the cup toward him. "Help."

Reluctantly, he took the warm cup and sipped. It tasted as zingy as it smelled, as well as warm and cool at the same time. He gagged a few times, but to his surprise, the drink stayed down. In fact, his nausea seemed to ease a little.

Alexandria had been watching his face carefully, and now she nodded. "Okay, Ian."

Her little brother almost instantly appeared at the bedside with a bowl of something yellow and a slice of bread. Behind him, Nik held the familiar empty bowl. Alexandria set the drink on the little table by the bed and handed Gil the food instead.

"Apple." Ian smashed his hands together to illustrate what had happened to the fruit.

One tiny bite at a time, Gil forced down the food. The three human children sat on the other bed and watched him intently. Helen continued to rummage through the bags and put things into the heat box.

Gil gagged once, and Nik was instantly at his side, but the food stayed down.

"Okay," Gil croaked.

More slowly, he finished the smashed apple and half of the bread before his stomach clamped shut. He pushed away the bowl and several pillows and pulled the blankets higher. Within minutes, he was asleep, trapped in the world of bad dreams.

Every time he woke, the humans made him drink, then eat more smashed apple, bread, and a kind of soft white grain. Nik ferried him to and from the hygiene room, and someone was always available to adjust his pillows or blankets or keep him from scratching himself.

By the time the light faded again, his stomach was calmer, though he still ached horribly and was once again burning. He panted, trying to cool himself, but it didn't work.

At a command from Helen, Alexandria donned the mask and slipped out again. She returned in only a few minutes with a bowl full of shiny rocks. After wrapping the glittery stones in small cloths, she laid the packets on his head and chest. Instantly, cold soaked into him.

"What magic?" he asked.

"No magic," Ian said. "Ahys. Cold hard water."

Like the frozen water in the elders' tales of the ice worlds? Curiously, Gil unwrapped one package and poked at the shimmery miracle. Imagine, ice! Wait until he told Miknon.

"Why face?" he asked Alexandria, covering his mouth and nose with his hand to clarify.

"You sick," Alexandria said. "Not want more people sick."

"Mask make not sick?" he asked.

He would wear one if it would cure him. It wouldn't be worse than wearing it to keep humans from screaming at him.

With the book of word pictures, Ian tried to explain, but it didn't make any sense. The humans seemed to think there were tiny beings, too small to see, that made them sick. The mask was to keep the "jurms" from traveling to new people. With his headache pounding every time he moved, it was easy for Gil to keep from laughing at the silly idea. If it were true, then whenever one person got sick, lots of people could get sick. That never happened with the fae. The healers cured the sick person, and that was the end of it.

"Why not sick before?" Gil asked to prove his point.

Ian took a deep breath and kept talking. He seemed to think it took a while for the "jurms" to get strong enough to make someone sick. Hmm. Did the fae healers destroy the jurms while they were still too weak to transfer to anyone else? Was there any truth to this, then?

Maybe, or maybe the humans were ignorant. But they were worried enough to wear a mask when they left this room.

What if they were right about sharing this illness? If he had somehow been invaded by these jurms, could Miknon have been also?

He closed his eyes and imagined her in the tiny message capsule on the back of the dragon. Alone, without a healer or treatment. He was miserable with this illness, and she was weaker. Could she survive without help until she reached the ship?

And what if she did have these jurms? Could she spread the illness to the entire ship? What if the healers couldn't treat it and everyone on the ship died?

His mother, his brother, his prince, his friends, all his people. All dead.

The rest of the fleet was waiting in the ring of stones. Though every ship had their own pilots, only *New Kunisu* had the navigation device that allowed them to travel between the worlds. If no one from the prince's ship could retrieve the fleet, they would all die without reaching the new world, either as accidents picked them off or as they ran out of food.

His entire people might vanish like they had never been.

Suddenly, his fever dreams weren't the worst scenarios.

Chapter 17

Waiting

June 26-27, 2022, Allentown, Pennsylvania

When Gil woke again, Ian instantly looked up from his scriptures. "Are you okay?"

They had stayed home from church to maintain quarantine, studying the Sunday School lesson about King David as a family instead. The quiet worship time had been periodically interrupted by frantic care of the sick werewolf.

Now in late afternoon, everyone had been reading silently or planning or napping, though Alexandria and Nikos also jumped to attention at Gil's movement.

Gil rubbed his bleary eyes. "Okay."

That was an exaggeration, but at least he wasn't delirious this time. Sometimes he had raved and fought them, and even Nikos struggled to keep him safely in bed, especially without harming his broken leg.

Gil reached for the sheet, and Alexandria immediately turned her back, using the excuse of waking Mom. Ian bit his lip to keep from laughing. His sister's modesty had been badly stressed the past two days. It was bad enough Gil was naked because he kept randomly shifting from wolf to boy at an instant's notice, but his raging fever also made him unexpectedly push away the blankets.

Nikos grabbed the towel they kept handy and wrapped it around Gil before carrying him to the bathroom. The others jumped into the familiar routine and were ready when they returned. Ian put cool water on the nightstand, Alexandria handed over lukewarm mint tea, and Mom got applesauce and hot rice ready to go.

With any luck, Gil had caught a human disease rather than bringing an alien one to Earth. Not that the option was any better for him, but it was a better prospect for humanity.

Ever since he collapsed Thursday night, he'd hovered apparently on the edge of death. They hadn't dared take him to a doctor — or a vet — with his shape changing so often.

Besides, as Alexandria had said, without knowing anything about alien anatomy and chemistry, what could a doctor do? A blood test was meaningless, and they didn't know his regular temperature. They couldn't give him medicines without the possibility of killing him, though Mom decided mint tea for nausea was probably harmless since Gil had eaten their food with no evidence of allergies.

For the first time all weekend, Gil ate rapidly and easily and asked for more. Mom gave him only a slice of bread.

"More later, if that stays down." She sighed. "We might as well start making dinner."

Ian jumped to his feet. "No more sandwiches?"

When Alexandria picked up supplies for Gil, which were currently stacked in every corner in the room, she'd also gotten food they could actually cook in the microwave. Fancy it was not, but at least it was a change.

"We'll still use sandwiches when we're gone for a meal," Mom said, "but yes, let's cook tonight."

"Yay!" Ian rifled through the closest food stash. "What about this one? The rice is flavored, but it's still rice, so maybe Gil could eat it? If his snack stays down, I mean."

"I bought canned chicken somewhere." Alexandria grinned and

raised her eyebrows. "We could add it after we remove some rice for Gil."

"Okay, that works." Mom frowned. "But do we have a big enough microwave bowl?"

Like a magician, Alexandria reached behind her and pulled out a large bowl.

Smiling like crazy, Nikos rubbed his hands together. "What do you want me to do, Mama?"

With all of them working together, dinner preparations went quickly, and the hot meal tasted heavenly after almost two weeks of sandwiches and cold snacks. There were no leftovers, especially since Gil managed to eat again.

Then he promptly shifted to wolf and curled up for another nap while the humans cleaned.

"Do you think he'll be okay?" Ian asked Mom.

Sure, he looked a little better, sort of, but he was as skinny as photos of starving African children, and he'd only managed to stay awake for an hour.

Mom touched Gil's furry head. "He's a lot cooler now, and he seems less distressed. It's too early to say, but I think it's promising. In fact, if he's no worse in the morning, I should go in to work before I lose my job. They weren't happy about me taking two days off right after I started."

"We can take care of Gil," Alexandria said. "No worries."

But she bit her lip as she always did when she was worrying, glancing at her notebook of lists and plans.

Ian nodded vigorously. "Sure, Mom; we'll be fine. If he gets bad again, we'll call you."

"No worries," Nikos echoed.

In the morning, Gil was doing so much better that both Mom and Nikos left. After dropping Mom at work, Nikos planned to go to his college to look for a job. Though he couldn't start until August, if anything was open to applications, he wanted to be at the top of the list.

Alexandria watched them go, then turned with a smirk. "I'm in charge, so you can make the beds."

Ian folded his arms. "Gil's still in my bed, and you can make your own."

Nikos, the overachiever, had already rolled up his sleeping bag, and Gil was sound asleep again, tail curled over his nose.

Alexandria rolled her eyes. "Whatever. I'm going to look for jobs online."

Stacking pillows next to the sleeping wolf, Ian relaxed with a book.

In a couple of hours, Gil woke, shifted, and requested the bathroom.

Alexandria bit her lip. "Nikos isn't back yet. I can text him, but I don't know how close he is."

Gil squirmed and plucked at the covers, gaze flashing from one to the other. No time to wait for Nikos. Ian rummaged in the corner for Gil's medical boot and discarded skirt.

"Turn around," he told his sister, then helped Gil dress. "Okay, Alexandria, it's safe. You take one side and I'll take the other, and Gil can hop."

"What if he breaks his other leg?" But she was already moving forward.

With her much greater height, she took most of Gil's weight on her shoulders, though she abandoned the boys in the bathroom and nearly slammed the door in her haste to leave.

"Sorry," Gil said.

Ian shrugged. "Sisters."

He managed to get Gil to the sink to wash his hands, then called Alexandria back in. They settled the alien back on the bed, reclining on pillows.

Unlike the past three days, Gil showed no signs of immediately going back to sleep. "Miknon say?"

"No," Ian said, "we haven't heard from Miknon."

"How many days?" Gil asked.

Reluctantly, Ian held up five fingers. They had hoped Miknon could send a message when she reached the ship, supposedly two days ago. That hadn't happened, so either it wasn't safe for her to communicate or something else had gone wrong.

Gil sighed and clamped his lips together. "Okay."

He ran his fingers through his messy hair and glanced out the hotel window, though Miknon was too far to see, wherever she was. As a distraction, Ian tried to improve their mutual vocabulary about health while Alexandria reviewed her lists and made a snack. Gil was still eating when Alexandria's phone rang.

"Hey, Mom," she said. "Sure, they can call me. Okay, see you tonight." She hung up. "The powers that be will call us with questions about the aliens."

"Sure, but why?" Ian said.

"Why questions or why us?" she said. "I thought both were obvious."

"I mean, why are they asking a couple of kids?" he clarified.

"If Mom gets too many calls at work," she said, "she'll get fired. Besides, Gil is here with us, and you're our best translator. She says we can handle the questions, and any adult decisions can wait until she gets home."

"Well, if you're going to be logical about it." He shut his notebook. "Hey, Gil, want to watch a movie or something? Um, magic pictures?"

"They aren't magic," Alexandria said.

"Can *you* explain how television works?"

"Not really."

"Then magic is as good a word as any." Ian grabbed the remote and flipped channels for several minutes, finally settling on a science channel as a happy compromise between practical and easier to explain. He didn't want to try justifying the wars on the history channel, not when they were trying to broker a peace treaty for Earth.

The phone rang again, and after a brief greeting, Alexandria put it on speaker. Ian muted the television.

"Hello," Mr. Riggs said. "I'm working on the high school setup. I know Pennsylvania requirements, of course, but I need to know what, um, our visitors are likely to know. What do they usually study in school?"

The State Department secretary sounded much more relaxed, so Ian assumed his boss wasn't leaning over his shoulder at the moment.

"Sure, let me ask Gil," Ian said. "It might take a while, so should we call you back?"

"No, I'll wait," Mr. Riggs said. "I have Ms. Maxwell with me, and she'd appreciate the opportunity to eavesdrop, if that's all right."

At Ian's nod, Alexandria set her phone on the bed between Ian and Gil. With the help of the picture dictionary, Ian questioned Gil. He didn't get far. Apparently, girls rarely went to school and were only taught domestic skills at home. For boys, it depended on their social class or race — Ian wasn't sure which Gil meant. Some boys got only job training with a bit of counting and gymnastics, while others also learned poetry and music. Only a few learned to read and write, even among their rulers. Either the language barrier had struck again, or Gil was being careful about how he spoke about the nobles and their habits.

"Oh, dear," Mr. Riggs said. "I hoped we could translate textbooks to their writing as soon as we learned it, but it sounds like we'll have to start entirely from scratch. Thank you for asking. Goodbye."

Alexandria retrieved her phone, and Ian unmuted the show, only to mute it again a few minutes later to search the internet for an answer for Gil. They bounced back and forth between the television and the internet for a couple of hours, then Ms. Stafford called with questions about clothing, food, and housing. She wanted to come in person to show photos, but Major General Anthony had denied her request until Gil was completely well.

While Ian and Gil struggled through the vocabulary to answer Ms. Stafford, Alexandria made lunch and presented it with a mocking bow.

"Thank you," Ian mouthed, catching her self-pity, though Gil seemed to think nothing of being served. Either he'd gotten used to it because of his leg or it was something cultural. Either way, he'd get a rude awakening at some point. Even if Ian didn't tell him, Alexandria was sure to get fed up sooner or later.

"I wish we had better answers," Ms. Stafford complained. "I'm used to refugees who are at least the same species."

"Too bad," Alexandria interrupted bluntly. "You'll have to make do.

Food and housing are the first priorities, and we can decide everything else later if we have to."

Wow. Ian raised his eyebrows at his sister's rudeness to an adult. Good thing Mom wasn't here to hear it.

"You're right, of course." Ms. Stafford sighed. "I'll go see what I can do with this information, though I might call back later."

She hung up.

"Can't believe she didn't argue," Ian said.

"But I'm right," Alexandria said.

And then it was time for them to help Gil hop to the bathroom again.

After, Gil took another nap, shifting first to wolf, and Ian used the time to update his vocabulary notes and sort them. Look at him, making as many lists as Alexandria!

His sister, apparently bored with her own notes, cleared a space near the door and practiced her judo. She had been a blue belt for a while, and Ian had suspicions about why she hadn't reached brown. The reason was probably spelled D-A-D, since the stinker had messed up everything else in their lives, too; though he wasn't sure if the lack of advancement was just from moving around a lot or if Dad had been more directly involved.

Honestly, he didn't know what Alexandria used to see in Dad. Maybe she had better memories from when Ian was too little to remember. Or maybe Dad was nicer to her because she was a girl or didn't get migraines or liked science instead of languages. Who knew? And nobody cared.

Ian violently crossed off a word he had moved to a new list. Languages were handy, so there.

He was better off with Mom, anyway. And Alexandria and Nikos. And now he had a dog — right, not a dog. Nonetheless, he brushed Gil's furry back and grinned.

He finished his notes and returned to reading before Gil awoke, but Alexandria was still practicing.

"Do Alexandria what?" Gil asked sleepily. "Warrior?"

"She fights with body," Ian said, but had to ask for the vocabulary to exclude weapons.

"Is my brother a warrior," Gil noted in his peculiar grammar that made it sound like a question though it wasn't. "Eat?"

The door opened, and Nikos and Mom walked in.

"Yeah, Alexandria," Ian said, "why don't you cook dinner for us?"

"Hey, Ian," his sister said, "why don't I hang you upside down? I'm not your servant."

"I'll cook," Nikos said. "It's my turn, yes?"

With all of them back together, dinner conversation was mostly coordination and updates. Nikos had applied for a couple of jobs and tracked down the bookstore, though it was too early to buy his books. Mom got a text from Mrs. Ortiz, the astronomer, saying there had still been no message on the reserved frequency, and passed the phone from person to person instead of reading it out loud where Gil could hear.

Alexandria chewed on her lip again, but said nothing.

Mom's phone rang, and after the greeting, she put it on speaker.

"Sorry to bother you again," Mr. Riggs said. "Ms. Maxwell is here with me. We want to know how soon Ian can start teaching the language to diplomats and potential teachers. We realize he'll still have to do a lot of translating once school starts, but the more people we have who can speak a little, the less time we'll have to infringe on his classes."

"I'm just hanging around here," Ian said. "Whenever is fine."

"Great," Ms. Maxwell said, "then we'll do some Zoom classes tomorrow."

"Sounds like a plan," Mom said. "And of course, he'll be happy to come help after school every day, once that starts."

"After school?" Mr. Riggs said. "We planned to leave time in his schedule to help during school. Assign classes strategically, so he can translate right then."

"I'm only in eighth grade," Ian protested. "I won't be in high school."

If he was lucky, he could talk Mom into home-schooling him again, since he was old enough to stay home by himself while she was at work and responsible enough to get his assignments done.

"Oh, dear," Mr. Riggs said. "Let me see if I can add an eighth grade."

"Will you have only humans in it?" Alexandria said. "Gil is the youngest person on the ship, and he's about fifteen. None of the aliens will be in junior high."

"But we need Ian," Ms. Maxwell said.

"I'm sorry," Mom said. "You'll have to manage with extracurricular time."

Mr. Riggs wheezed. "Oh, no. That's not what Mr. Compton said." He sucked in air loudly enough for it to echo across the phone. "Ian seems pretty smart to me. I'll see what I can do."

The phone disconnected.

"What?" Alexandria narrowed her eyes. "That almost sounded like he's suggesting—"

"Oh, no," Ian said. "I don't want to go back to public school. I miss so many days with my migraines that the teachers get upset, and I want to spend my extra time on languages, not their stupid requirements." He shoved his bangs out of his eyes and clutched Mom's arm. "Don't make me go."

Chapter 18

In Which Miknon Returns to the Ship

Partway through her trip, Miknon got cold without Gil's body heat. Fear of being caught when she returned to the ship made her stomach churn with nausea. Her joints ached from rattling side to side in the capsule, bouncing against the straps.

Eventually, the heat of the dragon seeped through the floor and warmed her. The heat rose and rose, and by the time she realized she was boiling from fever, not the dragon's warmth, delirium tugged her into darkness.

Periodically she woke, to sweat and freeze and ache and itch alone in the dark, for days, weeks, eternities. What was wrong with her? Had she been poisoned by the stench of the flying barge? Drunk bad water? The air spell couldn't have gone wrong, could it?

The dragon bumped to a stop, and she vomited at the jolt. From the stench surrounding her, it wasn't the first time, but she didn't have the energy to move.

Meeping and crooning filtered into her prison, and the baby dragon jerked more, though softly. Finally, it stopped moving, leaning at an angle that slid her against one wall. A steady humming vibrated the capsule from both sides.

Some time later, light stabbed her eyes. Weakly, she threw her arm across her face.

"Oh, no," someone whispered. "Hang on."

Miknon tried to see who was talking, but her eyelids were too heavy to lift and the whisper was too soft to identify the voice. Cloth wiped at Miknon's face, then hands scooped her from the capsule and into — a bucket, judging by the curved wooden sides so close to her. The magic talk box settled beside her, and a lid closed, dropping her back into darkness.

Banging and scraping noises echoed softly for a few minutes, accompanied by grunts.

Then her prison rose and moved. As the bucket swung, she tried desperately to keep her stomach under control. If she vomited on the talk contrivance, she might break it.

Since the person carrying her hadn't killed her, she could probably assume he or she was a friend. But who was it and where were they taking her? She should be hiding in the maintenance tunnels now, but she couldn't sit, much less escape the bucket. And she had arrived during a weighted shift, when she couldn't move the talk contrivance by herself.

With no other choice, she waited.

The bucket never stopped moving for more than a moment, and the trip seemed to take forever. Miknon wrapped her arms around her stomach and endured.

Finally, the swinging stopped. The bucket settled onto the ground. The lid disappeared, letting light stream in.

"What's wrong with her?" the prince asked.

"Sick, I think," Zak's voice said.

Ah, Zak, of course. The gremlin navigator would have known when the dragonet approached the ship, and he was Gil's friend even if he did spend most of his time alone in the tower of the ship. They must now be in the auxiliary nav room, where the prince had been hiding since the assassination attempt.

Gingerly, Miknon waved a hand, though she didn't bother opening her eyes.

"Did you get the capsule put away?" the prince asked.

"Yes," the navigator said, "and now that their baby is back, the dragons have settled down. I left them curled up together. That black box was in the capsule with Miknon. It must be a Ki contrivance of some sort. I wonder how it works."

"Don't touch," Miknon croaked.

"I'll be careful." The young gremlin's tone was hurt.

But if he bumped the dials, he could ruin the signal for Earth — Ki. Or accidentally send a message prematurely. Miknon's throat hurt too much to explain. "No touching."

He sighed. "I won't play with it. Can we at least move it so we can take care of you? I promise to touch only the box, not the controls."

"I'll do that," the prince said. "You go find a healer and get some food, water, blankets, whatever Shalla thinks we need."

Footsteps pattered, and the door opened and closed. The prince moved around the room for a few minutes, while Miknon kept her eyes closed and concentrated on keeping her stomach inside her body.

"Are you ready?" the prince asked. "I'll move you now."

"Mmm," Miknon said.

Warm hands slid under her, supporting her gently. The prince laid her on a blanket and tucked a corner of it over her. A minute later, he set the cold, hard box of the talk contrivance next to her.

"Sorry about the cupboard," he said, his shadow blocking some of the light. "We have to be able to hide you without warning. I got caught once, when the council was searching for you. The blue-winged spy, they called you." He snorted. "I cowered, face to the floor, and pretended I was frightened of those bullies. They were so pleased with my terror that they never made me stand and show my face. No wings, you see, and much too big to be you. Stupid. Do you want water?"

At her tiny nod, he helped her sip. Pausing to squelch nausea made the process take so long that the door opened before they finished.

"Ah, Merodach," the prince said. "I appreciate you coming so quickly."

His shadow vanished only to be replaced with another.

"Greetings, Miknon," the healer said softly. "You look terrible." He examined her with questions and touch, then nipped her arm for a blood sample. "No one is to come in here besides those who have already been exposed."

Exposed? Like a disease, not bad air?

The healer's voice changed to a chiding tone. "And I'm not happy about you being here, Shar."

"Too late." The prince didn't sound sorry. "I'm not busy anyway, so I might as well take care of her. And as soon as she's well enough to talk, I need her update."

"I'll hurry with the cure as fast as I can," the healer said. "In the meantime, keep her warm and clean and give her as much water as she'll drink."

The outer door opened and closed, and the cupboard door moved inward until most of the light was blocked.

"We're right here," the navigator said. "We won't leave you."

And Miknon let her misery sweep her back into darkness.

EVERY TIME the cupboard door opened, Miknon cringed from the light. Gil's friends gave her water and a little food, cleaned her messes without complaint, and soothed her bad dreams. She wasn't sure how long she was sick before the healer returned, but the boys only sounded worried, not frantic.

"Drink this." The healer helped her sit and held a small cup to her lips.

The water was bitter, and she gagged on the nastiness.

"I know, but drink the whole thing," the healer murmured. "We're lucky this is an illness we can treat instead of a poison."

She choked it down, then held her stomach and hoped it stayed there.

"Now you two," the healer said.

The sounds of more gagging echoed in the room. Miknon would

have felt sorry for them if she wasn't still struggling to keep from vomiting.

"I need to put the cure in the water supply," the healer said. "Do I have permission?"

"Yes," the prince croaked. "How will you explain the taste?"

"A diluted solution will be sufficient to prevent the disease. Few will notice the taste. Only those who were actually exposed need the stronger dose."

Exposed. He had said that before. She had exposed the prince to a potentially lethal disease, if the healer hadn't been able to make a cure. And if it was an Earth disease, it could have been incurable.

"Lucky us," the gremlin groaned as the conversation went on around her.

"I'll be back tonight," the healer said. "Keep doing what you've been doing."

"Will she die?" the navigator whispered, not quite softly enough.

Miknon squeezed her eyelids tighter. No, she wouldn't die, because if the treaty fell apart, her brother would be abandoned on a strange world.

But for now, she must sleep again. In the dark cupboard, she fought the demon illness as she slept, determined to win.

WITHIN A DAY, her brief, miserable periods of waking became longer and more pleasant. Her stomach settled, and her aches faded to a hint of misery. The fever and chills evened to a normal warmth, and her dreams faded to nothing, though a nagging worry took their place. Her skin stopped itching from the inside, though only a bath would erase the grossness on the outside. The ship sadly had no hygiene facilities like Earth, and her cleansing was limited to a bucket of cool water and a damp cloth.

When she emerged from the cupboard, cleaner and dry and dressed in a borrowed outfit, the prince and gremlin were waiting. The prince was still disguised as a girl in a flounced skirt and long ringlets.

He waved his hand for her to take a seat on the floor in front of him. "Are you back because you made a treaty, or are you running from something?"

Miknon grimaced at the need to answer his questions before she could mention her personal concern. "We have a preliminary agreement, though the humans won't finalize it without talking to you."

"Hyoomuns." The prince drew out the word. "I gave Gil authority to speak for me."

"He tried." Miknon shrugged. "They also want more mutual language capabilities, which is reasonable."

"We can't stay up here much longer," the navigator said, "language or not. Did you explain that to them? Must we send the army?"

Miknon nodded vigorously. "They are anxious to avoid a war. You really don't want a war with them, anyway. They have as much stamina as orcs or trolls, and they greatly outnumber us."

"How do you know how many hyoomuns there are?" the gremlin asked.

"They told me." At their skeptical looks, she nodded emphatically. "They did. They are so unconcerned, their numbers are not secret. I calculated they have the population of two hundred and seventy fleets."

"Ships," the navigator corrected. "We can match that."

"*Fleets*," Miknon insisted.

"You must be wrong," the gremlin said. "That's more than we had on all seven worlds before we left."

Miknon folded her arms. "I'm not wrong."

The prince shrugged. "Vast numbers or not, they didn't look any more impressive than a highborn."

"You don't understand," Miknon said. "Some of them run for hours for *fun*. They are stronger than you think. Maybe we could conquer them, but I doubt we could do so without severe casualties on our side. Especially since you would have to attack them while still weak from our journey. My brother broke his leg merely exiting a barge."

The navigator winced and wrapped his arms around his knees.

"The plan was to land on the dark side of the world and build our strength before attacking," the prince said. "Then their strength is irrelevant, and if we conquer one settlement at a time, their numbers won't matter."

"There is no dark side," Miknon said.

"Of course there is," the gremlin said. "There always is."

Miknon shrugged. "On our old worlds, yes. Not here. I saw their sun rise and set every day I was there. At first we thought it was magic, but they say it's not. Their world *turns*, I tell you. There is no dark side. And their people fill the whole world. We were a small target on the dragonet, and lucky, but if you try to land an army, you'll be spotted."

"I didn't want to fight anyway," the prince said. "But if we don't have a treaty, what choice do we have? We can't stay here."

"We have no treaty yet," she said, "but we do have a temporary truce and a plan."

"Tell me the plan," the prince commanded.

Gil's plan. Was he still working on it, or...

"They are setting up a school to teach us their language and their world," Miknon said. "I came back to get all the children on *New Kunisu*."

"We don't really have children," the prince noted. "Ram and Gil are the youngest."

"Yes," she said, "but they mean those who are not yet adults. They want to teach the young while some of the adults go to retrieve the rest of the fleet. That will already ease the food supplies a little, and the dragons can gradually bring down those left on *New Kunisu*. By the time the other ships arrive, we will have many people who can speak their language and understand their culture. They will even teach us their reading. Then we will be in a good position for a treaty."

"Reading?" the gremlin asked. "Really? They aren't worried about us learning their magic spells?"

"They don't think they have magic." Miknon shrugged.

"But we've seen in the scrying bowl," the prince said.

"Yes," she said, "and it's everywhere. Magic light, magic heat, magic barges — that fly without dragons — magic talking boxes, magic pictures, magic sunstopper in a bottle. But they say it's not magic, and they don't mind teaching us."

Both boys sat silently for a long moment, eyes wide. They looked like Gil had when Ian said he would teach him to read.

"It sounds very egalitarian," the navigator finally said. "My grandmother would have approved."

"As would my father." The prince sighed. "But I still don't like sending the children alone."

"We can fill the two largest barges," Miknon said. "Any space not needed for the children can be used for their parents or other adults you trust."

As nice as Helen was, Miknon would rather have her own mother with her. And if Mother helped, it would be easier to kidnap Ram.

"After all," she continued, "we don't want to leave either dragon for the council to take to Ki. Their only options must be to go after the fleet or starve. Surely even they are smart enough to make the right choice rather than die."

"It will take a long time to retrieve the fleet." The navigator counted on his fingers and mouthed calculations.

"Yes," Miknon agreed, "but if the lords take the minimum staff in one of the smaller barges, the lighter craft will fly faster than this ship."

"Even with the children and the pilots gone," the prince said, "there will still be too many left here to feed for long. Perhaps we should put non-essential personnel into hibernation for a while."

"Good idea. We should have done it earlier." The gremlin nodded, then froze. "Oh." His long, pointed ears turned orange in distress.

"What's wrong?" Miknon asked.

"My father will have to go get the fleet. He's the best navigator, and loyal to the prince."

"I regret the necessity to part you two," the prince said.

"Gil and I will stay with you," Miknon offered.

If Gil was around then. Despite the low weight pulling from the — the moon, the humans called it — she felt heavy enough to sink through the floor. The navigator rolled his shoulders but didn't say anything. His ears stayed orange.

The prince rubbed his chin. "Your plan is not as sure as I wish, but it will do. We will make it work. Your efforts are appreciated."

Miknon took a deep breath and choked back a sob. Now was the time to mention the concern that had been bothering her ever since she put together the possibilities.

"There is one more problem," she said. "I don't know if Gil also became ill after I left Ki. The humans know nothing about healing us. If he got sick, he might not survive. I might be the only one left who knows any of the human language."

Not that she knew it well.

"Nonsense," the prince said. "He might not even be sick. Shifters are hardy people, and something that fells you might not touch him." Despite his brave words, his forehead wrinkled.

The gremlin's gaze flashed from the prince to Miknon. "Yes," he said, "he's probably perfectly healthy."

They were only trying to make her worry less. They didn't know if he was well. He could have been as deathly ill as she was, with no healer to chase away the disease.

Even if the plan worked and she returned to Earth, even if the treaty saved him from a war, he might already be dead.

CHAPTER 19

PLANNING

"YES," Alexandria said into her cell, "we're expecting some kind of message or signal any day now. But Miknon might wait until the last minute to send it, if she thinks she might be detected." By Earth or her own people.

She peeked through the window into their hotel room. Gil and Ian were still watching television and learning new words like crazy when Ian didn't have a migraine. The werewolf was still sick but managing most of his own care now. His appetite had returned with a vengeance, and the grocery bill was through the roof.

He didn't talk about his sister, and nobody wanted to worry him by pointing out they hadn't heard from her in five days. Granted, they had expected three days of silence and wouldn't have worried about longer if Gil's illness hadn't raised the question of his sister's health. Or survival.

To keep him from overhearing messages that might unexpectedly be disturbing, Alexandria usually took her calls outside. At least today was merely hot instead of boiling like yesterday, thanks to the cloud cover, and the hotel was surrounded by shady trees.

"After she signals," she said, "it will take about three days from leaving the ship to landing."

With everyone on high alert the whole time. Especially if the plans for dealing with the aliens weren't finished before then. With Mom working and Nikos preparing for school and running errands, most of the coordination with the military, scientists, and State Department had fallen to her. Her notebook was full of lists and questions to tackle, and a lot had question marks by them even after talking to Gil.

"That's not much time," Allan Riggs fretted.

"No," Alexandria agreed. She didn't envy the job of the poor State Department under-secretary, but it would be nice for her life to get back to normal. In a week or two, her extra guests would be someone else's problem, and she could concentrate on her family. "How is the red tape going for the school?"

"We're going to move exchange students in the FLEX program to the new school," Mr. Riggs said, "which will account for many of the human students we need. For the rest, we've already started recruiting locally and among other exchange programs. We made dual language abilities one of the requirements, so that will help narrow the field. We still have to interview the students, of course."

"That's great," Alexandria said. "What's next?"

"A building and teachers." Mr. Riggs sighed. "I'm working on inter-viewing teachers, but there aren't many school buildings for sale or rent."

"Does it have to be a school building?" Alexandria asked. "They'll all graduate in three years or less, and after that it will be awhile before any more of them are old enough. By then, they'll be spread across the world and will go to their local schools, right?"

"Right!" Mr. Riggs said. "Of course. So any building will do if it meets the need. Good idea." A keyboard clicked on the other end of the line.

"Maybe an apartment building?" Alexandria suggested. "Or an old hospital? Anything, really, that has a pool and gym for physical therapy.

And maybe a yard or flat roof for the dragons to land, if we don't find anything better."

"Dragons." Mr. Riggs gulped. "Are there really dragons?"

"My brothers saw one," Alexandria said. "The baby was as big as a pickup truck."

"Oh, dear." More typing sounds. "An elevator for the wheelchairs, yes?"

"Yes."

"Two hundred dorm rooms?"

"If you can get more," Alexandria said, "I recommend doing so. Gil thinks they'll send more of his people later, so we'd better have enough capacity for all of them, eventually."

Mr. Riggs groaned. "Ten thousand? Where can I find a building to hold ten thousand?"

"What about neighboring buildings?" she asked. "A one-year lease would give enough time to make other arrangements. And there's only so many the dragons can bring at once, remember. If Gil gave us the right numbers, it will take a year to get everyone landed, so you can get one or two buildings now and keep looking for more."

"Right." Mr. Riggs cleared his throat. "I've been working with Clyde Farrell from the Office of International Affairs. We're trying to prepare the other countries for these refugees, without sounding like crazy idiots."

"Having any luck?" Alexandria asked dryly.

He wheezed. "Anyway, whenever this secret breaks, we don't want the rest of the world either expecting us to shoulder all the burden or accusing us of building a magical army. Heh. It's rather tricky. But I don't need to bother you with the politics."

Alexandria's phone buzzed. "Oh, Mrs. Ortiz is calling. Did you need anything else from me?"

"Not right now," he said. "Thank you very much for your help."

Mr. Riggs hung up, and Alexandria answered the astronomer's call.

"Artemis will check on them," Therese Ortiz said without preamble.

"Excuse me? What are you talking about, Therese?" They'd talked often enough to abandon formality between the two of them. Their mutual love of science, particularly astronomy, had sealed their friendship. In fact, Therese would love Alexandria's shirt today. If they didn't get together when she was wearing it, she'd have to send a picture.

Therese took a deep breath. "Artemis will fly by the moon in August. NASA has agreed to take some close-up photos for us and see if the alien ship looks okay. If they need help, it will take longer to send another spacecraft, but at least we'd have a chance to help."

"That's wonderful news," Alexandria said a little dubiously. If it took months to help, any emergency would already be over by the time it arrived. But the thought was kind.

"So..." Therese hummed for a second. "Were you able to ask Gil if my guess about their planetary system is correct?"

"I asked," Alexandria said, "but he doesn't know. He said you'll have to talk to the navigators."

"Oh well." The astronomer sighed deeply. "I suppose my curiosity will have to wait. But unless they've learned how to break the laws of physics entirely, I'm pretty sure I'm right."

Alexandria laughed. "I'm dying to know, too, so when you find out, let me know."

They chatted about various James Webb Space Telescope images and other news articles of scientific interest, then Ian tapped on the inside of the window and beckoned.

"Sorry, Therese, I've got to go see what the boys are up to."

"Au revoir, Alexandria."

Alexandria pocketed her cell and entered the hotel, interrupting Ian's funny grimaces at the window.

"What's up, twerp?" she asked.

The air conditioning hit her sweaty neck, and she lifted her hair to cool off faster.

"It's lunch time," he said. "We want food."

Putting her hands on her hips, Alexandria glared at him. "Did you break your fingers while I was outside? Should I call 911 or just Mom?"

Ian rolled his eyes. "I'll make the food. But the last time I picked something without asking you, I 'ruined your meal plans.'" He made air quotes around the words, backing out of swatting reach at the same time. "So tell me what's okay to eat, okay?"

"Fine." She thumped three different choices onto the small hotel table. "Any of these."

"Great." Ian snatched two and showed them to Gil.

Once a final choice was made, Ian kept his promise and cooked by himself, narrating through the steps like he always did so Gil could follow along and learn more words.

In the interest of family harmony, Alexandria set the table without comment.

After the three of them ate, Gil shifted to wolf and curled up for a nap. As weird as the idea was, the practice seemed to heal him faster. Even his injured leg hurt less, he said, though he'd broken it just over a week earlier. Her scientific brain badly wanted to compare the healing times of two werewolves, one who shifted and one who didn't, but she didn't have two werewolves, much less two with broken legs. And it wasn't ethical to wish for injuries for the experiment.

Since Ian had cooked, she washed dishes, then she reviewed her lists while Ian went over his alien vocabulary. Gil was still asleep, so she switched to judo practice when Ian winced and covered his eyes. Her new judo class didn't start for another month, but she wanted to be in shape so she could level up to brown belt as soon as possible. Her future college career depended on a scholarship, and her grades were only respectable, unlike brainy Ian's. But the air conditioning made it tolerable to struggle through her exercises in the small hotel room rather than go back outside.

The boys slept all afternoon, waking only when Mom and Nikos walked in.

Nikos hefted three flat boxes into the air. "We got pizza."

"Yay," Ian cheered.

The vegetarian pizza went to Gil, who ate it by himself with much finger-licking. Mom had one slice of pepperoni and one of pineapple ham, and the perpetually hungry teens polished off the rest of it. For once, the boys didn't fight over the last slice, and Alexandria managed to snag it.

With no dishes to wash, cleanup took seconds. Everyone was still chatting about their day when someone knocked on the door. Mom opened it wide, revealing Raquel Maxwell, the military linguist, and Mr. High-and-Mighty Compton himself.

Alexandria turned her head to hide her grimace. The State Department Secretary usually tried to avoid the actual work meetings, to everyone's relief. What did he want now? Behind Compton, his hulking bodyguard looked bored.

"May we come in?" Mr. Compton said. "We have a few questions."

Mom looked at the hotel room and bit her lip. "There's not a lot of room. What if we come outside? It's cooler than it was earlier. Or if we need a longer conversation, I suppose Gil is well enough to go to a library or something."

"We'll keep it short," Raquel promised, "so we don't cause a relapse."

The glare Compton threw her way didn't seem to faze her. Compton snorted but walked back and leaned against his car's hood. Alexandria didn't know enough about cars to know if she should be extra impressed with the convertible, but it looked like it had been freshly washed and waxed. His bodyguard didn't touch the car but constantly scanned the area.

Ian unfolded the wheelchair, and Nikos settled Gil in it, still bare-chested. In this heat, nobody wanted extra layers, and Gil was still shifting every few hours. Everyone exited the hotel and found a place to stand in the shade of the trees between the building and the sidewalk.

"Since we're in a hurry," Compton said, "I'll cut to the chase. Since we still haven't heard from the fairy, do we know if she made it back alive or if she died with the same disease he had?" He pointed rudely at Gil.

"I'm not translating that," Ian said. "If Gil hasn't wondered about that possibility yet, we won't mention it."

"Have a heart," Mom said. "That's his sister you're talking about."

Compton sniffed. "But what if she did die? What do we do then?"

"We'll try to meet the first ship coming down," Alexandria said. "Gil will help us talk to them."

And maybe it would be totally useless at that point, but they would try.

"Where will they land?" Compton asked. "What kind of ships do they have? What landing facilities do they need?"

"Hang on," Ian said. "I'll see what Gil knows."

He crouched in front of Gil's wheelchair and chattered away in a funny mix of English and Alienglish, looking very serious despite his floppy bangs.

Compton checked his watch, but Ian kept talking. It wasn't long before he stood, despite Compton's impatience.

"Can't help you on the landing site," Ian said, "but he says the dragon barges look like big boxes and must land on water. Actually, Miknon doesn't know where you want them to land, even if she's fine. You still need to pick somewhere."

Pulling out her phone, Raquel made a note. "The river, maybe? I'll see if there's a good spot."

"And how," Compton asked, "can we convince them in a hurry that Earth is different from their old world and not ready for conquest?"

"Well, the sun rises," Alexandria muttered, knowing it wasn't what the jerk meant.

After consulting with Gil, Ian said, "Put a woman in charge. He says women never lead in his society, so that will make them think twice about what else might be different."

Mr. Compton narrowed his eyes. "*I'm* in charge of this fiasco."

"Perhaps you could designate a woman to deal with the day-to-day decisions," Mom soothed. "Since you are very busy. Someone in the military, maybe, since Gil's people don't have female warriors, either."

Eyebrows lifted, Raquel made another note, then winked at Alexandria. Oh, ho, since she was learning the language, maybe she figured she'd end up in charge. Well, that was fine with Alexandria. The linguist was kind and easy to work with.

"Riggs is working on housing," Compton continued. "As soon as he finds a building, we'll move the boy over there."

"What?" Ian squeaked. "No way. He's staying with us."

"We're putting all the aliens together," Compton said. "We want to keep an eye on them."

"No fair," Ian whined. He translated for Gil, who frowned.

Nikos's phone beeped. He looked at the screen and headed inside. "Sorry, this is about an apartment. I'll be right back."

Raquel, who had been staring at Alexandria's red t-shirt during the whole conversation, suddenly laughed. "Oh, I get it. Blue shift."

Winking, Alexandria pulled the shirt taut to show off the words. *This shirt is blue if you run fast enough.* Half of her shirts had astronomy jokes on them, because why waste an opportunity?

"Could we focus on the problem?" Compton griped.

Ian folded his arms. "He says he'll do what the treaty requires. But I want to keep him!"

"Ian." Mom sighed. "We already talked about this."

"He's not a dog," Alexandria whispered. "You can't keep him."

"But Mom—" Ian whined.

Gil was still frowning, sadly instead of fiercely. His fingers were clutched together. Since Ian was busy arguing with Mom, Alexandria crouched to comfort Gil.

"It's okay," she said.

Gil nodded but didn't look at her. She touched his knee and tried to think of what else to say. If the treaty needed him to live with the others, how could they fight that? And what a hypocrite she was, since she was looking forward to getting his problems out of her life. But she didn't want him to be sad, either. Where was the answer?

A man parked one door down and got out. He examined Nikos's bright blue truck, reading the Colorado license plate, then slammed his car door. Compton's bodyguard examined the newcomer, sneering at the unkempt, skinny dude with his jeans hanging low.

"We'll visit," Alexandria offered Gil, then didn't know if that was on his vocabulary list yet. Drat, this language barrier was the pits! Uselessly, she patted his knee.

He untangled his death grip on himself and put a hand over hers. "Okay."

Great, now the sad alien was trying to comfort *her.*

The new hotel guest wandered down the sidewalk toward them. Those on the sidewalk split to either side to let the man pass. As he walked closer, he glared at Gil.

Alexandria glared back. Whether he objected to Gil's skin color, his wheelchair, or his skirt didn't matter; he should mind his own business.

At a yard away, the man screamed. "Go home, werewolf!"

Great, one of the kooks off the internet. Alexandria squeezed Gil's hand, hoping he didn't understand.

Then the man yanked a knife from behind his back and dove at the wheelchair-bound boy.

The bodyguard dragged Mr. Compton down behind his car. Raquel slapped at her belt and swore.

Alexandria's training kicked in without thought. She spun and lunged at the same time, ignoring fancy holds and throws. Her shoulder collided with the man's hips, and she wrapped her arms around his knees and threw herself sideways to knock him off balance.

Opponents rarely expected a girl to body-check them.

CHAPTER 20

IN WHICH BLOOD IS SPILLED

DAY 12 AFTER LANDING, KI

FINALLY FINDING HIS VOICE, Gil screamed.

Alexandria and the man hit the ground and rolled, knife flying to the side. As she let go and kept rolling, Mak-swill stepped forward and kicked the knife away.

Gil pushed himself up so forcefully that his leg stabbed with pain, knocking him back to his seat. The man crawled to his knees and staggered forward, clutching his ribs. Mak-swill punched him, but the man rocked sideways and kept going. He lunged forward and squeezed Gil around the neck.

Worse than the pain, Gil's air disappeared. He clawed at the man's arms, but his attacker didn't flinch. He stared down at Gil with hate in his eyes, and his hands tightened more.

Mak-swill pulled at the man from behind, and for one brief instant, the man let go. Gil sucked in air while his attacker punched Mak-swill in the eye. She staggered back. Before Gil had a chance to move, the man was back, both hands around Gil's throat again.

Helplessly, Gil clawed to free himself. His vision narrowed, black and spotty, and his chest ached.

Nik ran from the inn, reaching for Gil. "Stop," he shouted.

Com-tun's Companion shouted, "Down."

Helen pulled Ian to the ground, and Nik rolled for Alexandria, who was still struggling to her feet.

Desperately, Gil shifted to wolf and bit the first piece of his attacker's arm he could reach. The man staggered backward, and thunder roared.

The man wavered for a moment, then crumpled to the ground. A red spot on his chest grew bigger, and the tang of blood filled the air. His skin faded to pale blue, and his eyes turned dull. Like the poisoned baubau at the prince's attempted assassination. Unlike the baubau, red scratches criss-crossed his arms.

"Okay?" Ian crawled to Gil and patted his leg. "Okay?"

Gil shifted to boy form and burst into tears. His throat hurt, and his chest hurt, and crying hurt, and the man had tried to kill him, and now *he was dead*. Gil didn't even know him, so how were they enemies?

And Gil had bitten him. He bit him and scratched him! Blood was in his mouth and under his claws. His skirt was covered in red spots. The reek of blood was everywhere.

He gagged at the stench, then gagged again when his throat protested. He sucked in air and clenched his hands on his wheeled chair.

Ian kept patting him. "Sorry, Gil. Sorry. Okay?"

It was as well he kept to the easiest words, since Gil couldn't remember how to respond, even if he could make his throat work. He had bitten an intelligent being. Worse, maybe, he might have ruined the treaty before it was signed. He tried to spit out the blood on his tongue.

Mak-swill rotated, scanning the area. Com-tun's Companion put gleaming metal under his jacket and helped his lord stand and brush off his clothes. He had a weapon, then, that had killed the man without touching him.

With Nik's help, Alexandria rose. She shook her head and shrugged her shoulders, wincing.

"I'm okay," she said. "Nik? Mom? Ian? Raquel? Great. Ian, get water."

They all nodded, though Helen was silently weeping. Ian ran into the inn.

Alexandria nodded at the Companion. "Thank you."

Grabbing the white cloth sticking out of Nik's pocket, she limped to Gil. "Hey, Gil, it's okay." Her voice was low and soothing, shaking only a little. She crouched in front of Gil and examined his throat with gentle fingers. "Nikos, call 911."

How did one talk to numbers, and why? But the mystery must wait, at least until Gil could stop shaking.

"No," Com-tun said. "No poleese."

"Already am." Nikos held his magic talk box to his ear.

Com-tun reached for the box, and Mak-swill stepped in front of him, talking and pointing to inn guests who were emerging from their doors and peering curiously in their direction. Some of them had magic boxes, too.

Alexandria patted Gil's arm and shushed him the way Mother had when he was younger. "Okay, Gil."

Ian trotted out with a glass of water, and Alexandria dipped the cloth into it.

"Okay, Gil, let's wash you, okay?" She reached for his hand slowly. "Ian, more water."

Her brother dashed off. Gil let her wash one arm and then the other, then she carefully dabbed at his face and neck. As she worked, she rolled her shoulders and winced. Her impact with the ground must have left bruises.

When Ian returned with two more glasses of water, Alexandria made Gil rinse his mouth and spit. He drained both glasses before the nasty taste was mostly gone. Swallowing hurt, but so did breathing.

Mak-swill and Com-tun's Companion smiled blandly at the curious spectators. Com-tun examined his wagon, running his fingers along its shiny sides.

"Let's go inside," Helen said. "It will be more pryvut."

"Okay." Alexandria patted him again. "Okay, Gil."

She started to rise, and he threw his arms around her, fresh tears gushing down his cheeks. He bit someone! He had never bitten anyone before, except a few playful nips at his brother, which never drew blood. What kind of monster was he?

The memory of the metallic tang filled his nostrils, and he gagged again.

Wait, that blood smelled like Alexandria. Why would it have her scent? He jerked his arms away and looked at his hands. Red covered his palms.

"Oh, dear," Alexandria said. "I thought we got all of that." She reached for Nik's white cloth again, now a muddy red.

Gil tugged on her arm. "Okay?" he croaked, then winced at the pain in his throat.

"Yeah, we can wash it," she said. "Okay."

"*You* okay?" Gil tried again, despite the rawness of his throat.

"That's a lot of blood," Nik said. "You didn't miss that much."

His eyes widened, and he tugged her to her feet and turned her so the sunlight fell on her back. Helen gasped and pulled on Alexandria's shirt. A slash across the shoulders parted, though no pale skin showed through. Instead, it was as red as the shirt.

Instantly, Helen bunched the shirt and pressed it to her daughter's back. She shoved her daughter to the inn door, rattling instructions over her shoulder too fast for Gil to follow.

Nik grabbed the chair and yanked it out of the flowers, then pushed it full speed toward the door which Ian held wide open. Mak-swill headed toward the onlookers, a smile plastered on her face, arms outstretched to block the path.

And then Gil was inside, and Ian ran back for his boot before slamming the door. While Nik transferred Gil to the softer chair in the room, Helen dragged Alexandria into the cleansing room, scolding her the whole way. Gil didn't have to understand the words to recognize the tone.

Ian offered a clean skirt to Gil, which he accepted, though he changed and resettled his stiff boot without removing his gaze from the doorway of the cleansing room. Alexandria's voice mixed with Helen's, one cranky and one worried, too quiet and complicated for Gil to understand.

Was Alexandria okay? She had been injured in his defense, and though she was a warrior, she had no weapons. She was only a girl, though he knew this world had different traditions than his own. Makswill had also defended him.

He wanted to shift to speed the healing of his throat and soothe his breathing, but Com-tun and his Companion were still nearby, and the clean skirt meant Ian wanted him dressed, which meant no shifting.

A loud wail came from outside, and red and white lights flashed through the window. In a minute, blue lights joined them.

"Oh, good," Helen called.

Nik and Ian grimaced at each other, but Nik opened the door while Ian stayed with Gil. Two large rectangle wagons stopped outside the inn, red and white lights flashing over their orange stripes. Right behind it, smaller wagons squealed to a stop. These had red and blue lights and blue stripes.

Apparently, the humans knew these wagons were coming. That was probably why Ian wanted him dressed instead of shifting.

Men in blue clothes piled from the wagons. Those from the blue wagons, who wore blunt-arrowhead-shaped badges on their shoulders, spread out with shiny metal in hand, searching the area and sending the onlookers back inside their rooms. Com-tun's Companion took his own weapon from under his jacket and gave it to them slowly. Makswill started talking, gesturing toward the wagon the attacker had used.

At each orange wagon, the men with white circles on their shoulders opened the back and lifted down a narrow cot on wheels, which stretched its legs to be tall. They threw a large bag onto the cot, then a long shiny cylinder and a black and silver box with magic dials. At least, they looked like the dials on Zak's navigating contrivances and half the magic boxes the humans had.

Two men from an orange wagon hurried to Gil's attacker, while the other two dragged their wheeled cot to the inn. Nik waved at Gil and motioned toward the washing room. Gil transferred his gaze to the window so he could keep watching while the doorway was blocked. The men outside bent over the attacker, touching his neck and chest. They shook their heads and stood.

"Hey, Gil." Ian touched his shoulder. "Dokter help you, okay?"

"We're not dokters," one of the blue men protested.

He kept talking, but Gil didn't recognize the words, and he didn't care. Ian waved his hands and talked back, and Gil's attention drifted back to the window. The men with arrowhead badges were now unrolling a yellow ribbon across the road.

"Hey, Gil," Ian repeated. "Okay to help?"

If they would go away, he could shift. It had certainly helped his broken leg heal faster. But he nodded anyway.

One man turned Gil's neck and prodded at it, while the other strapped something around his arm and put a little box on his finger.

"What's your name?" the first man asked. He was tall and dark-haired.

"Gil," Gil croaked in a whisper, trying not to flinch as his sore neck was poked and bent.

"Last name?"

Gil looked at Ian.

"Family name," his friend clarified.

Gil clamped his lips shut. If he hadn't shared that with his human friends yet, he certainly wouldn't reveal it to strangers and open himself to their magic.

Ian shrugged, and the dark man raised his eyebrows but kept examining Gil's neck.

The other man, as short as Nik but with hair as pale as Ian's, hit something on the box attached to the strap around Gil's arm, and the strap tightened, first a little and then until it hurt.

"Ow." Gil swatted at the pale-haired man.

Ian grabbed his hands. "Okay, Gil."

"What happened?" the tall man asked.

Ian and Nik talked to him, and Gil gritted his teeth against the pain in his arm. It lasted a moment longer, then the strap loosened entirely.

The pale man listed some numbers, then glanced at the box on Gil's finger and said more numbers with a frown. He retrieved the shiny cylinder from the wheeled cot and stretched a clear mask toward Gil's face, with a long string running from it to the cylinder.

Gil flinched away, jerking hard enough to slip from the tall man's hands. Whatever magic was in that, he wanted nothing to do with it.

Ian sighed and reached for the mask. He pressed it against his face and inhaled. Exhaled. Inhaled again. "Okay, Gil. Help." He tapped his chest and inhaled again.

Narrowing his eyes and coiling his muscles in preparation, as if he could get away with a broken leg, Gil held still and let the man hold the mask to his face. To his surprise, it smelled like nothing but the mask. Air blew onto him, and when he inhaled, the ache in his chest eased a little. So this was the humans' air spell. No matter how many times Ian said they didn't have magic, it was obviously not true.

The pale-haired man put a cold metal circle on Gil's chest and back, listening through strings running to his ears.

"When is your burthdae?" The tall man reached for the contrivance still on the wheeled cot.

Gil looked at Ian.

"The day you were born," Ian explained.

Oh, that made sense. "One hundred fifty-seven conjunctions ago," Gil whispered.

Ha, he remembered the human words, too. Maybe he should say one hundred and fifty-eight by now. How long had he been on Ki?

The tall man blinked and puffed out his cheeks. Ian winced, and Nik covered a chuckle.

"Any ellurjies?" the man asked. "Medikuhl problems? Medukations?"

"He's been sick," Ian said, "but he's better now." He widened his eyes and smiled innocently at the man in blue. "Except for his leg." He pointed to the boot that protected Gil's broken leg.

The man grunted and pressed a sticky square to Gil's chest. The other man reached for Gil's finger, and before he had a chance to react, had stabbed him.

Gil jerked away again, clenching his fist to hide the bleeding finger. "No." He dropped the air mask and ripped off the sticky square. "No, no, no."

His throat hurt and his voice creaked, but this was enough. They could not have his blood for their magics.

"Oh, Gil." Ian sighed and picked up the mask.

Nik stepped forward and pointed toward the washing room. He spoke quietly and quickly, and Alexandria's name was in his plea.

"Yes," Ian said. "Help Alexandria."

Gil nodded emphatically, leaning away from the dokters. Alexandria had been cut by that man. She was certainly bleeding and might have damaged muscles, or worse. She needed help, and he was tired of these inadequate humans poking at him instead of just healing him.

"Oh for—" The tall man shrugged and headed for Alexandria, with his partner trailing him.

Nik turned his back to the washing room and leaned against the wall, shoulders tight as he looked out the window.

Ian offered the air mask again. "Please?"

Reluctantly, but remembering how the air spell had eased his chest, Gil pressed the mask to his face again.

From the washing room, Helen's voice spoke calmly. Alexandria answered questions in a tense voice frequently interrupted by yelps of pain.

Someone knocked on the door, and Nik opened it to more of the men in blue, this time with the arrowhead badges. After settling themselves, one in the chair and one by the washing room, they asked a lot of questions. Who was the man? Nobody knew. What did he want? No idea. Did Gil have enemies? Ian said no, and Gil kept his mouth shut. None of his enemies were on Earth yet.

What had happened? The humans recited the events over and over, and Gil happily used the air mask and his sore throat as excuses to say as little as possible. He didn't know anything anyway. Why did that man want to kill him? He had never met him, so how could they be enemies?

What kind of people were these humans? Com-tun's Companion had killed the man without blinking an eye and hadn't seemed a bit bothered afterward. Alexandria, at least, had fought to disable, not to kill.

Helen called Ian, who rummaged through Alexandria's bag and tossed a shirt at her. In a minute, everyone emerged from the washing room. A small lump showed under the back of Alexandria's shirt, stretching across one shoulder. She walked carefully, sitting on the bed instead of the empty chair. Ian sat beside her, touching his shoulder gently to her uninjured one until she leaned against him.

Finally, the questions ended. The dokters spoke to Alexandria, who shook her head.

Ian translated for Gil. "They want you to go to dokter place for more help."

Gil shook his head more emphatically than Alexandria had. If he couldn't have a proper fae healer, he would rather shift and take care of himself.

The tall man threw his hands into the air, and the dokters packed their contrivances. Gil handed back the air mask with relief.

Helen wrote on some papers and said, "Thank you."

The dokters left. The other men in blue talked more, and eventually Ian told Gil that the family needed to go talk to them somewhere else. Gil could stay behind, since he didn't speak enough of the language and could barely be heard anyway.

"Will you be okay here alone?" Ian asked.

Gil nodded wearily. All he wanted to do was shift and sleep. Actually, he would love to eat first, since he had already shifted twice without a snack, but his throat hurt too much to consider that.

Through the window, he watched his human friends leave in Nik's wagon, and the other humans take their own wagons without the lights and noise.

Gil unbuckled his boot and dropped it onto the floor. After removing his skirt, he dragged up enough energy for a shift, thanks to his regular diet on Earth. When he woke, he would be very hungry, but he would manage. He curled into a ball and wrapped his tail over his eyes.

Were all humans as willing to kill as the highborn, or were there few like Com-tun's Companion and Gil's attacker? Was this whole world full of enemies?

He was a fool for thinking this would be easy. Miknon had been right. This truce might be a bad idea, but he certainly couldn't cancel it without talking to Shar, and by the time the prince arrived, it would be too late.

His people were coming, like it or not. They must make the best of it. The humans might fear magic, but it was born into the fae to greater or lesser extent, and could not be gained by those without it.

But Com-tun's Companion had killed the man without touching him, and the weapon was small enough to hide in a pocket. If every human could use such a weapon, the fae would fall like ripe wheat.

They must have the truce, or they would all die.

CHAPTER 21

HOUSING

IN THE TRUCK on the way back from the police station, Ian folded his arms and glared at Alexandria. His sister was sitting gingerly next to him, shoulder leaning diagonally against the window so her wounded back didn't touch the seat. Every time they passed under a streetlight, he could see the pain on her face.

"What were you *thinking?*" he blurted. "What kind of idiot attacks an armed crazy? With no weapon!"

He'd been dying to yell at her for hours, but planning their conversation with the police had occupied their trip to the cops, and then they'd been too busy answering questions.

"Ian," Mom said, "leave her alone."

But Mom's lips were tight enough that Ian knew she was wondering the same thing. Nikos had been scowling since the paramedics arrived, though he'd managed to hide it while they talked to the police.

Alexandria sighed. "No, Mom, it's okay. I wasn't thinking, Ian, okay? I just reacted the way I was trained."

She could have been killed. His sister was a pain, but he would have missed her even more than Gil. Maybe more than his right arm. Ian sulked silently until they reached the hotel.

Nikos helped Alexandria climb from the truck. Ian hurried to open the door and turn on the light so she wouldn't stub her toe in the dark and jolt her back.

As soon as they opened the door, Gil woke and turned his head to look at them, ears pricked forward.

"Please shift, Gil," Mom said. "We'll make you a snack, but we need to talk."

Alexandria and Mom turned their backs to find food and allow Gil privacy. More slowly than usual, Gil shifted to boy and pulled on his skirt and his medical boot.

He looked terrible. His eyes were red from broken blood vessels, and bruises glowed red and purple on his neck, even with his black skin.

Once he was dressed, Alexandria took a seat on the bed she shared with Mom, sitting upright instead of lounging. Ian sat by Gil, and Nikos took the second chair.

"I'm so glad that guy is dead," Ian muttered. "Gil, if anybody else tries to hurt you, the law will punish him."

"Law?" Gil croaked.

That took a bit of explaining, since Gil was used to the law being whatever the lords said it was. Ian filled a clean washcloth with ice cubes and showed Gil how to hold them to his neck. With his free hand, the werewolf devoured apples and cheese sticks, though he winced with every swallow.

"Compare the law to Mom punishing us for misbehaving," Alexandria suggested. "He's seen that several times."

Her idea worked, mostly, though Gil kept asking who was in charge and how they decided on punishments. He perked up, though, when Ian explained murderers were usually locked away for a very long time.

"If know we killers, lock up the law them, yes?"

Untangling the sentence order took a minute. *If we know killers, the law lock them up?*

"Well, we'd try," Ian hedged. What killers did he know besides the dead attacker?

Gil nodded, then shifted the ice on his throat. "Want we this in treaty."

"We'll ask," Mom said, "but first, I have another question." Sitting on the edge of her chair, Mom clenched her hands in her lap. "Do we still want to let Gil and Miknon live in the school housing?"

Ian translated as fast as he could. Gil merely sighed.

Alexandria shrugged, then grimaced. "Ow. Look, I was all for dumping the aliens since we have our own problems, but when that guy attacked, I reacted like I would for any of my brothers."

"Brother?" Ian asked.

"Yes," she said, "somehow he feels like family, okay? I don't know when that happened, but I don't want to abandon them. We can't trust anyone else to take care of them right. What if the government decides they need to investigate the insides of aliens? Or they abandon the treaty because they think they can win a war? No, we stick together."

"Then do we want to split up and send Nikos to college by himself?" Mom leaned over to pat Nikos's hand. "Not that we don't love you, but we're putting you in danger. You'd be safer if you didn't live with us."

Nikos shrugged. "I don't care. You're my family now. Your danger is my danger. Do you think I'd feel any better if I heard about it after it was over?"

"Yeah," Ian said. "We're family. Nikos is my brother, and if Gil can't be my dog, then he's got to be my brother. And I suppose two sisters aren't any worse than one." He stuck out his tongue at Alexandria. "We're family, and we're sticking together. They don't know anybody else, and nobody knows their language. They need us."

He left the dog part out of his translation for Gil and didn't mention that once the rest of the aliens landed, Gil and Miknon would know plenty of people on Earth who spoke a common language.

"It's not much worse looking for a three-bedroom apartment than two bedrooms," Nikos said. "And two bedrooms will work if we can fit a bunk bed and a single into one room for the boys."

"But this time," Mom said, "let's leave Gil at the hotel until we think we have a final choice. We can take turns staying with him."

Alexandria raised a hand partway. "I volunteer for the next few days, actually. I think I'd prefer not to move around."

Ian glared at her again. "Maybe it will keep you out of trouble."

"Look, twerp," she said, "I'm alive and so is Gil. A little owie is worth that, don't you think?"

Ian exchanged a look with Nikos. Little owies didn't bleed all over. But Nikos looked concerned enough that Ian bet he'd be willing to help make sure Alexandria didn't lift anything heavier than her plate for a couple of days.

Pulling out his phone, Nikos tapped for a few minutes. "Must allow pets," he muttered. "Elevator if not on ground floor. Up to five people."

"Six," Alexandria corrected.

Nikos raised an eyebrow. "Nobody would believe about Miknon, and she doesn't need an actual bed."

"Gil could stay a dog all the time," Ian suggested. "Then we'd only need space for four beds."

"That's not fair to him," Mom said, "and he has to learn how to live in the human world."

"These don't list elevator status," Nikos said. "I'll email about my roommate needing handicap access. Okay, until we get a reply, that gives us two we can look at tomorrow. We'll need to go early, okay, Ian?"

"Gotcha, early." Ian yawned. They'd been at the police station for a long time, and his migraine was coming back. "Hey, Alexandria, how will you sleep like that?"

"Carefully," she said. "But Mom, can you help me with my pj's?"

"Of course," Mom said. "You boys can change while we're in the bathroom. Don't leave the ice on Gil, please, or the bed will be wet in the morning."

Mom grabbed Alexandria's pajamas and her own, and they both went into the bathroom. The boys were ready within minutes. Ian tucked Gil into bed and climbed in beside the wolf. Nikos waited by the door to turn off the light. Muffled whimpers marked the progress in the bathroom, and when Alexandria emerged, her eyelashes looked suspiciously damp.

Mom helped Alexandria lie carefully on her side, then took the other half of the bed. Nikos turned out the light, and his sleeping bag rustled.

Within minutes, deep breathing was the only sound, and Ian fell asleep while he was still imagining their new apartment.

IN THE MORNING, Ian and Nikos gulped their breakfast and left while their injured siblings were still struggling to lift or swallow their food.

"Remember to look for bugs, old outlets, and fire hazards," Mom said.

"Got it," Nikos promised, pushing Ian gently out the door. "We have two hours before Mama has to leave for work, so let's hurry."

Ian hopped into the front seat, gloating silently that his sister wasn't there to grab it. Nikos pulled up the first address on his GPS, and they wound through very narrow streets clogged by parked cars. The houses were old, antiques even, and if it weren't for the modern cars, Ian would have felt like he was a time-traveler or in a historical movie.

The first apartment was wheelchair-accessible but only had two bedrooms. The ceilings were too short for a bunkbed, and the rooms were too tiny to fit two beds or a queen bed for the girls. The boys were in and out in less than three minutes.

The next apartment was in a big building and had an elevator. All three bedrooms were big enough, but all the electrical outlets were two-prong, and when they turned on the water, it ran brown with rust.

Back in the truck, Nikos drummed his fingers on the steering wheel. "That didn't take long. Do we have other errands?"

"Groceries?" Ian suggested. "We always need groceries."

"Sure." Nikos pulled onto the crowded street and crept to the closest intersection. He put on his blinker to turn left, and the car across from him stopped and waved him on.

"Um, don't we have the stop sign?" Ian asked.

"Yesss." Nikos waited, and the other driver waved more energetically. "Okay?"

He turned left and continued to the closest Aldi. Without Alexandria's lists, they had to guess what to buy, but a lot of their purchases were always the same, and Ian had been the unlucky recipient of the empty jam jar that morning.

"And how are you today?" the customer behind them in the checkout line asked.

"Huh?" Ian blinked in surprise. "Um, fine?"

"Oh, that's great." The mom-aged lady beamed at him. "A lovely day today, isn't it?"

"Yes." Which was true. The temperature had fallen enough to be cooly comfortable.

"Did you find everything you need?"

Ian looked at Nikos in puzzlement. Had they run into an off-shift store employee?

"We're fine," Nikos said.

"That's great. Remember to get your quarter back when you return the buggy." She held her hand by her mouth and whispered, "You seem new here, so I thought I'd drop the hint, just in case. Oh, look, it's your turn." She smiled and waved her hands to encourage them forward.

Nikos paid for their groceries, waved at the lady, and urged Ian out of the store.

"That was weird," Ian said.

"I think it's called being friendly," Nikos said.

"Yeah. Weird." Ian tossed the groceries into the back seat and climbed into the front. "Colorado people don't talk to strangers like that."

Nikos laughed all the way back to the hotel.

Mom left for work, and the boys put away the groceries, refusing any help from Alexandria. For the rest of the morning and most of the afternoon, they watched the most amusing television documentaries Ian could find. Though Gil and Alexandria had a hard time laughing with their sore bodies, their smiles cheered him enough that he didn't mind making lunch and dinner.

Mom returned in time to eat dinner, and as soon as it was over, they headed out to look at an apartment that had texted Nikos during the day. The pictures looked so promising, and Alexandria and Gil were so antsy after a day locked in the hotel that they took the whole family.

Ian, Mom, and Nikos checked it first while the injured parties stayed in the truck. It had big enough bedrooms, modern electrical and plumbing, and decent wheelchair access.

"I think we should sign," Mom said, "but let's bring the other two in first. You go get them while I check the cupboards."

The boys dashed out and helped their siblings into the apartment. After showing them the bedrooms, they parked Gil in the kitchen.

"The paperwork is online," Nikos said. "We could fill it out right now."

"Go ahead," Mom said.

"Okay, my name…" Nikos muttered as he typed on his phone.

"Ha!" Gil exclaimed.

Ian turned in time to see him pop a big bug into his mouth. "Ew!"

"What?" Mom asked.

Everyone turned, and Gil crunched on another bug. Alexandria gagged. Nikos stopped typing.

"That's a cockroach," Mom squeaked.

Ian ran to Gil and knocked the next cockroach from his hand. "No!"

Pocketing his phone and grabbing the wheelchair handles, Nikos headed for the front door. "I think this apartment is not for us."

"Ew," Alexandria repeated.

They buckled Gil into the truck, and Ian pulled out the picture dictionary he always carried now.

He turned to the page on insects. "Bugs. Bugs not food!"

Gil shrugged and rubbed his growling stomach.

Alexandria covered her mouth. "Do you think he's eaten bugs before? Gross!"

Blinking back tears, Mom said, "He said his spaceship was short on food. How short?" She took a deep breath. "Maybe we should leave Gil home from now on."

Without further comment, Ian pulled a granola bar from his backpack and handed it to Gil. "I'm glad he found the cockroaches before we signed, but…"

"Ew." Alexandria's voice cracked.

Back at the hotel, they made a second dinner for Gil, then went to bed.

ON WEDNESDAY, Nikos and Ian spent the morning looking at apartments and houses for rent in every nearby town. Most of the houses had all the bedrooms upstairs, which wouldn't work for a wheelchair. A surprising number of them had a free-standing toilet in the basement, without an actual bathroom. Some of the apartments were too small, some too dirty or too smelly, and some had parking a full block away. Most of the prospective neighbors were friendly — weirdly friendly — so the few that were creepy were noticeable.

Not until the end of the day did the boys find something suitable, though it was in Allentown instead of Bethlehem. It was only twenty minutes from Nikos's college, and came with a bit of furniture — a table and four chairs in the kitchen, a sofa in the living room, and a queen bed in one bedroom and a twin in another. The third bedroom was empty, and they would need more chairs, more beds, and some odds and ends, but it was a start. With Alexandria's yard-sale skills, they'd be set before school started.

Nikos took photos with his phone, then called Mom and talked for a long time. While he waited, Ian made a list of what they needed for the apartment. Alexandria would appreciate it, since she always made lists. At least the cupboards were big enough to hold all the food Gil could eat, and they'd have a real oven for home-cooked meals.

Nikos hung up. "Okay, let's go. Mama is working on her part of the app already, and dinner is ready."

"Yay!" Ian hopped to his feet and raced Nikos to the truck.

At the hotel, Mom was submitting the application. Alexandria examined Ian's list with great interest, adding and amending before she nodded decisively.

"We should have an answer next week," Nikos said.

"Hey, Gil, we found a house for us," Ian explained. "All of us. Even Miknon, when she gets back."

Gil grinned and raised his hands for a high-five, absurdly proud of that new skill.

Alexandria bit her lip, and Ian could practically read her worry-wart mind. If Miknon got back safely. If nothing else went wrong.

Well, nothing else *would* go wrong! It would be fine.

Alexandria's phone rang.

"Hello, Therese," Alexandria said. "Oh. Oh, yes, please do." She put the phone on speaker and nudged Gil.

"The message was only one word," Mrs. Ortiz said, "and we don't understand it. What does 'ohKEEgoe' mean?"

All the humans looked at Ian. He shrugged and ran for his vocabulary list.

Gil cheered. "They come!"

"Therese," Alexandria said, "we can confirm a positive message. They have launched. Repeat, they have launched."

Ian bit his lip to keep from asking if it was Miknon's voice on the radio. If she had sent the message, wouldn't she have used English?

"Thank you." Mrs. Ortiz hung up without a goodbye.

Now they only had three days until the aliens landed.

"Are we ready?" Alexandria asked.

"I just have one question," Ian said. "Gil, what they say?"

Gil wrinkled his forehead. "Earth words. You know."

"No?" Ian paused, vocabulary page half-turned.

Gil held his throat and laughed.

CHAPTER 22

IN WHICH THEY LEAVE THE SHIP

DAY 12-14 AFTER LANDING, *NEW KUNISU*, PARKED ON EARTH'S "MOON"

HEARING someone at the door of the room, Miknon reached for the cupboard door and heaved with all her might. Even with the light moon-weight, she only had it halfway closed when the outer door opened and Zak walked in. The apprentice navigator was talking over his shoulder. Miknon froze. Moving the door more might attract attention, but surely the navigator would be careful whom he brought in while she was hiding.

"Shar will join us soon," the navigator said, holding the door open.

The prince had sneaked out a while ago on an unspecified errand, despite the risk of someone recognizing him through his disguise.

A stream of people bounced into the room, and Miknon held her breath until she recognized the king's secretary, housekeeper, and naga chief guard, Merodach the healer, a highborn mage, a pilot, and Zak's father. The secret council of the hidden prince. They must have decided it was time to move on with the evacuation plans.

Any mage allowed in must be trusted, so she let go of the door and flew out of the cupboard.

"How do you feel?" the healer asked her. He eyed her from head to foot and nodded.

"Just a little weak." She wasn't lying, though she would have if that's what it took to get a healer to Gil as soon as possible.

The door opened again, and the prince slipped in. Behind him came Miknon's mother.

"Oh!" Miknon flew to her adopted mother's arms.

Though she had been gone less than two fae weeks, if she had the time conversion correct, it felt like an eternity.

"Miknon," Mother whispered in her ear. "I'm so glad you're well. How's Gil?"

Miknon shrugged and pressed her lips together. "Talk later?"

Mother nodded and sat with the others, Miknon on her lap.

"As you can see," the prince said, "Miknon was not swept from the ship in an accident in the dragon hold. Neither was her brother or the dragonet, and the dragon didn't make his way back randomly. In fact, it was a planned escape to Ki, and though we regret the distress it caused the adult dragons, it was almost entirely a success."

"Almost?" the secretary asked.

The prince shrugged. "Gil broke his leg, and the truce is only tentative for now. But he made friends and a plan. We are putting non-essential passengers into hibernation long enough to take the youngest fae to Earth in the dragon barges to learn their language. This will leave the council no alternative except to pilot a barge to the stone ring to retrieve the rest of the fleet."

A murmur of surprise ran around the circle for a moment.

"Why didn't we try hibernation earlier?" Mother asked.

The prince grimaced. "The army was training." He cleared his throat. "By the time the fleet returns, we will have Ki speakers to finalize the treaty. However, the plan is complicated by several factors."

Someone snorted, but when the prince raised an eyebrow, no one spoke.

"First," the prince continued, "we can't tell most of our people lest the secret leak. Second, we have to take enough of the pilots with us that the council can't move this ship, only a smaller barge."

The pilot raised his hand. "I can tell you who can be trusted to leave and who will need to be taken in hibernation."

The prince flashed a smile. "I hoped you could. Third, we have one hundred and fifty of our people on board who have not reached the age of adulthood. They will fit in two barges, but we must include some adults as well, which makes space tight. We can't leave any dragon drivers behind, even without the dragons, and we need a mage for the shielding spell."

"And we must send guards and healers with you," the naga insisted.

"I will stay behind," the prince said, "to take the greatest risk."

"You should go," the naga argued. "You are not yet an adult and have no acceptable heir."

The king had appointed Lord Kishar as the prince's temporary heir until he fathered children, to prevent a civil war. But if Kishar actually became king, fae society would deteriorate to the old ways, forfeiting the king's promises of equality. The prince knew that, so if that didn't convince him to go, he needed another reason.

"But, Sire," Miknon said, "Ki won't finalize the treaty without you. You must go."

The prince bowed his head for a moment. "Very well," he finally said. "With the addition of food and water for a day and a half, that doesn't leave us much room."

"Excuse me," Miknon said. "Our trip took two days, though perhaps only because the dragonet is smaller."

The prince sighed. "We will reduce the passengers to allow for more food and water, then."

The highborn cleared his throat. "We can save space by including more mages."

"Sending more people saves room?" the prince asked.

"If we use mages and elementals to clean the water and deal with hygiene," the highborn said, "as well as work the spells for air, shielding, heat, and cold, we can take less water and reduce facilities. And if we put most of the passengers in hibernation, they won't need any food or as much water."

"They will be quite hungry when they arrive," the healer said. "Will there be a problem feeding them when they wake?"

Miknon shook her head. "The truce includes food and housing."

"In that case," the housekeeper said, "we can put more than one person to a bunk and convert the cargo area for more bunks. If they are sleeping, the tight conditions won't matter."

"We can put fifteen or twenty of the smallest fae in the message box on the dragonet," Miknon said, "and put hibernation over them."

"Very well," the prince said. "Nik, please make rosters for who goes and who stays. Once you have the required passengers, I suggest you consider the parents of the children going. I expect everyone to cooperate in their suggestions to you. Balasi, Amarud, starting with you."

The mage and the pilot nodded, and the secretary patted his slate. Miknon should tell him she knew a Nik on Earth. He might find it as amusing as Gil to find the same name on an entirely different world.

"And Shalla," the prince said, "I need you to come with me to keep track of everything. You can also sing to us on Ki to learn our new world faster."

The housekeeper pressed her lips together and nodded.

The prince took a deep breath. "Nik, I regret I must leave you behind to run this ship in my absence. You must make sure the council has no option but to retrieve the fleet. Remind them that without dragons, they cannot land on Ki, so they must go after the dragons on the other ships. We will keep our dragons on Ki until you signal that the lords have left."

"No," the housekeeper cried. Her pretty face puckered, and she put a hand on the secretary's arm.

Miknon looked away. Poor man. Trying to influence the council was the most dangerous job in the plan. The secretary was clever and subtle, but if hints and logic failed, the council lords were as likely to fill his lungs with water as to listen to a direct command.

The secretary patted the housekeeper's hand before removing it from his arm. "Yes, Sire."

"Izdu," the prince said, "I leave you in charge of the navigators and pilots. Make sure that if the council leaves this ship, they take no one but those necessary to retrieve the fleet, and go nowhere else."

The chief navigator and contriver nodded, one hand clasped tightly around his son's. "I must stay anyway, to transfer the navigation contrivance to a barge and care for it after. Though the fleet has others who can serve as pilots, we have the only navigation system. Zak and I are the only ones who understand it well enough to reassemble it elsewhere, and Zak must go to Ki."

Zak's face was wooden, but his ears were bright orange with distress. Without his father, he would be an orphan on Earth. Not even his grandmother had made it to Earth. She had been killed in the "accident" that had taken Gil's father and both of Miknon's parents. The accident certain lords had arranged to get rid of the female navigator they did not like.

One of these days, Miknon still intended to bring justice to those lords. Somehow.

"I can also open the hold door when it is time," the navigator said.

The prince nodded. "Taras, you and your men are in charge of converting two barges to hold as many passengers as possible, regardless of comfort. Make sure your work is undetected."

His naga Companion nodded. "Yes, Sire."

"Remember," the prince said, "tell no one unless they are both essential and trustworthy. We will tell everyone else who is going right before we leave."

Mother sighed. "Sire, you had better not tell Ram at all. You know he believes the lords and is ready for war."

"I don't want to leave him behind," the prince protested.

"No, kidnap him at the last moment," Mother said.

Miknon hid an urge to giggle. Gil's twin would be positively furious, but she agreed with Mother. Unfortunately, her other brother was no longer trustworthy. With any luck, living on Earth would soon convince him of the wisdom of colonization instead of war.

"Truly, Sire," the naga said, "we must kidnap many of the passengers. I'm afraid the secretary may face much anger when the parents wake and discover their children are gone."

The prince rubbed his face. "It can't be helped. Report back twice a day, or more often if you run into trouble."

The others bowed and left, including Zak. Only the prince and Miknon were left in the auxiliary navigation room.

"Well, Miknon," the prince finally said, "are you ready to signal Ki that we are coming?"

"No, Sire."

"No?"

"Not until we leave. Ian said the signal runs on the same system as their music, which the navigators can detect on their contrivances. I won't take a chance on the council having a spy among the navigators."

"I see," the prince said. "I agree. But how will you keep them from overhearing when you do signal?"

Miknon grinned at him. "They might, but they don't speak Ki and won't have time left to investigate."

Since Miknon had to stay in hiding along with the prince, she heard every report as it came in.

First, the king's secretary rearranged the deck assignments, claiming the army needed more room to practice and putting non-essential personnel and most of those who would be leaving on the third and fifth floors. Those deemed essential for running the ship and everyone aware of the escape plans were moved to the seventh deck. The highborn remained on deck nine. Ram had already moved to the seventh deck to sleep with the army, which occupied his time so much he didn't notice when Mother moved to the same floor on a different work and sleep schedule.

As the lower decks noticed they were all oddly on the same sleep shift as their entire floor, filling every available room, several trusted mages crept into the makeshift dormitories and put them into hibernation. They would wake in a few weeks before they had time to starve, but it would buy time for the escape and reduce food needs for a short time. Then the mage put the entire second-deck zoo to sleep so the animals wouldn't have to be cared for while help was short.

"And when the highborn notice we're gone," Mother gloated to

Miknon, "they'll have to do more work. If they get too hungry, they can put themselves into hibernation."

With no one left to notice their frequent trips to the dragon hold, the guards stripped the lower decks of materials to remodel the barges they intended to take. Miknon snuck through the maintenance tunnels in the walls and ceiling to check their progress. They had added travel bunks as closely packed as possible, filling the cargo areas and narrowing the aisles. Only the front of each barge had room to move around for the mages and elementals who would take care of the various spells needed for the trip.

When she got back to the auxiliary navigation room, a mage was with the prince.

"I've selected two magic-workers for each task in each barge," he told the prince. "That way, they can take turns sleeping. I've got people for water, air, heat, cold, shielding, and hibernation, as well as healers and pilots to smooth the landing if needed." He grimaced. "I haven't had a chance to talk to the dragon drivers yet."

The prince shrugged. "That may have to wait until the last minute. Well done. How much more time do you need?"

"I think haste is our friend, Sire."

The prince turned to Miknon. "And are the barges ready?"

"Almost," she said. "The guards are installing the last of the bunks right now. We can start taking down sleepers whenever you want."

"Bal," the prince said, "go ahead and check the sleep spell. I'll send the guards to you within the hour."

The mage bowed and left.

The prince sighed. "What about the highborn children? We couldn't put them to sleep."

"Gil could have gotten them to come with him," Miknon said, missing her brother fiercely. "Everyone liked Gil."

"Yes." The prince rubbed his chin. "Perhaps a ruse."

Zak entered the room and checked his contrivances.

"Ah, Zak," the prince said. "I have a task for you. Please go to the ninth deck and summon the highborn children to the third floor. Tell them… tell them we must test their magic in preparation for assignments in the new colony."

"What if they have questions?" the navigator asked.

The prince smiled. "Why would a mere messenger have answers? If they want to know more, they must come to the third floor."

The navigator twitched and left, scowling over his shoulder.

"Miknon," the prince said, "please hurry to Balasi and tell him to be ready to sleep-spell the children when they arrive. He must be swift, before they notice anything awry."

"What about Ram and the other young warriors on deck seven?" Miknon asked.

"I'll think of a plan while you're gone," he promised.

Miknon sneaked through the maintenance tunnels and delivered the message to the mage. To her surprise, soon after the last of the highborn youth collapsed, young warriors started appearing. They fell asleep just as quickly, until Ram arrived.

"What is going on?" her brother protested. He hovered in the doorway and glared at the mage. "Taras ordered us here, but I don't see why." He glanced at the rows and rows of sleepers. "What are you doing? I'll tell Lord Kishar."

He turned to flee, but bounced off the naga Companion who suddenly appeared behind him.

"Now," the Companion said.

The mage took one long bounce forward and pressed a hand to Ram's neck. Miknon's brother wavered and fell softly to the floor.

The naga threw him over one shoulder. "That's the last of them."

"I'll tell the prince," Miknon said through the grille.

She scuttled through the tunnels as fast as she could move. She popped back into Aux Nav, which was full of the prince's secret council. Those leaving already had small bags packed. Miknon beckoned, and the prince nodded.

"It's time," he said.

Most of the people quietly exited, including Mother and the prince. Zak and his father did not. Miknon hovered at the entrance of the tunnel. Was something wrong?

"Don't get lost on the way to the fleet." The young navigator took his father's hand and sniffled.

"Don't lose track of when I'll return," his father replied.

They threw their arms around each other and embraced, then Gil's friend slowly pulled away. Without a word, he left the room. His father bowed his head and rubbed his eyes. Miknon shut the tunnel grille silently.

Poor Zak. Miknon's family would be with her, but he wouldn't see his father again until the fleet reached Ki and landed at least nine or ten conjunctions from now.

And if she didn't hurry, she would make the barges late for her return to Gil. She hurried to the bottom deck and fluttered from the tunnel right into the middle of an argument.

"I won't go!" one of the dragon drivers shouted at the king's secretary. "You are disobeying the council!"

His silvery-brown hair marked him as lesser among the highborn, though obviously his talent for mind touching was powerful enough to communicate with a dragon.

"Lock the doors," the secretary commanded.

Guards closed the inner doors to the hold and stood in front of them. The prince leaned out of the barge, curls bouncing. He opened his mouth, and Miknon barreled into his chest.

"Hush," she commanded.

"But—" He pulled on the doorway as if to exit.

"No." She scrambled up his bodice and pressed both hands to his mouth.

They weren't out of danger yet, and he must not be identified. If the escape failed but the prince stayed safe, they could try again.

From behind, the naga gently grabbed the prince and escorted him to a bunk. Miknon stayed to watch the argument. The dragon driver squared his shoulders and pushed off toward the door.

"I'm going," the other driver said.

He had the same color hair, which he wore unusually short. His resemblance to the first was striking, though he was shorter and slimmer. The first one flailed his arms and bounced off the wall instead of ramming the warriors.

"What?" He gently floated to the floor and gaped. "Why?"

"The king promised us changes in the new world," the second one said. "The council tried to ruin that, so I'm taking the chance of a new life." He folded his arms. "We've talked about this, brother. I'm going."

The first driver opened and closed his mouth several times, then huffed. "I suppose this is more of a chance than an armed rebellion. Let's go."

Once both drivers were inside their assigned barges, the secretary waved the guards toward the barges. With their help, most of the passengers were strapped into their bunks.

"Here." The secretary held the magic talk box toward Miknon. "Are you ready?"

She flew toward him. "You should keep it in case you need to send a message later. Don't touch anything except this bump, ever. When you are ready to speak, hold in the bump, then let go when you stop."

When he pressed the bump, she spoke two Earth words. If the council heard her, they wouldn't understand. She nodded at the secretary, who let go of the button and escorted her to the barge.

Miknon took her place next to the young navigator, who already had the maps secured for her.

The king's secretary and his housekeeper stood at the door of the barge, him outside and her in.

"Nik," she whimpered, reaching down to touch his face.

"Shalla, I will come," he promised. He inhaled and closed the door.

The housekeeper crawled into her bunk and turned to the wall. The naga nodded briskly to the dragon driver, who closed his eyes and whispered. Miknon clenched her fists on the straps at her waist.

In a few minutes, the outer hold doors ground open. The barge bounced gently forward, then swooped from the ship.

Soon, they would all land on Earth. And what then? Was Gil still alive? Was Earth ready for them?

CHAPTER 23

LANDING

June 29-July 1, days 14-16 after landing, Allentown and Bethlehem, Pennsylvania

Alexandria put her fists on her hips and watched Gil laugh. When he choked from his sore throat, she brought him a glass of water.

"So, what did Miknon say?" she asked.

Relief still flooded her from head to foot. If those were English words, then surely Gil's big sister had survived. None of the other aliens would know English.

"Oh-kay." Gil emphasized each syllable. "Go."

Ian smacked his head. Alexandria and Nikos laughed.

Well, duh! Easy words, but Miknon's pronunciation had never been as good as Gil's. For that matter, her vocabulary wasn't as extensive as her brother's, either, but it was hard to mess up two short words.

The phone rang again.

"Mrs. Ortiz called," Major General Anthony said. "Two or three days, she said. We've picked a landing site, but we'd like Gil to give an opinion on its suitability and how to mark it."

"Sure," Alexandria said. "We can take a look at the landing site first thing in the morning." She raised her eyebrows at Mom and Nikos, who nodded.

"I wish I knew what to expect," Anthony said. "Flashing lights? Flames? How do we keep the public from panicking? Sorry, Alexandria, that's not your problem. I was thinking out loud."

"What about the Bootids, sir?"

"Who booted whom?" The general sounded confused.

Alexandria chuckled. "No, the Bootid meteor showers. They've been falling all June and don't end until July 2nd, though the heaviest night was two days ago. Have NASA play up the fun of watching falling stars, so if people see anything, they'll think it's a meteorite. The Bootids are bright and slow, which will match the re-entry better than the faster showers. If NASA talks about all that, nobody will think twice about seeing a flaming object or two in the sky. And the new moon is tonight, so even in three days, the sky will be pretty dark. Nobody will see the dragons after re-entry."

"What if they don't land until the third or fourth?" Anthony asked. "If something goes wrong."

"I don't think that's too likely, but the Bootids are famous for being unpredictable. Have NASA lie about them going a little long this year."

"Good idea," the general said. "Meet us at Bethlehem Sand Island tomorrow. Eight o'clock?"

"Oh-eight-hundred, yes, sir." Alexandria hung up.

The phone rang almost immediately, and she fielded call after call while Mom and the boys got ready for bed. Ms. Stafford wanted to know what to feed them the first day. Vegetarian was safest. Mr. Compton had more questions about housing. They were used to cramped quarters and would be fine doubling up. Therese thought the Bootids were a fabulous distraction.

Finally, the phone was silent. Mom helped Alexandria into her pajamas to spare her slashed back, and everyone went to bed.

Lying carefully on her side, Alexandria stared at the wall through the darkness. Three days left. Or two. Or four. But soon! Gil and Miknon would no longer be the only aliens on Earth. Who knew how many had fit in the barges, but probably at least a couple hundred.

Would they be more like Gil, more like Miknon, or completely different? Gil seemed to recognize most of the pictures in the mythology book Ian got for him, though he thought they were amusingly inaccurate. Obviously, the stories of werewolves were almost completely wrong. What was the truth? Were vampires and elves, trolls and centaurs real? What other creatures might exist?

"Alexandria?" Ian whispered.

"Go to sleep," she whispered back. As if she could take her own advice.

"But—"

"I know," Alexandria said. "But it will wait until the morning."

Ian grunted and rolled over, rustling the sheets. "Spoil sport."

She closed her eyes and took slow breaths, trying to force herself to sleep. Eventually it worked, though she dreamed of legends all night long.

In order to get out the door on time in the morning, everyone had to scramble. Gil could dress himself but not walk alone, and Alexandria could walk but not dress herself. The resulting dance of the able-bodied helping the injured was chaos in the small hotel room and single bathroom. Everything took longer than expected, and in the end, they ate bagels and fruit in the truck on the way to Bethlehem.

"Cross the bridge to Sand Island," Alexandria read off the GPS. "Then turn right and drive under two bridges."

Within minutes, they could see a boat ramp on the left.

"There," Ian said. "Parking on the right."

Nikos pulled in next to several cars and a Jeep. As soon as he turned off the engine, people poured from every vehicle. Only Compton and Farrell hadn't come, and Anthony had a few extra military with him.

Raquel Maxwell, the military linguist, helped Nikos with the wheelchair and Gil, while Ian and Mom helped Alexandria slide from the truck.

"Thank goodness River Days are over," Ms. Stafford said. The refugee specialist surveyed the river, hands on her hips. So many trees lined the river that half the water reflected green instead of blue. "The last thing we need is lots of boats, tubes, and tourists."

"But this should work." Major General Anthony pointed west. "If the barges land right after Lehigh Mountain Park, they'll have a long stretch of straight river to slow them down. With any luck, they'll stop before the bridges and we can use this access point, but if they go farther, we can go after them."

"What about the island in the middle?" Alexandria asked Gil, pointing to it. "Will the barges fit on either side?"

Gil squinted at the tiny island. "Okay."

"How will we signal them to land here?" Raquel asked. "What might they recognize?"

"Lights?" Nikos suggested.

"With all the city lights?" Mom protested.

Anthony rubbed his chin. "What if I arranged a city-wide blackout for a few minutes? If we timed it right, we would have the only lights on as the barges approached."

"Can you make shapes?" Ian asked. "Make them like this." He drew a rayed circle in the sand.

"Brilliant," Alexandra said.

The symbols meant nothing to most humans, but Miknon would remember she had taught the Fitches the alien figure for a thousand. Ian grinned, and she ruffled his hair, shoving his floppy bangs over his eyes.

"All right," Anthony said. "We've got work to do. Ortiz, you're handling NASA's announcement of the star shower. Stafford and Riggs, you deal with food and housing. My men will assemble the lights and take care of transportation and the perimeter. Maxwell, you're in charge of the landing as far as the aliens are concerned, and you contact me when you need lights out. I will take care of the blackout personally. Everyone dismissed!"

The military saluted, and the civilians straightened their shoulders. Alexandria winced and immediately relaxed hers again. Darn that crazy man with the knife!

Her family piled back into the truck and dropped off Mom at work.

Nikos took Alexandria, Ian, and Gil to the hotel, then left for more job research.

Ian and Gil continued their language studies, and Alexandria examined her lists.

So much to do in so little time! They certainly had two days, but after that, it was up in the air. She giggled to herself. Up in the air, indeed, all the way up in space. But if she didn't concentrate, she'd get in trouble.

As if to echo her thought, her phone rang. Caller ID said Riggs. She took a deep breath, settled in the chair so her injury wasn't touching anything, and tapped the green call button.

THE NEXT TWO days went by in a blur, but by Thursday, everything was supposedly ready. Gil threw a fit about the bruises on his neck until Mom covered them with a scarf. The whole family drove back to Sand Island and waited impatiently in the blue truck. The parking lot was full of buses and trucks, and four miles of the river was lit with rayed circles, like thousands of tiny suns. How did they make so many lights in two days?

The military personnel waiting to help the refugees were dressed discreetly in civilian clothing or fatigues, unlike Raquel Maxwell in her full uniform.

Unable to help with the physical tasks, Alexandria was in charge of the phone tree. She anxiously watched the Bootid star shower, looking for a flash to change direction. Every hour, she texted Therese at NASA and Riggs or Stafford at the "school" he had finally obtained. After seeing the school's daily schedule, they were lucky their new apartment was close by, or they would have had to find another one. And somehow in this chaos, they'd have to find time to move in once their lease started.

Nothing yet

she texted.

Therese always texted back.

No signs here.

Mom and Nikos reclined their front seats and catnapped. Halfway through the night, Ian and Gil fell asleep in the back seat. Unable to find a comfortable position next to Ian, Alexandria fidgeted, watching the lights reflect off the river.

When dawn finally crept over the horizon, Raquel tapped on the truck window. "Go home," she murmured. "Get some sleep. We'll try again tonight."

Yawning, Nikos started the truck and headed for the hotel.

Alexandria ate cold cereal for breakfast with everyone else, then curled up in bed and pulled the blanket over her head.

When she woke in late afternoon, the boys were napping. Sensible, really, if they were going to be awake all night again. She made sandwiches for dinner and woke the boys to eat when Mom walked in.

After eating, they all took a nap, though anxiety kept her sleep light until her phone alarm went off at 7:45 pm.

"Let's go, let's go," she called, then darted for the bathroom before Ian could reach it.

By eight o'clock, they were loaded in the truck, arriving at Sand Island by sunset. Gil again wore Mom's scarf around his neck.

Yet again, trucks and buses filled the parking lot, and numerous military pretended to be casual visitors.

Yet again, everyone waited. And waited. And waited. Occasionally, a meteor flashed by, jerking everyone to attention, but then it continued on and faded away. The hourly texts were nothing but confirmation that people were still awake.

Hours passed with no sign of the barges. Alexandria found herself dozing, only waking when her wound touched the back of the seat.

Her phone rang. "Therese, what's up?"

"Do you see anything?" The astronomer's voice was tense. "Look now."

Alexandria tumbled from the truck, knocking her back against the door jamb. "Ow, ow, ow."

Ignoring the searing pain, she peered at the sky. All around her, other doors opened and closed. Raquel Maxwell rapidly texted on her phone.

"Do you see anything?" Nikos asked.

"There!" Alexandria pointed westward to a meteorite blazing brightly. In a moment, it split into two flames, and each curved slightly away from the other.

In the truck, Gil closed his eyes and clenched the ring hung on the chain around his neck. His lips moved silently. The falling stars curved again to head toward them. The glow faded slowly.

"Was it a meteorite?" Mom whispered.

"Did they get lost?" Ian asked.

Raquel looked up from her phone. "NASA is computing for me based on their original speed and last known location." She squinted at the screen, lips compressed. "They should be using the second map now." In a few minutes, she said, "Third map." She texted, then put the phone into her pocket. "Now they'll be relying on our signal for the exact landing site. Any minute now."

Nothing happened. Had everything gone wrong?

And then the city lights went dark. The rayed circles along the river shone like the biggest Christmas lights in the world.

"Shar," Gil chanted quietly in the absolute silence. "Shar, Shar, Shar."

Alexandria looked at Ian, who shrugged. Not a word they had gone over in vocabulary lessons, then.

They kept waiting.

The city lights went back on, and Raquel inhaled loudly. "Ten minutes. I hope that was long enough."

In the sudden illumination, something glittered in the sky like jewels on a velvet tablecloth.

Gil cheered. "Out," he cried. "Chair."

Nikos ran to the bed of the truck and grabbed the wheelchair.

"All right, folks," Raquel shouted, "this is it. Everyone into positions!"

The military slipped on medical masks and lined up by the buses. Frantically, Nikos settled Gil in his chair. Alexandria ran to help but backed off at Nikos's fierce glare.

The jeweled sparkles spiraled in the air, lower and lower until the shape of massive wings became clear. Two large dragons turned in line with the light-etched river, with a much smaller shape drifting behind them.

"Wow." Ian's mouth hung open after the exclamation.

Alexandria nodded mutely. Dragons! Real dragons would land right in front of them. Behind the great wings, dark shapes flew as if they were planes instead of boxes. When they had time, she'd have to ask Gil what kept them up in the air.

The dragons swooped lower and lower, following the lights. Would they land before the bridges? They did see the bridges, didn't they?

Right in front of the sandy access point, the water sprayed upward in a million sparkling drops of light, and Alexandria sucked in her breath at the unexpected beauty.

Then the dragons folded their wings and drifted to a stop. Slowly, the first one swam to the sand, pulling the floating barge behind it. It crawled onto land and stopped with the barge just past the water. Everyone stared, frozen. The smallest dragon splashed into the river and scrambled onto land, huddling at the side of the larger dragon. Its hide was equally bright and sparkling, like a mosaic of stained glass or gems.

With Ian pushing his chair, Gil barreled past Alexandria. "Azidaka," he shrieked.

He stopped by the small dragon, which was suddenly much larger with him for scale, and patted its head. After chattering at the dragon, he said something to Ian, who beckoned the closest soldier and bossed him through unlatching the coffin-sized box on the dragonet's back.

When the lid was eased back, the soldier swore. "What the — Are they dead?" He lifted out a limp body the size of a doll.

That stung everyone into motion. The military swarmed the dragons cautiously, removing the box and the tiny figures from the small drag-onet and hauling the first barge farther onto the sand. Gil borrowed a hammer and banged on the door.

While they waited, Gil showed the soldiers how to unharness the dragon, and he coaxed the huge beast farther up the shore. As soon as the space was clear, the last dragon swam up and dragged his burden to the edge of land. It, too, was unharnessed and led away, leaving only the two barges side by side.

Slowly, the first barge door opened a crack, then stopped. Ian and Gil rolled to it, and Gil stuck his mouth against the line and started talking rapidly. Ian looked at Alexandria and shrugged.

After a few minutes, Gil and Ian moved to hammer on the second barge, and the military closed in on the first. They pushed the door wide open, then flinched back.

The smell drifted to Alexandria, and she gasped for breath. Though she didn't know what she had expected. The barge held a hundred or more people, crammed into bunks so crowded they looked like a concentration camp. By rights, after three days like that, they should have smelled even worse.

Most of the people lay still, sleeping or possibly dead, but a few near the door struggled to sitting positions on their bunks. A tall man with reptile-scaled skin and yellow eyes drew a knife, and the beautiful woman next to him began to hum. All of them, male and female alike, wore either some kind of skirt or a long tunic.

"No pants." Ian giggled. "That explains a lot, doesn't it?"

Alexandria nudged him. "Manners."

Gil returned, smiling widely and waving at his people. He chattered again until the snake-man put away his knife, then nodded at Raquel.

The military linguist waved her people forward. "Remember that they have fragile bones," she called. "Be careful! And don't be alarmed at anything you might see. Regardless of their looks, they are friends. Top secret friends for now, so keep your mouths shut when you go home."

The soldiers and Nikos lined up to remove each alien, waking or sleeping, and carry them to the buses in the parking lot. Mom followed to offer a friendly face and a limited vocabulary in their own tongue. Though her injury prevented Alexandria from helping physically, she walked forward to stand with Ian and Gil and show another smile.

As each wakeful person was carried out, Gil greeted them with a few quiet words and sometimes a soft touch. One of them, with dark silver hair and ears more delicately pointed than Gil's, clutched at the werewolf's sleeve for a moment. Gil nodded, and with the help of Ian, directed the soldier carrying the man to take him to the first large dragon. The alien stroked the dragon's head and spoke to it, and soon it followed him like a puppy into the back of a semi-truck, accompanied by the little dragon.

"Nikos car..." Gil half-said, turning his hands on an invisible steering wheel. He raised his eyebrows in a request for the missing word.

"Drive," Ian said.

"Drive Nikos car," Gil corrected. "Drive *him* dragon."

The werewolf kept craning his neck to look inside the barge. To keep the operation as secret as possible, the military hadn't turned on any floodlights, and the river lights were behind the barges. A few vehicle headlights lit the area enough for the walkers to find their way, and the barges had only a faint light inside.

Alexandria bent and whispered in Gil's ear. "What's wrong?"

"Where is family?" Gil croaked. "Miknon, Mother, Ram?"

"Maybe in the other barge?" Alexandria suggested. "It looks like they have it open now. Do you want to go over there?"

Gil clutched her arm. "Yes."

As Nikos passed, Alexandria snagged his sleeve. "Hey, let's take Gil to the other barge and see if we can find his family."

If they had escaped safely. If not, Gil always had a home with her family, but she hoped he wouldn't end with the parent-sized hole that still ached in her chest.

CHAPTER 24

IN WHICH THE FAMILY IS REUNITED

Day 16 after landing, Ki

FLANKED BY HIS NEW FRIENDS, Gil moved to the second barge, where the other hibernation spell had ended and the sleepers were stirring. The Earth warriors were moving his people to the long, human wagons, and the second dragon was on her way into her transport with her driver. The humans wore expressions of curiosity, surprise, confusion, and sometimes fear, but they kept their mouths shut and carried the fae gently, sometimes teaming up to carry a larger body.

Nik stopped the wheeled chair out of the way, and Gil craned his neck to see into the barge. Shalla, Merodach, and the king's Companion had been on the first barge, so Shar was probably still in there some-where, but Gil wanted his family first.

He spotted familiar red hair and slapped Ashur's shoulder as he was carried past. "Greetings, Ash! Are you well?"

The warrior carrying his friend paused and turned until his burden could see Gil.

The dryad groaned and rolled his eyes. "I'm so heavy. And hungry."

"No worries." Gil raised his voice so more fae could hear, despite the pain lingering in his throat. "These people will carry you to their wagons, to transport you to where you'll live for a while. Don't be alarmed at the noise of the wagons, and please cooperate with your helpers. There will be food when you arrive."

"Will they carry us forever?" Ash asked.

Gil patted his wheeled chair. "If your size permits, you'll get one of these later, but they take too much room on the wagon. Are you ready to go?"

"Food, you say?" Ash licked his lips. "Very ready."

"Okay," Gil said in Human. "Go."

The warrior nodded and continued toward the wagon.

"I still can't see my family," Gil fretted. "Was Mother unable to get Ram on board?"

Ian darted through the stream of helpers and looked from another, closer angle. "I think I see your mother."

Gil leaned forward until his head almost touched his knees. "Yes, there she is! And Ram."

"Where?" Ian asked.

"Right next to her."

Ian's forehead wrinkled. "But he's white."

Gil nodded. "He looks like Father."

Ian translated for his family, who looked as confused when he finished.

"What's wrong?" Gil asked.

"That's not the way color works for humans." Ian shrugged.

"Alexandria has dark hair like your father's," Gil said, "and yours is pale like your mother's."

"Yeah..." Ian shrugged again.

"Never mind," Nik said. "We will figure it out later."

He patted Gil on the shoulder and slipped into the line of warriors moving fae. When his turn came to enter the barge, he crawled over empty bunks toward Gil's family. Stopping by Mother, he spoke softly, gesturing toward the doorway.

Gil couldn't hear what he said, but Mother's ears pricked toward the entrance, and she hesitantly nodded, reaching to Nik. They locked arms, and he backed up, pulling her over the edge-to-edge bunks until he reached an aisle. Once he could stand, he scooped Mother into his arms and walked out.

Gil's wheeled chair started to move forward. Ian shouted and ran back to Gil, grabbing the chair from Alexandria.

"No pushing," Ian said. "I can do it."

Alexandria sniffed and moved to Gil's side. Subtly, she rolled her shoulder, wincing.

But before Gil had time to scold her for hurting herself again, Nik was there with Mother.

"Gil," Mother whispered, reaching for him.

Nik knelt on one knee, supporting Mother on the other. She embraced Gil, and he leaned into her arms as joy flooded him like the heat of the human sun.

They said nothing, merely held each other until Alexandria cleared her throat.

"Ram?" she asked.

Reluctantly, Gil sat back. Mother touched his short hair with pursed lips, but the scarf successfully hid his bruises. He would tell her about them later, when he could tell the whole story, including Alexandria's heroism. Nik smoothly rose to his feet as if Mother was no burden.

"I'll be back." Nik hurried toward the Earth wagons.

He returned before the warriors reached the back corner where Ram lay. When he emerged from the barge with Gil's brother, he was frowning. He stopped by Gil's chair and bent, showing Ram still deeply sleeping.

"The others wake," Nik said. "Why he sleep?"

Gil shrugged. He suspected Ram had an individual sleeping spell on him to keep him out of trouble, besides the general one on the entire barge, but he would have to ask the mage to be sure.

"Fix later," he said.

Nik nodded and headed for the long wagon.

Ian crouched by Gil. "Miknon?"

Yes, where was his sister? "Look?" Gil begged.

Ian nodded and ran inside the barge. He returned in a few minutes, shaking his head.

"Let's try the first barge again," Alexandria said.

Immediately turning the chair, Ian pushed Gil forward. They reached the other barge as the final people were removed.

Gil waved at Shar and Zak. "Miknon?" he asked.

Zak pointed toward the barge. "She went that way."

Ian grunted, and the chair zoomed up the path. At one of the long wagons, Nik waved his arm. Ian headed toward him, and as soon as they screeched to a halt, Nik lifted Gil up the stairs of the wagon. Alexandria and Ian crowded up after them.

Mak-swill stood in the aisle, directing the placement of fae into the last few empty seats. She nodded at Gil but stayed at her business.

He spotted Shalla and Ashur. And there was Miknon, sitting with Mother and the still-sleeping Ram! His family was here, safe at last. Relief fizzed in his veins like the sparkly drink Ian liked.

But he still had a job to do.

He raised his hands for attention. "You are safe," he said to the fae on the wagon. "As I'm sure Miknon told some of you, we have a truce and are working on a formal treaty. You will play a part in that, which I'll explain later. For now, let me introduce Mak-swill, who is our liaison to the humans — the people of Ki."

At her name, Mak-swill saluted. When Gil stopped talking, she said, "Welcome to Earth."

Gil translated that, ignoring the shocked looks from his people.

"Is she a woman?" Zak asked, proving they were worried about more than him using Mak-swill's name in public.

Gil nodded.

"Where is the real leader?" Zak demanded.

"Things are different here," Gil said. "We want you all to learn fast, before the rest of the fleet arrives. You also need to know Nik."

He patted his human carrier on the shoulder. The sooner the fae got used to hearing names, the less they might fuss when he told them the humans expected names from them.

"And his siblings Ian and Alex." He pointed to each of them.

"Hey," Alexandria protested.

He beckoned her closer and whispered in her own language, "With long name and touch, can see magic people your thinking. Please use short name."

He didn't have the vocabulary to explain about thought mages, but he made pleading eyes at her. She scowled but nodded.

Gil turned back to his people. "Alex has stonegazer eyes but is our friend." He didn't mention she claimed she had no magic. For now, the belief in her power would keep her safer. "Their mother is Helen, and I'm sure you'll meet her later."

"Where are they taking us?" Shalla asked.

"To school, to learn the Earth language, reading, and their magic."

Astonished gasps echoed through the wagon.

"What about the commoners?" Shalla asked.

"All of you," Gil said. "School is required here."

"What about the girls?" Zak asked.

Gil grinned. "Girls too."

Zak narrowed his eyes. "Will we learn about their contrivances? These wagons, the talk box Miknon had, everything?"

Gil shrugged. "Yes?"

Ears green with excitement, Zak stared out the window at the other wagons.

"Are they keeping the adults with the youngsters?" Shalla asked.

"You will all live together for now," Gil said, "though as more join us, housing assignments may change. In fact, any adult who wants to attend the school may do so for as long as they like, but only the children are required to stay until they come of age."

Shalla sucked in a breath, then started to cry. Alexandria wriggled past Nik and Gil and hurried to Shalla. In bad fae vocabulary, she comforted the king's housekeeper, arm around her shoulders.

Mak-swill glanced at the contrivance on her wrist. "Ready? You tell others same?"

Gil nodded. "Everyone, please stay in your seats. The humans will help you disembark when it is time. Don't be alarmed at the sound or vibration. All is well. I will see you again when we reach our destination." He winked at Mother, then patted Nik. "Okay, ready."

Together, he and his human friends gave a shorter version of his speech to the fae in every wagon. By the time he finished, the fae barges had been loaded onto giant, flat wagons and covered. The rayed circles of light had been collected. The site looked untouched, except for hundreds of footprints in the sand.

Nik loaded Gil and his chair into his bright blue wagon, and the family followed the long line of wagons through the darkness.

"Wow," Ian said. "You all look so different."

"Wow," Gil said. "You all look so alike."

Ian laughed. "Okay, okay."

Nik stopped his wagon in front of a large building blazing with lights from every window, far enough from the other wagons to not interfere with unloading. Even with unpacking the wheeled chair, the family made it inside before many of the fae were carried in.

Mak-swill stood in a large room full of wheeled chairs, directing her warriors as soon as they deposited each person into a chair. "Girls to the second floor from that elevator, boys to the fourth up that one, families on the third." She paused. "Gil, how many families have we?"

Her accent was terrible, but the words were understandable, especially considering how little time she had been studying.

"Few," he said.

He didn't know yet which parents had been left behind, either because they were essential personnel or untrustworthy, but lack of space limited the number that could come, anyway. He was lucky his mother had been included. In fact, Gil needed to ask Mother…

Mak-swill nodded and kept pointing one way or the other down the hall as fae came in. He helped Mak-swill send fae to the correct locations, particularly when gender was unclear to human eyes, until his family arrived.

Ram was finally awake, jaw clenched so tightly that Gil feared for his teeth. Miknon looked exhausted but well.

"Mother," Gil said, "Miknon and I are staying with Ian's family." He glanced at Miknon to make sure she agreed, and she nodded. "Do you want to live with us? Our new home will be ready in a few days."

Mother sighed. "I think we'll stay here, as long as we can see you often. I'd rather be among our own people."

"They're my friends, Mother," he said. "And humans will be joining you here in a few conjunctions anyway."

"Friends!" Ram grunted. "They are not fae. They cannot be friends."

"This will give us time to adjust to the changes," Mother said. "And…" She glanced between Ram and the human warrior pushing his chair. "It will be better."

Oh. She was worried about what Ram might do. Gil sighed. "I'll see you every day, Mother."

He hugged her and Ram, despite his brother's stiffness, and moved Miknon to his lap before escorting them to a room. Though small, they would have it to themselves. Compared to the single bed they had shared as a family on the ship, it was spacious.

When he made it back to the entry room, he was just in time to see Ash, Zak, and Shar settled in wheeled chairs. Mak-swill directed Ash and Zak to the boys wing and Shar to the girls.

Gil bit his lip. "Nik, hurry, catch that girl!" He pointed at Shar while he called after Zak. "Navigator, wait!"

Zak turned his head, and his escort stopped pushing his chair. Nik pushed Gil fast enough to catch Shar.

Shar still wore his feminine disguise, a bodice and flounced skirt like Mother, with his hair curled in long ringlets. Zak wore the usual cast-off tunic from his father, hair bound tightly against his head in braids as Gil's used to be.

"It's time to end the secrets," Gil said in his native language. He pointed down the hall and put a hand on Shar. "Boy." He touched Zak and pointed the other way. "Girl."

Nik and their escorts shrugged and nodded.

Miknon choked, then buried her face in Gil's shoulder. Faint giggles still made their way to his ears. Apparently, she had never guessed about Zak.

"What did you say?" Shar asked, unable to understand the human language but obviously sensing something with his mind-touching.

"Don't worry," Gil said. "You don't need to be a girl now. You can't hide anymore, anyway. We'll put you in a room with Ash, so you can decide when to reveal your rank. I only revealed your proper genders, nothing else."

Zak turned sickly orange from neck to hair. "Genders? Plural? No!"

Shar jerked to stare at the navigator. "What?"

"You're wrong about me," Zak insisted.

"You'll be sharing a room," Miknon said, "and not with your father. Do you prefer to share with a girl or a boy?"

Gil nodded vigorously. That was why he had revealed her secret.

Zak's lips pressed together. "A girl," he — she gritted between her teeth.

Shar stared at Zak, eyes wide. "You're really a girl? But you've always been a boy."

Zak glared at him. "My father's been disguising me since I was a baby, to protect me from the same fate as my grandmother."

Her grandmother, the inventor of the new navigation system, had been killed in an "accident" arranged by some of the lords to remove her from her position of authority. Her only female apprentice, Gil's father, and both of Miknon's parents had been in the same accident. And since Earth believed in bringing murderers to justice, Gil planned to do something about that when the fleet returned. Miknon would certainly agree as soon as he told her about "the law."

"Don't worry," Gil said. "Girls are worth as much as boys here. Remember, the girls are going to school, too."

"How did you know?" Zak continued. "Nobody ever suspected."

Gil laughed. "I've known since we were little. I have a very good nose. Mom said to never talk or think about it, so I didn't. Grandsire knew, I'm sure, but I don't think Ram or anybody else does. You avoided most people."

"But—" Shar spluttered. "A girl?"

"Shut up." Zak folded her arms and looked away.

"Don't worry about it now," Gil said. "Get some sleep. I'll come see you when the sun rises."

"The sun doesn't rise," Zak said. "Worlds rise, but in this system, they are mostly too far away to notice."

Gil laughed. "Oh, you have so much to learn about this world. We all have much to learn before the council returns with the rest of the fleet." He yawned. "But I really do need sleep. Go to bed, and I'll be back in the morning to help with the rest of the details, including what to call you."

"You aren't staying here?" Shar asked.

"I'm staying with my friends," Gil said. "It's easier for Ian and me to learn each other's languages if we live together. But we'll be here most of the time. I promise, I'll be back in the morning. You won't miss me until after breakfast."

"I doubt that," Shar said.

"Breakfast?" Zak asked.

"Breakfast," Miknon repeated. "And the food is good."

"No bugs," Gil said. "I told you, things are different here." He looked at the chair-pushers, still waiting patiently, and waved one arm in each direction. "Ready."

As the chairs disappeared in opposite directions, he cupped his hands around his mouth. "I'll be back in the morning!"

The last of the fae were heading to their rooms. Lights went dark one by one, and Nik spun the chair around. Mak-swill checked her list and rubbed her eyes. Helen and Alexandria were sitting in two extra wheeled chairs, leaning against each other for support. On his lap, Miknon sat down and leaned against him, eyes closed. Beside him, Ian yawned noisily. Behind him, Nikos sighed.

"Go home," Gil said.

"Okay." Ian cheered and ran to collect his mother and sister.

Home. What a lovely word. Gil grinned as they headed into the night.

Epilogue

School

Standing outside the front door of the new school, Ian shifted his weight from foot to foot. Why did he have to greet the new students? Mom and Alexandria were perfectly capable, since the humans were required to speak English, and he'd be more useful inside with Gil and Miknon and the others. Lucky Nikos was at his new job, far away from the impending chaos. Lucky Gil, inside with the air conditioning instead of broiling in nearly ninety-degree heat.

"Ian, where's your ID?" Alexandria hissed, elbowing him.

Ian pulled his new identification tag from his pocket and glared at it. Mom's ID said "faculty," since they gave her a job teaching history. Nikos had a "visiting faculty" badge, though he was doing more studying of mythology than teaching, comparing Earth legends with the apparently original stories. Ian and Alexandria got an invented "student faculty" badge. Reluctantly, he hung it around his neck.

"I can't believe the state high school requirements are different *again*," Alexandria complained. "Everywhere we move, they're different. I hate having to catch up on classes. And I'll be so busy translating, I'll only be getting half my credits the first semester. We'd better not move again, or I'll never graduate."

Ian rolled his eyes. Okay, yes, she had a problem, but at least she belonged in high school. He was only thirteen, but they'd made him skip eighth grade to be here. If only he'd flunked the placement exams, he could have gone back to homeschool for at least another year. But no, he passed, so now he was stuck. And he would be as busy as she was, translating for the English and alien language classes while she helped the science and math classes. If they could cram it into his schedule, they'd make him translate for the other human language classes, too, even the ones he didn't speak.

They had students from all over the world, and he only knew ancient and modern Greek, Russian, Japanese, Spanish, and a bit of French and German. No Chinese, no Arabic, none of the Indian or African languages, not even Italian or Portuguese. And his Alienglish wasn't great, either.

Of course, he'd only been learning it for two months, and nobody knew it better. His family wasn't learning it as fast, and the professional linguists brought in by the military and State Department were weeks behind him and slower than he expected professionals to be. In his spare time, he was supposed to *teach* the new language to the other linguists. He was just a kid! Who would listen to him?

As for the alien side of things, Gil was the most cooperative in the language exchange, and he lived with the Fitches. The others didn't like talking to the humans, so though they'd spent the last six weeks working on English, they weren't learning as fast. He couldn't get a lot of answers from them, either. How was he supposed to teach the language if he couldn't learn it?

"Oh, here they come." Mom juggled the welcome packets in her arms.

Several cars pulled into the parking lot, and people pulled luggage from trunks and back seats. Alexandria straightened the list of room-mates on her clipboard and clicked her pen a few times.

"Hey, isn't that Mrs. Ortiz?" Ian asked.

"Yeah." Alexandria ran her pen down her list. "Well, there's an Ortiz on the freshman list. Ooh, and she's Zee's roomie. If she's as nice as Therese, Zee will be relieved."

Few of the fae had given the humans their names, instead accepting nicknames. Zee was a particularly odd case, since she had apparently been accepted as a boy on the spaceship.

The dark-haired girl with Mrs. Ortiz moved faster than the other arrivals and reached the bottom of the steps first. She detoured to drag her wheeled suitcase up the new ramp covering half the stairs. Her mom — the resemblance was strong — followed close at her heels, slowed a little by her narrow skirt and dress shoes and the duffel bag she carried.

"That's handy for the luggage." The girl held out her hand to shake. "I'm Gaby Ortiz."

Ian giggled. It did make dragging suitcases easier, but that wasn't why the military had built it.

Alexandria elbowed him and offered her own hand. "I'm Alex Fitch."

Ian bit his lip to avoid another giggle. All that time fighting her nickname, and now she was stuck with it anyway.

Alexandria stepped on his foot. "This is my brother U.N. and my mom, Helen Ellison. Hello, Therese."

Gaby jerked to look at her mom, eyes narrowed. "You know—" She examined Ian's family from head to toe, especially their ID badges. "Student faculty?" she murmured. "What?" She raised her eyebrows at her mom. "So, can I know stuff *now*?"

Mrs. Ortiz shrugged.

"Here is your orientation packet," Mom said, "and a copy for your parents." She handed the second folder to Mrs. Ortiz. "Once you say goodbye to your mother, we'll introduce you to your roommate."

"You've got a good one," Alexandria said. "Um, U.N., make sure to explain the one thing, okay?"

"Sure," he said.

Zee had been having a hard time adjusting to her new identity among her own people, so maybe it would be easier with a stranger who didn't remember her being any different. And if not, Gaby deserved to know why her roommate was so nervous.

"Do you like technology?" Ian asked.

"I like math," Gaby offered. "That's used in tech."

"Close enough." Ian smiled at her.

Mrs. Ortiz put down the duffel bag. "Au revoir, ma chérie. Écris-nous souvent. Et sois sages."

Automatically, Ian tried to translate. *Goodbye, dear. Write to us often. Behave yourself.*

"Quand est-ce que je ne suis pas sage?" Gaby said.

When do I not behave?

"Amuse-toi bien. Je t'aime." Mrs. Ortiz embraced Gaby, kissing her on both cheeks.

Then try to have fun. Ian choked back a giggle.

Gaby shot him a suspicious glance, and he smiled blandly.

Mrs. Ortiz left, and the next student and parents clacked up the ramp. Ian scooped up Gaby's duffel bag and bolted for the door. If he was helping Gaby, he had the perfect excuse for not being out front.

"So, I guess French is your second language?" Politely, he held open the door for Gaby.

"And Spanish." She crossed the threshold and stopped, staring around her. "This looks like a hotel, not a school."

"We converted it." Ian nudged her farther inside.

Mr. Riggs had bought three old hotels in the area, though the others were still waiting for occupants. The signal indicating the next landing had come the night before.

"Cafeteria, classrooms, and offices are on the first floor," he explained. "Bedrooms are second through fourth floors. The laundry and gym are in the basement, and the covered pool is between the wings."

"Ooh, aren't we fancy," Gaby muttered.

"It's for physical therapy." Ian guided her down the hall.

"So the ramp—" Gaby said as they entered the cafeteria.

Silence fell, and half the wheelchairs spun so everyone was facing the doors. The variety of skin tones and sizes was still amazing, even after seeing them every day, to say nothing of the various wings, horns, pointed ears, and other inhuman features.

Gaby's suitcase fell over as she staggered backward. "Gah."

Ian put a hand on her back. "You okay?"

"I—" She sucked in an uneven breath.

Gil hopped forward on crutches, with Miknon on his shoulder. He'd only been out of his cast for a couple of days, and his grin seemed stuck in "beam" mode.

"Hello," he said cheerfully. "Welcome to school. I am Gil. This is Miknon."

He looked at Ian from the corner of his eye, and Ian nodded approval of his pronunciation. Gil beamed harder.

Slowly, Gaby offered her hand. "Gaby Ortiz."

Ian nudged her. "They don't shake hands," he whispered. "It's considered rude to touch without permission."

"Oh." Gaby examined her new classmates and gulped. "I guess there's a reason they didn't name the foreign language we're learning?"

Ian shrugged. "Yep. They haven't told us what it's called yet. Now, let's introduce you to your roommate, Zee."

He pushed Gaby gently toward the short gremlin, pulled her into an empty seat, and prepared to translate the introductions.

Well, I am so relieved that everything will fall into place now.

Will it, dear reader?

Yes! The school is set up, the treaty is coming. Everything will be fine! Why are you looking at me like that?

Are you sure the lords go along with the plan when they land on Earth? Turn the page for a sneak peek at The Academy of the Fae.

The Academy of the Fae

At a secret high school for human and fae students, the top subject is the fate of Earth.

An advance ship of space fae volunteered their teens for an exchange program. Humans and fae must learn the others' languages and cultures to make a treaty when the rest of the fleet arrive from their old planet. A little friendship wouldn't hurt matters, either.

But not everyone is willing to play nice at recess.

Though some are taking advantage of the new lessons, others prefer their old ways. Bullies, prejudices, and private agendas threaten the tentative peace. The fae must be kept secret until graduation, but the teens face tests on every side.

Flunking is not an option. Too bad cheaters might ruin everything.

Imaginative world-building combines myth and reality at a boarding school where magic and monsters are in every classroom. **The Academy of the Fae** *is the third book in the* **Return of the Fae** *series of clean YA contemporary fantasy with a dash of sci-fi & mythology, from the author of* **Unexpected Heroes***, and is best read in order for the most enjoyment.*

Still want more? Get free stories by joining my newsletter. Every two weeks, I chat about my current writing or my life & offer book news and deals. And did I mention free stories?

Sign up at MCLeeBooks.com.

Free story #1: Spotting the Fae

Zak is considered too young to navigate the spaceship, even though he's the best among the fae.

On Earth, Gaby loves math and helping her astronomer Mama with her data.

When Mama spots a new asteroid heading toward Earth...

Everything will change.

The author of **Unexpected Heroes** *returns with a startlingly plausible blend of sci-fi, mythology, and the modern world.* **Return of the Fae** *is a clean YA contemporary fantasy series where fae from space don't match Earth's legends.*

Free Story #2: The Cat's Fortune

On another world, so long ago that truth has faded into legend, a cat and a boy seek their fortune together. You think you know the story, but do you?

Orphaned and homeless, young Aktar travels to the city of Rapata for a better life.

But it seems the rumors of gold-paved streets are false. Can he find a home and a job before he starves? Maybe with the help of a foundling kitten.

A retelling of Puss in Boots and Dick Whittington, with timeless themes of belonging, courage, and self-discovery, set on the fantasy world of Kaiatan, home of the **Unexpected Heroes**.

Please leave an honest review on any retailer or reader site. Seriously, it would really help me. :)

If you found a typo, you're welcome to report it at mcleebooks.com/report-a-typo/

Character List

Humans
James Anthony: Major General
Nikolaos Antonakis: 18-year-old Greek student, semi-adopted by Fitches, "Nikos" or "Nik"
Emil Compton: US State Dept
Helen Ellison (Fitch): Alex and Ian's mother
Clyde Farrell: Office of International Affairs
Alexandria Fitch: 16-year-old student
Ian Fitch: 13-year-old student
Troy Fitch: Alexandria & Ian's father
Raquel Maxwell: Military linguist & principal
Gabriela Ortiz: 14-year-old local student, "Gaby"
Therese Ortiz: astronomer & Gaby's mother
Allan Riggs: Compton's secretary
Tricia Stafford: refugee specialist

Fae
Arishaka: prior king of the fae
Ashur: dryad, Gil's friend
Azidaka: baby dragon
Dagan: prior chief guard, Gil's grandsire
Gil: wolf shifter
Izdu: gremlin, chief navigator, Zak's father
Kishar: fae lord, Arishaka's cousin
Maia: wolf shifter, Gil's mother
Merodach: fae healer
Miknon: pixie, Gil's adopted sister
Nashuja: hydra
Nik: pukel, king's secretary
Ram: wolf shifter, Gil's twin brother

Shalla: sirin, king's housekeeper
Sharrukin: fae prince, "Shar"
Taras: naga, king's Companion (chief guard)
Zaidu: fae lord
Zak: gremlin, youngest navigator

Places
Ki: the intended new home of the Fae; Earth
Kunisu: the old home of the Fae
New Kunisu: the flagship of the Fae fleet

ACKNOWLEDGMENTS

Thanks to my critique group for their usual spot-on comments: Carol Malone, Donna Gonzales, Gail Porter.

Also thank you to my fabulous alpha and beta readers: Jessica Ecklund, Lea Carter, Molly Morrison, & Virginia Cummings.

Special thanks to Hanna Mecham for Pennsylvania color, Medic 313 for EMT advice, Robin Cranney for more military expertise, and Ruth Ramirez for French corrections. If there are still mistakes, they are my own.

ABOUT THE AUTHOR

 Marty C. Lee told stories for most of her life, but never took them seriously until her daughter asked her to write one for her. Between writing and spending time with her family, she reads, embroiders, paints-by-number, and gardens.

She has lived in five states (including Colorado), seven cities, and eleven houses so far. She knows bits of two extra languages, but some days can't even speak her native tongue fluently. She isn't any kind of athlete but does have sneaky ninja (or fairy) feet. Though not an extrovert, she does have friends besides her books. You are welcome to write to her as a new friend. :)

You can find her at MCLeeBooks.com and on Facebook and book sites.

www.ingramcontent.com/pod-product-compliance
Lightning Source LLC
Chambersburg PA
CBHW030806020726
47499CB00006B/1788